A NEXT GENERATION NOVEL

CONSUME *Us*

J.M. WALKER

IBSN: 978-1-989782-39-2

Consume Us (Next Generation, #9)

FAMILY TREE

Angel and Genevieve "Jay" Rodriguez
(Grit, King's Harlots #1/Grim, King's Harlots #3)
Angelica "Gigi"
Ryder
Meadow

Asher and Meeka Donovan
(Stain, King's Harlots #2)
Aiden
Ashton

Coby and Brogan Porter
(Rude, King's Harlots #4/For You, King's Harlots #7)
Zachary "Zach"

Dale and Maxine "Max" Michaels
(Numb, King's Harlots #5)
Piper

Vincent "Stone" and Creena Stone
(Rust, King's Harlots #6)
Luna
Vincent Junior

Greyson and Eve Mercer
(Greyson, Hell's Harlem #1)
Jaron

Tray and Zillah Lister
(Tray, Hell's Harlem #2)
Beatrix "Bee"

John and Beatrix "Trixie" Butcher
(Hell's Harlem Series)
Cyrus
Samson "Sammy"

WARNING

Please be advised that this book does talk about cancer and alcoholism.
Example: Cancer survivor, mention of cancer, etc. A side character deals with alcoholism, and it's mentioned and shown a lot throughout the book.
Also, there is a mild and short sexy scene regarding the breeding kink/fetish.
But please be rest assured that no one gets offed in this book.
I'm saving that for the next one.

DEDICATION

To you and your love of books.

PROLOGUE

ASHTON

THE SCENT OF SOMETHING sweet wafted into my nose. It reminded me of the girls I used to run into at bars. With their made-up faces, too tight and barely-there clothes, it was like they bathed in perfume. A lot would say that guys did the same with cologne but several women I had come across were just as bad. If not more so.

Before I rolled over, I knew that I wasn't alone in bed. I thought back to the night before and what had gone down, but came up short. Only snippets filled my head, and they were nothing worth thinking about.

Not giving her a chance to wake up, I slipped out of the random woman's bed, pulled on my clothes, and grabbed my keys out of the pocket of my jeans. I didn't bother waking her because there would be no point. It would end up being the same conversation we always had.

She wanted more.

I didn't.

She would ask again because she always thought that by asking me more than once, I would give in.

I would tell her no and that I laid out the rules from the very beginning.

She would accuse me of leading her on.

I didn't.

She would still try and press for a relationship.

I would respond with I wasn't relationship material.

She would get upset.

And I would say or do something stupid that I would regret later on.

These feelings rushing through me were new. I never used to care how they felt. As long as I got what I wanted, that was all that mattered. All of the women I had been with knew ahead of time that I didn't want to commit. It wasn't in my nature. I was too young to settle down. That last part was a lie.

Truth was, I hadn't found my person. The one I wanted to spend the night with only to wake up the next morning and do it all over again. The one I wanted to cook breakfast for, take on dates, have her on my arm when others had tried but failed.

I *was* ready to settle down, but I never told these women that. Most of them were clingy, trying and begging for more from me. They wanted things I couldn't give them. I was saving that part of myself for that special someone. I just hadn't found her yet.

I didn't even tell the people I had grown up with that I was ready for a family. They probably wouldn't believe me anyway seeing as I gave a few of them a hard time. But I was ready to right my wrongs and show them, all of them, even my own brother and parents, that I needed more. That I was ready for more. No matter the cost. I needed to find me a woman who could tame this raging beast within me because I knew that if I didn't, karma would come back to bite me in the ass.

ONE

ASHTON

MY BROTHER INSISTED ON going out for drinks tonight. Really, he shouldn't be drinking at all, but I could only do so much. He didn't listen to anyone when they told him so. Hell, he didn't even listen to me. And we were twins, so you would think he would. Or that he would know how I felt about his little problem without me having to say so.

"I'm not really feeling it tonight," I told Aiden, shoving my hands into the pockets of my blue jeans. Although I said those words, I still followed him across the parking lot to the front door of the bar. If he wanted to go out for drinks, I would go with him every chance I could. Then he would at least get home safely.

"I need to take the edge off," he said, which was his way of saying that he needed the noise in his head to stop. I didn't know what his deal was. He wouldn't tell anyone. All we knew was that he had joined the Navy like our father had and was discharged after his first deployment. Something happened but he wouldn't talk about it. Aiden ended up with a drinking problem as a result of it.

"Can't we find something else to take the edge off?" I asked him. "We also have to work tomorrow. We can go to the gym or go for a run. Or do something else."

Aiden stopped, eyes that mirrored my own, connected with mine. "Since when do you want to go to the gym instead of finding some easy pussy? And us having to work the next day has never stopped you before."

"You never mentioned pussy," I corrected him. "You mentioned drinks."

There had been a time, not too long ago in fact, where I would go out, have a drink or two, and bring a woman home with me. It had been a routine of mine for as long as I could remember but watching our friends get married and have kids of their own, sparked something in me. I often went back and forth on if I was ready to have a family or not. One moment I thought I wasn't and then when I saw the people I had grown up with having families of their own, it made me long for the same.

I was in my thirties and never had a serious relationship. Ever. I had been known to try and destroy the relationships my friends had. It wasn't something I was proud of, but it happened. Nothing I could do about it but to apologize and move on. Not that I ever said I was sorry. I needed to fix that but at the moment, I needed to make sure my brother didn't get beat up tonight.

"Drinks usually mean pussy to you, brother," Aiden mumbled, pulling me from my thoughts and taking a step toward the front doors.

I grabbed his arm, stopping him. "Why don't we do something else tonight?" Even though he was right in the fact that it had never mattered if we had to work the next day and we would still go out the night before, I was telling the truth when I told him that I wasn't feeling it. Our dad had already given us shit over the fact that we weren't really good at keeping up with the business he left us now that he retired. Thankfully, we had some good guys who worked with us and helped us run Rod's Construction.

Aiden's brows narrowed. "Why?"

"I just…" I wasn't sure why exactly, but something told me, something deep in my gut said, that maybe we should call it a night. Maybe we shouldn't have drinks like my brother wanted. Maybe the universe was trying to tell me something. But then on the other hand, I didn't know how to say no to him either. Whatever he was going through, he asked me to be there with him. Even if he never gave me any of the gritty details, it meant something. So instead of arguing any more about it, I caved. "Fine. Just behave tonight. I don't want to have to bail you out of jail again."

Aiden grunted, running a hand through his dirty blond hair. "That was one time."

"Yeah, one time too many," I mumbled. "You didn't have to deal with Mom. I wasn't even scared of Dad. It was her I was more worried about. I thought she was going to kick my ass just because I look like you."

"I don't even remember what happened or why I ended up in jail in the first place," Aiden murmured, a far away look taking over. I learned he did that a lot. It made me uncomfortable because I didn't know how to help him. I wished I did but it was next to impossible when he didn't tell me anything.

"Of course, you don't."

His eyes shot to mine. "Lay off, Ashton."

My jaw clenched, the muscles jumping as I ground my teeth together. I had been told time and time again to back off where my brother was concerned. He couldn't be helped if he didn't want to help himself. Same shit, different day. But he was a selfish bastard and he needed to learn that the world didn't revolve around him.

"You know what, Aiden? You can drink by yourself tonight." I went to turn and walk back to my car when something caught my eye in the window. It had been so quick, I wasn't even sure what it was or what had my attention, but for whatever reason, I needed to find out. All I knew was that it was pink. It had been brief, so my eyes could have been playing tricks on me. I believed it was pink. It had to have been. Why else would I think of that color?

"On second thought…" I pushed past my brother and headed into the bar, but I had no idea what I was even looking for.

"Ashton?" Aiden came up behind me. "What's wrong?"

"Nothing." My eyes scanned the area. We had been to this bar quite a few times even though we didn't live in the neighborhood. It helped that we could usually throw back a couple hundred dollars worth a night. Add to the fact that we did some reconstruction on the place for the owner as well.

"Ashton." Aiden went to the bar and sat on a stool. "Sit. You're making me nervous."

I was about to head to the bar to sit beside him when a woman came out from the back. She was followed by another person, but I couldn't see if they were a man or a woman because she had me struck stupid. Literally. I had stopped in my tracks at the mere sight of her. But when she laughed at whatever was said to her, I was done.

She was it. This random woman I didn't know. She would be mine.

The woman walked back and forth behind the bar serving drinks, chatting with customers, and doing her job. While I stood there and stared at her like a dumb fuck.

She was wearing high-waisted blue jean cut-off shorts with a green and black plaid shirt tied in a knot just under her full tits. Several of the top buttons weren't done up, revealing pale cleavage that I wanted to sink my teeth into.

Taking a step closer, I let my eyes travel up to her face. She had pouty rosy lips with a white diamond sitting in the middle of the bottom one. Blood pumped through me, wondering how much of her was pierced.

I was in a trance as I sat beside my brother.

This woman was stunning. She wasn't normally my type. Especially with her pastel pink hair, dark roots, and tattoos that covered a lot of her exposed skin, but people could change. *I* could change.

Her pink colored hair was pulled high on top of her head in two buns with strands of hair falling down around her face. Her lashes were long and thick, heavy black eyeliner circled them. I would give anything to see what she looked like in the morning. Makeup free, exposed skin, and with a glow in her cheeks that I put there. I wanted to hear my name on her lips. I wanted to lick my tongue along that piercing in her lip as she shuddered beneath me. I wanted *her*.

"What'll you two have?" Natalie Moore, the regular bartender who always served us, and who had warmed my bed a handful of times, asked.

"Beer and a shot of tequila," Aiden answered for both of us.

I didn't give a shit what I had to drink. I just wanted to find out that pink-haired beauty's name.

"Same for you, Ashton?" Natalie asked, stepping in front of me. She leaned across the bar top, the movement pushing her full tits together. Another time and I would have had her in the back, bent over the nearest hard surface, but that was then. This was now. And I really wanted to know where that beauty disappeared to.

"Yeah, sure," I told Natalie, attempting to brush her off but when her hand reached out to cup mine that was resting on the bar, I flinched. "Not happening tonight." Or any night for that matter. Not again.

I could feel Aiden's eyes burning into the side of my head, but I ignored him.

Natalie frowned but when another customer called out her name, she shook it off and went to serve them.

"What was that about?" Aiden asked me.

"Just not feeling it."

"Since when?"

"Since now." Not that it mattered or that I had to explain myself, but I had been known to be a player, a womanizer, whatever word you wanted to use to describe it. I didn't treat women overly well and the one woman I could have had, ended up marrying someone else. Most of the women I was actually interested in before now ended up with someone else. It was like I was cursed or like that guy in that movie who fucked women and they ended up finding their true love after.

Trying not to make it obvious, I scanned the room around us looking for that woman, but when she was nowhere to be seen, I sighed and took a long swig of my beer.

"You're being weird," Aiden pointed out, throwing back a shot.

"I told you I wasn't feeling it tonight." That wasn't the complete truth, but it didn't matter. I wouldn't leave until I found out that woman's name.

"Where would you like this, Nat?"

My head snapped up, my eyes landing on *her*.

She was holding a crate of empty glasses, waiting for Natalie to give her instructions.

"Just over there." Natalie nodded to the spot in front of me and Aiden. "Then I can put them away in a moment."

"I can do it." The pink-haired beauty walked past her until she stopped directly in front of me.

Talk to me, Kitten. I want to hear your voice again.

When she crouched in front of me and started putting the glasses away, I cleared my throat. She paused, her gray eyes slowly lifting to meet mine.

A hot shiver raced down my spine, this sudden reaction not something I was used to. I was vaguely aware of Aiden talking to someone from beside me but all I could focus on was the woman staring up at me. It was a position I wanted to see her in again but only next time, I wanted her naked.

"Ashton, you listening to me?"

A voice pulled my head around.

Aiden frowned. "Daydreaming?"

"No, sorry. What did you say?" I asked him, glancing back at the woman in front of me. She was no longer looking at me but she was still there.

Which would do.

For now.

"I asked if you were going to drink your shot."

A full shot glass sat beside my pint of beer.

Instead of waiting for me to answer, Aiden took it and downed it back before turning it over and slamming it upside down on the counter.

The woman's eyes shot to mine. She looked between us both. "Did you want another?"

"Ashton," I added.

She stared at me, raising an eyebrow. "Excuse me?"

"My name. It's Ashton," I told her.

"I never asked you for your name," she said, the bite in her tone scraping along my skin. "I asked if you wanted another drink."

"You're right. You didn't ask for my name, but you also didn't ask if we wanted another drink either. You said, 'Did you want another?', which technically, was wide open." I tapped the rim of my glass. "So, you can understand why I would be confused."

She rose to her full height, her lips pulling into a thin line. "Forgive me. Would you like another *drink*?"

"No, thank you but I would like to know your name." It wasn't smooth on my part.

She laughed. She actually fucking laughed. She shook her head, blowing a pink strand of loose hair out of her eyes. "You're funny." She poured two more beers, placing the glasses in front of me and Aiden. "Anything else?"

I could think of many other things I wanted but for once in my life, I decided to keep my mouth closed.

Looking directly into her eyes, I waited. For a sign. A flinch. A damn hint that she felt it, whatever this was, snapping between us. But when she only raised her eyebrow even higher, I knew right then. She was the one. I wasn't sure how in fact I knew but I did. And I was determined to show her that this was right.

"Tabby, Scooter needs help in the back," Natalie called out as she walked to a table holding a tray lined with plates of food.

My eyes slid back to the woman standing in front of me. "Nice to meet you, Kitten."

"That's not my name." She scowled. "You just heard her say my name."

"Yeah, I did, and *Kitten* is actually fitting," I threw back at her.

She huffed, spun on her heel, and headed to the back of the bar, but not before I caught her giving me one last glance over her shoulder.

"What the hell was that?" Aiden asked, pulling my gaze away from Tabby.

"I have no idea," I told him.

"She doesn't seem like your type, Ashton," he reminded me.

"Nope, she doesn't." I drank down half of my beer, suddenly feeling parched.

"She also doesn't seem to like you very much," he pointed out.

"She definitely doesn't like me." I chuckled.

"So, what are you going to do about it?"

I looked at him then. He was staring down into his glass that was now empty, a longing expression on his face. I didn't know what it meant but if he needed my help, he knew where to find me.

"Ashton?" He looked up. "You didn't answer my question."

I drank down the rest of my beer, mulling over his words. "Marry her," I finally said. "That's what I'm going to do."

He laughed, shaking his head. "Right."

"You think I'm kidding?" I signaled Natalie over. "Just wait, brother. My ring will be on her finger some day. Just watch."

"You just met her, and she never even told you her name when you asked."

"You're right." I gently nudged him in the shoulder. "She didn't."

When Tabby came back out to the bar area, she walked past me and bent over to pick something up from one of the lower shelves.

I tried not to stare at her ass, I really did, but it was hard not to when her perfect little body was right in front of me.

Once she stood back to her full height, my eyes stopped at two tattoos on the back of both of her thighs. They were black bows with lines leaving from the center of them, and going down the length of her legs before disappearing into the heels of her black combat boots.

"Fuck me," I muttered, never seeing something so damn hot before. I didn't have any tattoos or piercings myself and I didn't have anything against them, but they had never really been my thing. Not until now. Not until they came with her. Tabby. *Kitten.* It was the perfect nickname.

A throat clearing made my head snap up.

"My eyes are in my fucking head, asshole," Tabby all but growled.

I opened my mouth to comment but nothing came out.

She huffed, stomping out from behind the bar and slamming her way into the back, leaving me speechless.

"Huh…guess there's a first time for everything," Aiden said from beside me.

He was right.

For the second time that night I was wrong.

I took a deep breath, giving myself a shake. "I think I just fell in love."

TWO

Tabatha

HE LOOKED AT ME like I mattered. Like I was the very reason he breathed. It didn't make sense when we had only just met. I had seen him come in with his brother from time to time, but I always stayed in the back. I was never needed out front until tonight. Life was funny in a way. I wasn't looking for anything. Not a relationship. Not even a fling. Random sex was dangerous.

I tried convincing myself that I didn't like the way he looked at me, but truth was, I did in fact like it. I liked it a lot and I didn't know why. I had never technically met him before, but Natalie seemed to know him very well. Add to the fact that he had a twin. The world didn't need two cocky fuckers like him. But his brother appeared to be quieter. So maybe they just looked alike and weren't actually similar when it came to their personalities. Thank the universe for that.

When he told me his name was Ashton without me having to ask for it because he had assumed I wanted to know, his deep voice sent a shiver down my spine. But I had dated guys like him. I also had my heart ripped out by guys like him too. Hell, even the guys I lived with were like him. The kind that wanted easy pussy and wouldn't think twice about kicking them out of their beds only to add that single notch to their bedpost.

When I reached the stock room, I left the door open to let some air into the small space. The building was old, so the single window in the room was sealed shut. It was stuffy and the air was thick, so I always left the door open. Made me feel less claustrophobic that way.

"Tabby, you good to stay an hour or two extra tonight?" came Scooter's deep voice from the doorway.

"Yup, that's fine." I needed the money anyway and it was Friday, so tips would be extra decent tonight.

"Perfect. Thank you. I'll tell Toya that she can leave early to pick up her son. Thanks again, sweetheart."

"Of course." I paused in filling up the crate of glasses and found Scooter still standing at the doorway. "What's wrong?"

"Have you talked to your brothers?" he asked, flipping through the pages on his clipboard. I found that he did that whenever he was trying to not actually look you directly in the eye but was waiting for a response anyway.

"Not since this morning before they left for work." I frowned, my heart skipping a beat that something could be wrong with one of my three foster brothers. "Why?"

"I've been trying to get a hold of Phoenix. There's a fight tomorrow night and I want to see if he'd be interested in going with me."

"No, you want him to fight, so you can make a shit ton of money off of him," I corrected him. He may have been my boss, but I had known Scooter for a while. His bar, Scooters, was only a front for the real activity that went on behind closed doors. While he never talked about it, bikers used this place after hours to get some business done. I never saw anything, but I had heard their deep voices when I was quietly working on the books for Scooter.

"I have no idea what you're talking about." Scooter crossed his thick tattooed arms across his chest. "If you talk to him, tell him to come here. I'll be in my office for a while."

Before I could say anything more about it, he turned on his heel and left the entranceway. The sound of his office door closing a moment later, echoed down the hall.

I pulled my phone from my back pocket and texted Phoenix, letting him know that Scooter was looking for him.

Scooter or Brian Charron, was the owner of the bar I worked at. He was in his mid-to-late forties and I had heard the guys tease him from time to time over his graying hair but most of the women I had seen him with, loved the silver fox look. Who wouldn't? Scooter was a lot older than I was and even though I considered him family, I could still admit that he was a good-looking man.

Scooters may have been a biker bar but anyone and everyone frequented the establishment. I had been working there for as long as I could remember and loved it. The pay wasn't the best, but it was better than nothing. It also helped that Scooter paid under the table when needed, too.

When I went back to stocking the crates to bring out to the bar, a throat clearing at the doorway, made me jump. My head snapped up, finding *him* standing there.

"Sorry, I didn't mean to scare you." Ashton shoved his hands into the pockets of his dark blue jeans. Much to my dismay, I couldn't help how the movement made my eyes drop to his crotch. The fabric of his jeans tightened over what was hidden beneath them and I knew that if a guy like him caught me staring at his package, I wouldn't live it down.

Quickly averting my gaze, I cleared my throat and rose to my full height. "You shouldn't be back here."

"I came to apologize," he said gently.

"You couldn't have waited for me to go back out to the bar?" I asked, raising an eyebrow.

"I know the owner and Natalie. They don't care if I come back here, as long as I don't get into shit."

I stared at him, looking for a sign that he was lying. "I know you."

"Uh…" He ran a hand through his dark blond hair. "You do?"

"I know who you are I mean. I know your type." I had never seen him with Natalie but I had heard her talking about a blond she let into the back so she could have some fun with him.

"Oh. Well…" Ashton only shrugged.

"Natalie seems to know you very well. Why don't you go bug her?" I was being a bitch, but I could read him even before he opened his mouth. Maybe I shouldn't have judged so quickly but with the things Natalie told me, he was far from being a nice guy.

"Not interested, Kitten," he said, stepping farther into the room.

"My name is Tabby," I corrected, not liking how the pet name sent a flutter through my belly.

"Tabby like tabby cat." He smirked. "So, calling you Kitten works."

"No." I placed my hands on my hips. "It does not work, Ashton," I growled. "My name is Tabby."

"Fine, Tabatha." His smirk grew. "Or I'm assuming Tabby is short for Tabatha. Am I right?"

I huffed. "Why are you being difficult?"

"I'm not sure." He ran two fingers along his full mouth, his eyes roaming down the length of me. "But I do like that feistiness in you. Kitten is definitely a fitting nickname."

I rolled my eyes, going back to doing my job and trying hard to ignore him, but it didn't work when he hovered over me. And it also didn't work when I could smell his spicy cologne. It was mixed with the scent of him, and it made my heart skip a beat. I had never had this reaction when it came to guys before. Even with the few exes I had, while they were good-looking and treated me well at first, this feeling was never there. But with Ashton, it was, and I wasn't sure how I felt about that.

"What do you want, Ashton?" I asked, keeping my voice monotone. I didn't need him to see how he affected me.

"I want to ask you out."

I laughed, shaking my head. "Right. Is that your polite way of saying that you want to fuck me?"

"Well." He coughed. "I want that too, but I would like to take you on a date first."

"Is that what you usually do? Do you take women out on dates first?" I didn't want to be that woman. The one who was used, fucked within an inch of her life, only to be kicked out after. I did that before and got the t-shirt to go with it.

"Geeze, woman." He laughed but the amusement wasn't there. "What the hell have I ever done to you?"

The hurt in his voice made my chest ache. "I've been with guys like you, Ashton."

"You have, have you? And what kind of guy am I exactly, Kitten?" His words were clipped and to the point, the hurt no longer there.

Call me a masochist but the fact that he seemed pissed, sent a rush of excitement through me.

"I bet you have at least a hundred notches on your bedpost and maybe a few dents too." I took a step toward him, letting my eyes roam up and down the length of his hard body. "If it's not that many, you would never say because you don't want to seem less cool," I mocked, using air quotes. "You also can't settle down because you are not made for monogamy. You've often wondered if maybe you have an addiction. If maybe you have too much sex. You've tried watching porn, but it doesn't do shit." I tilted my head, watching him, studying his reactions to see if I was right. When his jaw clenched, I knew I struck a nerve, so I kept going. "I'm also not your type. You go for tall, slender women usually. You don't really care what color the hair is on their head as long as they have holes for you to fill." I closed that final distance between us, placing my hand on his chest. His heart pounded beneath my palm, his muscles tight. "Your friends are getting married, having kids, maybe not in that order. Oh and your brother is holding you back. Maybe you're worried about him. Maybe you aren't." I went to pull away from him and go back to finishing stocking the crates when his hand caught my wrist. My eyes flew to his, expecting him to yell at me or demand to know how the hell I knew the shit I had said. I only knew it because I lived with and dated guys like him.

Ashton tugged me against him, the movement so quick, it forced a small squeak from my lips. He smirked and leaned down toward my ear. "You may think you know me, Kitten, but I promise you, you don't."

"Tell me I'm wrong then." I turned my head, our lips a mere inch apart. "Tell me that what I said, wasn't right. Tell me you don't have women begging to go home with you. Tell me that I'm wrong and that you do actually want to settle down."

"I didn't want to settle down. At all."

"Exactly. I told you—"

"No." His mouth found the side of my neck, sending a hot shiver down my spine. "I didn't want to settle down until now."

I frowned, leaning back. "What are you talking about?"

Ashton kicked the door closed, spun me around, and pushed me up against it. "I'm talking about how I didn't want to settle down until I met you. Might have been a bit before but it was definitely when I met you at least."

"You just met me tonight." I tried pulling my wrist from his grip, but he was too strong for me. Truth was, I liked his hands on me, but I just wouldn't tell him that.

"Exactly." When his mouth found the side of my neck again, a low growl left from somewhere deep in his chest. "I want to see how many piercings you have. I want to lick along every single one of your tattoos. I want to see if your gray eyes change color when you scream my name. But most of all, I want my ring on your finger."

My eyes widened at what he was suggesting. "You can't be serious."

"I am." Ashton pulled away from me, straightened his shirt and stared down at me. "You will marry me. Not now. Not tomorrow. But one day, you will."

"You're hilarious." I rolled my eyes. "Did you know that? You should be a damn comedian with how fucking funny you are." Spinning around, I went to open the door when a heavy hand slapped it closed. All breath left my lungs.

"Marry me," Ashton murmured.

"No," I murmured back.

He chuckled, placed a soft peck on my temple and moved his hand from the door.

I opened it, needing to put some distance between us before I did something stupid like saying yes to his proposal.

Ashton walked around me, looking down at me over his shoulder. "I don't know who hurt you, Kitten, but I'm not him."

Before I could say any more or argue that he *was* him and that they were all the same, he left, taking all of the air in my lungs with him.

THREE

ASHTON

WHEN I LEFT THE stock room, I stomped my way out to the bar to meet back up with my brother. He was still sitting where I had left him when I went after Tabatha and thank God for that. His head lifted as I approached, his eyes glossy. I noticed the empty shot glasses on the bar top in front of him, the sight alone making my jaw clench.

"We have to go," I told him. There was no way I was sticking around. Not tonight. I needed to go home and take a cold shower. My lips tingled with the memory of pressing them against Tabatha's throat. Feeling her tremble was not a reaction I was expecting. Especially when she seemed to know me so well and assumed the worst.

"I'm not leaving," Aiden slurred, picking up an empty shot glass.

"Fine." I threw some cash on the bar just as Tabatha rounded the corner. "Make sure he gets in a cab," I told her, my tone leaving no room for argument.

She looked between me and my brother. "Why can't you make sure he gets home yourself?"

"Because I need to leave." I went up to my brother. "You fucking call me if she doesn't get you a cab."

He nodded.

I kissed the top of his head and left the bar.

Once I stepped out into the cool evening air, I blew out a slow breath. It wasn't enough but it would have to do until I could get home. My body vibrated with a need I had never felt before. Add to the fact that I had proposed to Tabatha right away and I was on the verge of losing it. Especially when she told me no.

"Ashton."

Spinning around, I found the very reason I was leaving, rushing toward me.

"What's going on?"

"I can't stay," was all I said. Even though I didn't know where I was going, I began walking across the parking lot.

"Ashton."

"What?" I spun around. "You seem to think you know me so damn well already, so tell me, Tabatha. What do you want?"

"I just want to know what's going on and why you can't stay to make sure your brother gets in a cab yourself." She placed her fists on her hips. "And don't call me Tabatha. My daddy called me that and you are not my daddy. So, you haven't earned that right."

"So I was right, it is your name." Point one for me.

"That doesn't matter." She huffed. "Like I said, only my daddy called me that."

"Well, Tabatha." I took a step toward her. "That's not really a kink I've explored but feel free to call *me* Daddy."

Even though the only light surrounding us, was from the interior of the bar, I could still see the red in her cheeks.

She scowled. "Just answer my question."

"I can't stay because if I stay, I'll kiss you and I don't want to kiss you because I don't want you to hate me more than you already do. Since you seem to think you know me so fucking well already, Kitten. There, does that answer your damn question?" I walked away from her, not needing this. For the first time in my whole entire life, I was seriously crushing on someone, only for it to blow up in my face. Especially since she all but laughed when I proposed to her. It wasn't like it was planned. Hell, I'd only just met her tonight and already I was popping the question.

"Where are you going?" she asked, following behind me.

"You don't want to follow me, Kitten." I shoved my hands in my pockets, hoping that it would stop me from doing something stupid.

"Ashton."

Taking a deep breath and then another, I stopped and slowly turned toward her. "What?"

She grinned, crossing her arms under her full chest. The movement pushed her tits up even higher.

"I'm losing my fucking mind here and I only just met you," I mumbled, my blood pumping through every inch of me.

"I'll make sure your brother gets in a cab, Ashton." She came up to me, the air crackling around us the closer she got to touching me. Once she stood about an inch away, she grazed a finger down the length of my forearm. Goosebumps followed in its path, sucking all the saliva from my mouth. My tongue felt thick, my throat dry as hell.

"Do you really want to kiss me?" she asked, her voice breathless.

"Yes," I croaked.

She tilted her head back, her gray eyes connecting with mine. "What if I told you that I wanted you to kiss me?"

A breath left me, my dick jumping against the fly of my jeans.

"What if I told you that I wanted to feel your mouth on mine? Your tongue deep between my lips. Your breath mixing with mine." She stepped closer, her body brushing up against the side of mine. "What if I told you that I hope you take your shower and think of me while you touch yourself."

"Fuck." I breathed, pulling my hands from my pockets and dropping them in front of my waist.

She caught the movement, her eyes twinkling. "I hope you *do* think of me, Ashton." She took a step back, gave me a wink, and turned before walking back toward the bar. "Have a good shower," she called out, waving a hand over her shoulder.

"Geezus." I swallowed hard, gave myself a shake, and headed home. The walk didn't actually take too long because all I could think about was Tabatha and her full lips. Her beautiful eyes. Her curvy body. And that delicious bite in her tone. I loved how she spoke her truths and didn't hold back. I also liked how even though we didn't know each other, she wasn't scared to knock me down a peg or two. Lord knew I needed it.

Once I stepped foot into the apartment I shared with my brother, my phone vibrated in my pocket. Fishing it out, I saw a text from Aiden.

Aiden: It's Tabby. Your brother started passing out on top of the bar, so I just called him a cab before Scooter kicks his ass out.

I sighed, rubbing the back of my neck. I respected the hell out of Scooter and liked that he gave us work from time to time but it still pissed me off that he always threatened to have my brother thrown in the drunk tank. I got it. I did. Maybe it was what Aiden needed. But no one could force him to sober up. So, they needed to back the fuck off.

Me: Thank you, Kitten.

Unknown number: You're welcome.

I raised an eyebrow.

Me: Texting me from your phone now?

After I sent the text, I quickly added the number to my phone.

Kitten: Figured it was easier this way. Also didn't want Aiden to see the texts in the morning and get upset by them.

My heart warmed that she cared when she didn't know either of us enough to.

Me: Why do you care?

I knew the question was going to come out wrong, but I had to ask anyway.

Kitten: I know people who have...issues. Not with drinking but other stuff. Took them a long time to see it but they finally did.

Me: Looks like we have at least one thing in common.

Kitten: Looks like it. Have a good night, Ashton. And I meant what I said.

Me: I meant what I said too.

Kitten: Prove it.

I went to type something else and ask her how but decided not to. Instead, I put my phone away, locked up, and waited for my brother to come home.

Grabbing a bottle of water and some meds for the headache I knew he was going to have in the morning, I put them in his room on his nightstand.

It had been the same routine for a while now. We would go out, he would get shitfaced, come home, and I would take care of him. If he didn't pass out, we would bring women home with us. Sometimes we'd have a threesome. Sometimes we didn't. I often wondered why he even agreed to sharing women when he never seemed into it.

I never even saw him bringing someone home until I started doing it. Maybe he felt like he had to. Which he didn't. I didn't judge or even give a shit if he wanted to remain celibate or do something else. I wished he would talk to me about it, but he didn't.

A hard bang sounded against the door, indicating my brother's arrival.

Letting out a heavy sigh, I went to the door of our apartment and opened it. When Aiden's body toppled over, his soft snores the only sound, it was on the tip of my tongue to yell at him to wake the fuck up and put himself to bed. But I didn't because he was my brother, and I knew that he would do the same for me if the roles were reversed. It was also better that I take care of him than our parents. Dad was getting sick of his shit and Mom was trying to be the referee between them.

Dragging Aiden's body into the apartment, I shut the door and locked it back up. I did what I did every night and put him to bed, took off his shoes and tossed the covers over his unmoving body.

My phone dinged off in the distance, every cell in my body hoping it was Tabatha texting me. Closing the door slightly to Aiden's room, I went back to my own and checked my phone. My stomach sunk when I saw that it wasn't her.

Natalie: You down for some company?

My jaw clenched, a sour taste filling my mouth.

Me: Not tonight.

Natalie: Why not?

Me: Gotta take care of my brother.

Not that it was any of her business.

Natalie: Since when has that ever stopped you from getting your dick wet?

Leave it to her to remind me how my morals had been low for a while now.

Me: Not that I need to explain myself to you, but I am not interested. Go find another dick to bounce on.

Natalie: You're grumpy. Let me take care of you.

"Fucking women," I growled.

Me: Lose my number.

Tossing my phone on the bed, I slumped onto the edge and dropped my head in my hands. My phone dinged again, pulling my eyes to the small screen. "Fuck." Another text came in but from a different woman this time. My reputation was catching up with me and it wasn't something I was proud of.

Before I could think twice on it, I picked up my phone, went through my contacts, and started deleting and blocking every woman's number I had. Unless they were family, an actual friend, or Tabatha, they were getting removed.

When I was finally done, I slumped back onto my bed and stared up at the ceiling. I didn't even need a cold shower now. Never, not once in my life, had I thought about removing women's numbers from my phone. It was my little black book and had been so for as long as I could remember. Tabatha had me unraveled and I didn't even know her. Not really. But I knew that she wouldn't take my shit. I learned that rather quickly and fuck me, it turned me on.

She wanted me to prove it. Prove what exactly, I wasn't sure, but I would. If I spent the rest of my days proving it, I sure as fuck would. No matter how long it took.

FOUR

Tabatha

ASHTON: WHAT ARE YOU wearing?

Me: Nothing.

Ashton: Marry me.

I couldn't help but laugh at his demand for marriage. It was flattering to say the least. But still odd as hell.

I had known Ashton for a week.

Seven days.

One-hundred and sixty-eight hours.

He texted me every day and proposed.

Every. Single. Day.

Most would think it was innocent but my assumptions about him had been correct. He *was* a player, never having had a serious relationship in his whole entire life. Why he felt the need to pursue me, was enough to drive me mad. Maybe he lost a bet.

I tried not to think about him. I tried not to think about how this beautiful but frustrating man, proposed.

After a week, the texts became more. He would wish me a good morning and tell me to have a good day and then I wouldn't hear from him for a few hours when he proposed again. Then he would text again later at night to tell me to sleep well.

I found that I looked forward to them even though I really wished I didn't. It had been something small and even though that had been the case, I could feel a piece of my wall cracking.

Ashton hadn't shown up at the bar since the first time I met him, but his brother had been there. I quickly learned that drinking was like a noose around Aiden's neck. It wasn't my business, but I still found myself keeping an eye on him anyway.

One night, Natalie had me working behind the bar. I had spent my whole time working at Scooters helping the cook and just staying unnoticed in the back. But we were suddenly short-staffed, so she had me helping out front every chance she could. I tried arguing with her originally, saying that no one wanted the pink-haired girl with all of the tattoos serving them food and drinks. It was a lame argument on my part but it had been worth the shot.

Scooter kept a close eye on me, Natalie, and a couple of the other girls who worked there. It helped that my brothers showed up from time to time as well. I had tried fighting Natalie at first but apparently people liked the pink-haired, tattooed girl. Tips were high which earned me praises from my co-workers and Scooter himself.

"Woman, get us a drink. Us men are thirsty."

I rolled my eyes and began pouring three pitchers of beer. "Must you be a chauvinistic pig, Beck?"

He chuckled, sitting on the stool across the bar from me. "Phoenix has a fight this weekend."

My eyes shot to his. "Scooter was able to get a hold of him finally?"

"Sounds like it." My oldest foster brother, Beck Rhodes, reached across the bar and grabbed three glasses as he was joined by our other foster brothers, Jonah Scott and Phoenix Vos.

"Hey, Sis," they both said at the same time.

"Hi." I placed the pitchers on the bar in front of them. "Just in time. Because apparently you men are thirsty."

They laughed, which only made me smile in return.

"So, Beck told me you have a fight this weekend," I said to Phoenix.

He looked down at his beer, giving his shoulders a small shrug. "I guess. I'm sure it'll be an easy win. Scooter doesn't like giving me a challenge."

"You guys need to get your brewery up and running, so you don't have to do this shit to make ends meet," I told them, pointing out the obvious.

Phoenix grunted, licking along his lip piercing. "Yeah, well. A little pain never hurt no one."

"We're trying to get our brewery up, but these things take time." Beck looked down at his phone. "Which reminds me. I need to make some calls." He left the bar to go outside while I went about serving other customers.

About an hour later, I was placing another round of pitchers in front of the guys when the hairs on the back of my neck tingled. I looked up, finding Ashton looking directly at me. His brother headed to a stool at the end of the bar.

"Hello, Kitten," Ashton purred, his light blue eyes dropping to my mouth.

As soon as that pet name left his mouth, I winced.

"Just who the fuck do you think you're calling Kitten?" Beck demanded, shoving from his stool.

"Shit," I muttered, rushing around the bar.

Beck got in Ashton's face. "Answer the damn question."

"Beck, stop." I grabbed his arm, trying to pull him away from Ashton, but of course he was too strong for me.

"I don't know who the hell you think you are, but you need to back off," Ashton growled, stepping toe-to-toe with him.

"Guys, a little help here?" When neither Phoenix nor Jonah moved from their stools, I let out a huff. "Fine."

"It's warranted, Tabs," Jonah finally said.

"No, it's not." I pushed my way between Beck and Ashton. "Stop this now. This is my place of work." I was vaguely aware of the other customers watching the whole exchange.

"Problem?" Scooter asked, taking that moment to join our little party.

"Nope." Ashton looked down at me, his finger brushing along the side of my hand. "No problem."

Beck's eyes dropped, catching the movement. "Outside."

"No." I pushed him back and spun on Ashton. "Stop pissing him off."

Ashton only smirked before pulling away to join his brother at the other end of the bar.

"What the hell was that?" I asked Beck.

"Who is he to you?" he asked me instead of answering my question.

"No one." I went back behind the bar. "I met him here one night. Not that I have to explain myself to you."

The guys grunted.

"Fucker keeps looking at her," Phoenix grumbled.

Jonah leaned over, looking down the length of the bar. "I don't know. He seems harmless."

"Did you see the way he looked at her?" Beck threw at him. "That shit isn't harmless. It's how I look at women when I want to fuck them."

"I'm right here." I slapped the bar top when none of them looked my way and only continued talking amongst themselves.

"Not used to this shit. Usually Tabs tells them to leave her alone," Jonah muttered, sipping at his beer.

"I don't like it." Phoenix shook his head. "I don't like it at all."

"We can't have some fucker looking at her like that." Beck scowled. "It's not right."

"Hey, assholes." I slapped the bar top again. "I'm right here. And what goes on in my personal life is none of your business."

The guys looked between each other, back to Ashton, then to me, then to each other.

"It *is* our business when one, you live with us, two, Sarge asked us to look out for you and three..." Jonah thought a moment. "If this guy is anything like Beck, we have bigger problems than we thought."

Beck only shrugged. "It's true, Tabs."

"Doesn't matter if it's true or not..." I looked down at the end of the bar.

Ashton was talking to his brother. His head turned, his light blue eyes connecting with mine.

My heart jumped, thumping hard in my chest the longer he stared at me. I couldn't explain it but there was something about him that I liked. Especially when he was willing to go toe-to-toe with my brothers.

Moments like that, I wished I had a female friend I could talk to. I got along well enough with the girls I worked with but most just wanted to get close to me so they could get closer to my brothers.

"Tabs."

The abrupt bark of my name, pulled my head around.

I found my brothers staring back at me.

"Leave it alone, guys," I mumbled, going back to serving customers. When it was finally time for my break, I made sure the guys were stocked up on their drinks and headed out of the bar area and to the back. Once I was outside, I breathed in a lungful of fresh air. Something was in the water because the guys usually weren't so damn protective. They had their moments of course but none of the guys I had ever dated had them reacting this way.

Pulling my phone from my back pocket, I started playing one of my many games when a dark shadow loomed over me.

The spicy scent of cologne wafted around me, forcing me to lift my head, and I was met by the bluest eyes I had ever seen.

"You shouldn't be out here," I said but still liking the fact that I was finally alone with Ashton.

He smirked, giving his shoulders a small shrug. "Free country, Kitten."

"You need to stop calling me that. Beck almost ripped your face off because of that nickname," I reminded him.

Ashton chuckled, taking a step toward me. "He could try."

"What do you want?" I asked, my voice not coming out as sure as I had hoped.

"I want to take you on a date." He pulled away from me and moved to the picnic bench sitting by the wall. He sat on the table top, patted the empty spot beside him, and waited.

Swallowing a sigh, I joined him. Part of me wondered what the hell I was getting myself into but then the other part, the part that had been lonely for years, appreciated the attention. I longed for a guy I could go home to. One I could curl up with at night, read books with, joke and laugh about nothing at all, yet someone who could fuck my brains out just the same. But then the sensical part, the part I tried to ignore, knew it could never happen.

"Who are those guys to you?" Ashton asked, his knee brushing against mine.

I opened my mouth with the intention of telling him that it was none of his business but then his words from the first time I met him, slid through my mind.

"What the hell have I ever done to you?"

Nothing, he hadn't done anything at all, but it still didn't mean I couldn't be cautious and maybe give a little at the same time.

"Beck, Jonah, and Phoenix are my brothers."

"Huh."

I looked at Ashton then, wondering what that single word meant. "Why?"

His head slowly turned in my direction, his eyes dropping to my mouth. "I thought maybe you dated the guy who got in my face, but I think them being your brothers is worse."

I laughed, shaking my head. "Yeah, they're a little protective but no, I haven't dated them. We grew up together."

"You grew up together." He frowned. "What do you mean?"

My cheeks heated at my slipup. "They're my foster brothers." I jumped off the table and put some distance between us. I didn't like how easy it was to talk to Ashton. I didn't like that no matter how hard I tried pushing him away, I wanted him close instead.

"What's wrong?" he asked, pushing off the table. He took a tentative step toward me, his big body shadowing over me. "Tabatha."

"I don't know you." I was suddenly feeling cornered. The hairs on my body tingled, my heart racing to the point I was surprised he couldn't hear it himself.

Ashton took another step closer. "No, you don't know me, and I don't know you. But we will get to know each other. Even if I have to come to this bar every damn night while you're working. Or if I have to play nice and befriend your brothers, I will."

I frowned, staring up at him. "Why would you do that?"

"Because there's something about you that I need." His voice was gentle, low, and smooth. He stood about a foot away from me but a part of me, that dangerous part that didn't know any better, wanted him closer.

"I don't want a relationship," I told him.

"What *do* you want?" Ashton reached out and pushed a strand of my hair behind my ear. "If you could have anything at all, Kitten, what would it be?"

I licked my lips, my mouth suddenly dry. I wanted to be healthy, but I didn't know him well enough to tell him that. "Happiness."

He tilted his head. "You're not happy?"

I shrugged because what more could I do? He was practically a stranger, a pushy one mind you, but a stranger nonetheless. The guys would kill me if I gave in and told him my deepest darkest secrets and so soon.

"I'm happy enough," I told him, stepping away from him. But I wasn't quick enough when Ashton caught my hand. "Ashton."

"One date." He linked his fingers in mine, that single touch sending a hot shiver down my spine. His big hand engulfed mine but it made me feel safe. I had always felt safe with my brothers but this was different. I had never felt safe with any of the guys I had ever been with, so I was always the first to break it off before they could. It also saved my heart from getting hurt in the process.

"Why?" I asked, looking up at him then.

"Because I like you," he murmured, his voice low. His thumb brushed back and forth over my wrist.

"You don't know me," I reminded him.

"Nope." He leaned down to my ear. "But you seem to know me very well. You had me pegged for an obnoxious asshole the first time we met." His mouth ran along the shell of my ear. "Isn't that right, Kitten?"

"I wasn't wrong though, was I?" I turned my head, our lips lightly grazing each other.

"You weren't but it doesn't mean I like being called out on my shit." His mouth slid down the length of my jaw.

A husky laugh left me. "Looks like someone doesn't like being reminded of his faults."

He grunted. "Could say the same for you, baby girl."

"I have no faults." I pushed away from him then, needing some space between us. "I'm perfect." I winked.

Ashton chuckled. "Alright, Tabatha. I'll give you that."

"I was kidding." My laugh deepened. "I'm not perfect at all."

His eyes roamed down the length of me. "From where I'm standing, all I see is perfection." He gave me a wink himself and walked away from me, leaving me standing there wondering what just happened and why the hell I wanted to follow him.

FIVE

ASHTON

TABATHA WAS GOING TO be a tough one to break. She had walls built up higher than most of the people I knew. Hell, more than even myself. Not that my walls were up for any reason in particular. They were just…there.

She had been right in saying that I didn't want a relationship. I wasn't built for it. My dad had been the same way before he finally admitted his feelings for his best friend, which happened to be our mother. But I never wanted more than a hard fuck. Not until I met Tabatha. She still hadn't agreed to go on a date with me, so I needed to figure out another way to get her to crack. Maybe I would just have to hang around like I said I would.

After I left Tabatha out back, I went to join my brother back at the bar. But what I found instead was him chatting it up with Tabatha's brothers. When I neared them, all heads turned my way.

The guy I now knew as Beck, narrowed his brows in the middle, crossing his arms under his chest.

Tabatha had given me the names for the other guys, Jonah and Phoenix, but I didn't know who was who.

"Making new friends, Aiden?" I asked my brother, sitting on the nearest stool beside him.

"Just playing nice while you sniff around their sister," he threw back at me.

"Ass," I grumbled.

His lips pulled up into a small smile.

I stared at him. That single move had been something I hadn't seen in such a long time, I wasn't sure if I was seeing things. My brother had…issues, to say the least, and smiling was something he hardly ever did anymore.

When he caught me staring, that smile fell.

My stomach sunk but at least it was a start.

The hairs on my body tingled and I knew that Tabatha was around. Was it like this for everyone? Could they sense each other in the same room without even having to look? Was that even possible?

All of the people I had grown up with were either getting married or already married, and most even had kids. Aiden, myself, and another guy we knew and used to hang around were still single. But I knew that it wouldn't last long for that mutual friend of ours.

A melodious laugh brought my head around. Tabatha was chatting with her brothers, laughing at whatever shit they had to say to her. It was nice to know that I didn't have to worry about any of them being exes of hers but being family could be worse. I clearly had my work cut out for me.

"Ashton."

I grimaced as Natalie approached me.

"How's it going?" she asked, sitting on the stool beside me. Her knees brushed my outer thigh. She leaned forward, pulling her long blonde hair over one shoulder. Her top left little to the imagination when the deep vee in the white fabric showcased full breasts. The shirt was tucked into tight blue jeans that I was sure would cause a reaction in most men. It did for me at one time or another, but not anymore.

"You free tonight?" Natalie asked instead of waiting for me to answer her first question. She licked along her full bottom lip, her green eyes zeroing in on me. She was beautiful and she sure as hell used to be my type, but it was like as soon as I met Tabatha, my dick no longer worked for anyone but her. And we hadn't even fucked yet.

I suddenly felt eyes on me. Several pairs of them in fact. It was like everyone stopped talking the moment Natalie sat down beside me.

Tabatha's brothers were watching the whole exchange and so was she. She pretended to be focused on making drinks, but I could see her looking my way every so often.

"Ashton." Natalie placed her hand on my inner thigh. "I've missed you."

"And clearly you've become desperate too." I removed her hand from my thigh.

Her eyes widened a bit, her cheeks turning a dark shade of red.

"I told you that I'm not interested. What part of that wasn't clear?"

"I thought you were kidding," she confessed. "And I thought you'd be bored by now and would want some fun."

"If I said that to you, I would be considered a predator. It's the same thing, doesn't matter that you have a pussy, Natalie." I shot up from the stool. "No means fucking no." Instead of waiting for my brother like I usually did, I left the bar, slamming the door open. The sun had finally set, much like my mood.

"Ashton."

I spun around, finding Tabatha running toward me.

"Are you okay?"

"Why do you care?" I asked, my voice curt. It wasn't fair of me, but it also wasn't fair of her to assume I was like the previous guys she dated. Even though it was true, I was trying to change.

"I deserve that." She took a deep breath, looking back over her shoulder toward the entrance of the bar. "Natalie comes on a little strong."

"She texted me the other night. I told her that I wasn't interested, and I also told her to lose my number. I ended up deleting all of the women's numbers I had in my contacts list." I shoved my hands in my pockets and started pacing.

"Why would you do that?" Tabatha asked, taking a step toward me.

"Because I don't want you thinking that I just want to go on a date so I can get a piece of ass. Have I done that before? Yes. I won't lie to you and say I haven't. But people can change, Kitten. And you make me want to be a better man. For you. I don't give a shit about anyone else." I stopped pacing, waiting for her to respond. "Was that too honest for you?"

Her lips pressed into a thin line when a laugh bubbled through her. "I wasn't expecting that actually. Most people keep those truths locked up tight. Or at least for a while. But we met, what, a week ago? Maybe a little longer? It's refreshing actually, hearing you tell me how you feel."

I shrugged. "I meant what I said, Kitten. I like you."

"You don't even know me to like me. I could be a raging bitch or a lunatic or…" She chewed her bottom lip. A lip *I* wanted to bite.

"I know you enough. Is this all new for me? Yes. It is. And it's making me lose sleep at night." I had never meant to confess that last part. Tabatha was right. I didn't know her, but I wanted to. Fuck me, did I ever want to get to know her.

"You're losing sleep?" She tilted her head. "How come?"

"Don't play innocent with me, Tabatha. You know exactly why I'm losing sleep." My dick swelled the longer we stood there in silence, staring at each other.

With my hand in my pocket, I shifted from one foot to the other. My pants tightened, my finger grazing over the length of my cock.

Tabatha's eyes fell to my waist, her lips parting.

Clearing my throat, I smirked.

Her gaze shot to mine. "Ashton."

I chuckled, shaking my head. "Can't help how my body reacts to you, baby. My dick likes what he sees."

"Your dick needs to move on," she mumbled.

"Not happening." If I had to beg at her feet, I would.

"Well…" She looked back at the bar. "I don't know what's going on between you and Natalie." She met my gaze then. "But it isn't right for a woman or a man to press for something when you clearly said no and that you're no longer interested."

At the mention of Natalie, I scowled. It changed the mood from light and flirty to dark and disturbing.

"It just pisses me off that some people think they can get away with it. Yes, I have a reputation. I know that and I'm not proud of that fact, but I'm trying to change things." I took a step toward Tabatha, needing her eyes focused solely on me and me alone. I wasn't sure why, but I craved her attention, her touch, her using my name whether it be because she screamed it or used it when she was annoyed with me. I didn't care.

"You don't have to change for me," Tabatha murmured, her voice soft.

I closed that last little bit of space between us and cupped her jaw. "I'm not changing for you. Yes, you're part of the reason, but I'm mostly doing this for myself. My mom is on us to give her grandbabies. Not that I'm thinking about kids yet, but I did mean that question I've asked every day since I first met you."

She swallowed hard. "The answer is still no."

"For now." I kissed the soft spot by her ear. "I know when no means no. Unless it's when we're fucking and no actually means to go harder and faster."

"Why, Ashton. Whatever do you mean?" She laughed. "I'm a good girl."

"Sure, you are." I scoffed. "I bet you're fucking filthy in bed, Kitten."

"Hmmm…" Her gray eyes flicked to mine. "Guess you'll just have to wait and see but I could be boring. A lazy lay."

"Ha." I tapped her nose. "You're funny. I have a feeling that you're nasty as fuck."

Her cheeks turned pink, a grin spreading on her face. "I have no idea what you're talking about."

I chuckled, mentally patting myself on the back that I was slowly getting through to her.

"Come back inside. I can get you a beer. On me."

"I'd love to drink a beer off of you." I waggled my eyebrows.

"That's not what I meant." She laughed, linked her arm in mine, and started leading us back to the door to the bar.

"Why, Kitten, are we becoming friends?" I pulled my arm from hers and wrapped it around her shoulders before placing a kiss on top of her head.

"Maybe we are, Ashton." She smiled up at me. "Maybe we are."

(Tabatha)

I couldn't help the friendship brewing between Ashton and I. Even though I had only just met him, there was something about him that made me feel like I was at home. Add to the fact that he proposed the first night I met him and every day since, it sparked something in me I had never felt before. I was still cautious, especially due to my health and my personal history with abandonment issues, but everyone could always use a new friend, could they not?

Once Ashton and I stepped into the bar, all heads turned our way. Beck stood from his stool. Jonah chuckled. Phoenix just shook his head.

I rolled my eyes.

Ashton hugged me into his side closer, trying to bait the guys into doing something, no doubt. His lips brushed along the shell of my ear. "I've never been into public displays of affection but if they don't stop glaring at me every time I touch you, I'll do more than just hug you in front of them."

I stared up at him. "You don't need to pee on me to stake your claim, Ashton." Pushing away from him, I went back around the bar and ignored the incessant stares coming from the guys.

Thankfully, the rest of the night was drama free from my foster brothers. They only continued to get drunk and by the time my shift was over, Jonah and Phoenix had to hold Beck up as he stumbled between them.

"See you at home," I called out to them as they practically dragged Beck home.

"See you later, Tabs," Jonah said, placing a wad of cash on the bar top.

"Be safe."

"We will." Phoenix gave Ashton a final look and left the bar with Beck and Jonah.

"Alright, Aiden, we should go." Ashton helped his brother to his feet.

He wobbled, pinched the bridge of his nose, and let out a slow breath. "I think I drank too much."

Ashton didn't say anything, but I could see the look on his face where he wanted to tell his brother that he had, in fact, drank too much. But if Aiden *did* have a drinking problem like Ashton said he did, telling him so might not end well for either of them.

"Have a good night, guys," I told them.

"What time are you done?" Ashton asked me, holding his brother up beside him.

"I'm technically done now but I usually stay and help Scooter with some paperwork," I told him. "Why?"

"How are you getting home?"

"I usually walk." I only lived a couple of blocks from the bar. In the neighborhood I lived in, everyone knew everyone, so we watched out for each other.

"I'll bring Aiden home and then come pick you up."

"Oh." My heart jumped. "Okay. Thank you."

Ashton nodded once and left the bar with his brother.

Would this be Ashton's way of taking me on a date? Not that much was open at this time. There was a deli close by that was open all night, but I wasn't hungry. If Ashton wanted to get to know me like he said he did, going somewhere that could possibly be loud and busy, wouldn't help.

"Are you seeing Ashton?"

My head lifted, finding Natalie scowling at me with her hands on her hips.

I looked around the bar, realizing that we were alone minus the few customers who always stayed until Scooter kicked them out.

"Tabby."

I raised an eyebrow at the rough use of my name. "Whatever you're implying, Natalie, it hasn't happened. Even if it had, it's really none of your business." I always liked her, but I didn't appreciate being accused of something I hadn't done.

"I like him," she told me, the hard lines of her face softening.

"Have you told him that?" A sour taste filled my mouth at the thought of Ashton and her being together. Well, that was new.

"I tried but he's not interested." She sighed, slumping down onto a stool. "I thought we had a good thing, but I guess I got my hopes up. I'm sorry. I shouldn't be a bitch to you. It's not your fault. And it's not even his. It wasn't like he wasn't honest with me and told me what he wanted and didn't want."

"Could have been worse I guess," I said, not liking this sense of jealousy rushing through me. "He could have lied and led you on."

"Yeah, I know. Oh well." She clapped her hands together, rising from the stool. "I'll find someone else to warm my bed at night."

I laughed, shaking my head. "I'm sure you will." She was beautiful and I knew that a lot of the customers who came into Scooters would love to have a night with her. She always turned them down and now I understood why.

Making sure to check in with Scooter himself, I found him in his office, slumped over a pile of paperwork. "Did you need my help?"

His head lifted. "Nah, go home, darling. Just be safe."

"Always." I gave him a small wave and went to quietly shut the door behind me when his next words stopped me.

"Actually, can you ask Natalie to come see me please?"

"Of course." Grabbing my things from the staff room first, I made my way back out to the bar and relayed Scooter's message to Natalie.

Her face fell, almost like she just got caught with her hand in the cookie jar. "Did he say what he wanted?"

"No, just that he wanted you to come to his office." I paused. "Is something wrong?"

She laughed, rubbing the back of her neck before smoothing down her t-shirt. "Wrong? No, nothing's wrong. At all."

Instead of saying more, she quickly left the bar and headed down the hall that led to Scooter's office.

I shouldn't have followed but curiosity got the better of me, so I did.

Natalie stood outside Scooter's office door. She took a deep breath and then another before knocking.

When the door opened, a hand reached out, capturing Natalie by the throat.

My eyes widened, my chest tightening that something bad was about to go down.

Scooter stepped out into the hallway, crushing his mouth down hard on hers.

She melted into him, snaking her arms around his neck.

He cupped her ass, picked her up, and carried her into his office. Once the door slammed shut a moment later, a breath of relief left me. I didn't think Scooter had been that type of guy but I had never seen him with anyone either. So, I was thankful that my assumptions about him being a good man, were true.

I had never been into voyeurism, but I swore that was the hottest thing I had ever laid eyes on. I had no idea that Scooter and Natalie had a thing. Maybe he found out about Ashton and was pissed. I wasn't sure but I made a mental note to see if I could ask Natalie about it.

Shoving aside my creepy stalker tendencies, I said goodbye to everyone and left the bar.

I walked one block before a dark car pulled up beside me. My heart jumped to my throat, a tremor of fear slicing over my skin.

"Kitten."

A breath of relief left me at Ashton's voice.

"Sorry I'm late," he said from the driver's side. He pulled the car to a stop.

"Everything okay?" I asked, slipping into the passenger seat.

"Yeah." He gave me a small smile. "Nothing to worry about."

"You sure?" I asked, noticing the tension rolling off of him.

His jaw clenched, his hand gripping the steering wheel. "I am," he finally said, pulling the car away from the curb.

I wasn't sure where he was taking me, but I found that I liked this. Being alone with him. We didn't have to worry about my family, or Natalie, or anyone. It was just us.

Even though he told me he was sure, I could still see the stiffness of his body. "Give me your hand."

Ashton frowned but did as he was told.

I linked my fingers in his, holding his hand on my lap.

He let out a sigh. "Thank you."

"You're welcome." Leaning my head against the seat, I watched the world outside pass us by. "Everything okay with Aiden?"

"For now." Ashton pulled his hand from mine, placing his on my inner thigh.

Clearing my throat, I shifted in the seat, trying not to make it obvious how I noticed that his grip was firm. Or the fact that I was wearing shorts and his touch heated my skin.

Ashton brushed his thumb back and forth over my inner thigh. "So, tell me, Kitten. How many tattoos and piercings do you have?"

"It's a secret," I laughed, giving him a wink.

He chuckled.

"You never know, Ashton. Maybe one day I'll let you count them."

His head whipped around. "Don't tease me like that."

A giggle escaped me.

"Fucking women," he grumbled.

Turning my body toward him, I wrapped a hand around his forearm. "Where are we going?"

"I'd say we're going on a date, but you haven't given me a yes yet. I'd take you to get fucking married, but you haven't given me a yes there either. So, for now, we're just driving until you tell me to pull over somewhere."

"What would you want to do if we did pull over?" I asked him, running my hand down his arm and pushing his hand higher up my thigh.

"Uh…" His eyes dropped to my lap. "I feel like I'm twelve again and have no idea what to do when a beautiful pussy is near."

"How do you know it's beautiful?" I teased, pulling his hand even higher until the backs of his knuckles pressed against my center. It had been a long time since I had done anything sexual with a guy. A little fun wouldn't hurt either of us. I didn't want a relationship. It didn't matter that he was now ready for one because I never would be.

Ashton also needed to learn that he couldn't get everything he wanted when he wanted it.

"Every pussy is beautiful, Kitten," he said, his eyes flicking between where his hand rested and the road in front of us.

"Keep driving, Ashton."

"You're killing me here," he mumbled.

"Good." Pushing his hand away, I unbuttoned my shorts and slid them down my legs.

His eyes dropped back to my center, his throat working over a hard swallow.

"What do you like, Ashton? Do you like being in control?" I grabbed his hand, placing it high on my inner thigh. "Or do you like being the one controlled?"

"I like being in control," he answered. "But that's hard to do while I'm driving."

"Exactly." I leaned back against the door, a soft sigh leaving me as his fingers grazed over the crotch of my black thong. "Most of my tattoos are hidden. I got them for me and any that you can see are because I want you to see them."

"I like the ones I can see. Especially your bows."

I only smiled, knowing the day would eventually come where I felt his mouth grazing along every single black line on my body.

"The guys have a poker night every Wednesday," I told him. "You should come over. Since you want to take me on a date and all."

"I want to date you, not your brothers." He brushed his knuckle along the crotch of my thong.

"I know but I need to make sure that they…"

"Approve of me?" Ashton asked, pulling his hand from between my legs and reaching for the waist. He hooked his fingers into the band and lowered the tiny fabric as I lifted my hips to help him. He took the fabric, reached over, and popped open the glove compartment. "For later." He winked, putting my panties away and closing the door.

"What do you have planned for later?"

"I'm going to jerk off with your panties wrapped around my dick."

"Oh." I swallowed a gasp. "Is that all?"

"You never answered my question." Ashton cupped my knee, sliding his hand ever so slowly up my inner thigh.

Bringing my feet to the cushion beneath me, I pulled my bent knees up to my chest. "They never approved of anyone I've ever dated, so yes, I need them to approve of you."

"Fair enough." Ashton nodded toward me. "Hold on to your knees and bring your sweet pussy closer."

My core clenched at the soft but curt demand. Inching my ass a little closer, I held my knees against my chest and leaned back against the door.

"Fuck," he groaned, his eyes dropping to the apex between my thighs.

"Is it beautiful like you said it would be?" I purred.

"It's more." He licked his lips, brushing the tips of his fingers along my slit. "So much more."

Chewing my bottom lip, I closed my eyes as the surge of pleasure erupted through me.

"Definitely more," he growled, shoving two fingers into me in one smooth move.

I cried out, my eyes popping open.

"So damn tight, Kitten." He pumped his hand against me. "My dick is going to break your cunt whenever we get a chance to fuck."

It was on the tip of my tongue to be a brat and argue with him but by the way his fingers stretched me, I could only imagine that the rest of him was big too.

"You thought you were in control of this, didn't you?" he asked, slipping another finger into me.

I whimpered, glancing down between my legs and watching his fingers slide in and out of my body. "I was trying to be in control but god, Ashton, that feels good."

"I need to pull over."

Before I had a chance to argue, the car swerved off to the side of the road. Ashton had his hand removed from between my legs and, the next thing I knew, my door was opened.

"What are you doing?" I reached for my shorts that were on the floor of the car when he pulled me into his arms.

He lifted me out of the car and dropped me on the hood at the same time he crushed his mouth to mine.

I sighed, my eyes fluttering closed. The kiss turned deep and frantic fast. I ran my hand through his hair, wrapping my legs around his waist.

"I need to taste you," he whispered, sucking my lip piercing between his teeth.

A hot shiver trembled through me. God, I wanted that too. I wanted him. I wanted it all. But it was too soon. I wasn't new to having one-night stands, but I didn't want that. Not yet anyway.

Ashton lifted his head, staring down at me. "What's wrong?"

"Nothing." I looked away, not liking how his eyes appeared to be searching for something.

"Tabatha, talk to me." He kissed the side of my neck, sinking his teeth into my jaw. "Words, baby."

"I don't want to be another notch on your bedpost," I blurted, my cheeks heating.

"You won't be." Ashton kissed me softly on the mouth. "I don't want you to be a notch either and besides, we're not having sex tonight."

"Isn't that what you want?" Because I knew I sure as hell did. No matter how hard I tried denying it, I was definitely attracted to him.

"Of course, I want it but not tonight. I do want a little something though." His mouth found the side of my neck. "How many piercings do you have, Kitten?"

A breathless laugh left me, knowing he was about to find my favorites. "You're about to find out."

Ashton's chuckle vibrated against my skin. "Let's take a look." He moved down the length of me, pushing my shirt to just beneath my breasts. When he glanced down, his eyes shot to mine. "Fuck."

A laugh bubbled through me. "Like them?"

He looked down again. "I've never...I didn't feel them when I fingered you...I just...*fuck.*"

"The two between my legs are my favorites," I told him, breathless.

A wicked grin spread on his face before he lowered to his knees.

SIX

ASHTON

I HAD NEVER BEEN with a woman who had any part of her pussy pierced, let alone two parts. I didn't know what they were called. One was just above her clit, and one was directly in that beautiful little nub. The pain she went through must have been intense, but I didn't judge. Especially when it was hot as fuck.

I made a mental note to Google the names for them later but for now, I was going to get acquainted with every inch of Tabatha's pussy.

She also had three diamonds lined diagonally in her left hip, just above an infinity tattoo, which was also hot as hell.

Lowering my mouth to her inner thigh, I brushed my lips up the length of it. I wanted to savor her, get used to her scent and flavor but I was obsessed and needed to know what she tasted like. Hooking my hands under the backs of her thighs, I pushed her knees higher and shoved my face against her.

Tabatha cried out, a soft curse leaving her as a surge of wetness coated my tongue. I licked along the diamonds that started from the top of her mound, down to the last one sitting just beneath her clit. She moaned, a hard shiver trembling through her.

Oh yeah, these piercings were definitely my favorite.

Her flavor exploded on my tongue, the acidic scent of her making me dizzy. I had never tasted something so damn good.

"Ashton," she moaned.

Flicking my tongue back and forth along the piercings and her swollen clit, I held one arm against her legs and pushed them higher up toward her chest.

The movement made her open even more for me.

"God, Ashton." She trembled beneath me.

"I want your cum soaking the hood of my car, baby." I slowly thrust my thumb into her.

Her chest rose and fell with ragged breaths, her gray eyes searing into me.

I was thankful I left the headlights on so I could see the flush in her cheeks.

"Please." She arched her back, lifting her hips up and down in tune with the gentle thrusts of my thumb. "God, that feels good."

I growled, shook my head against her, and slipped my thumb from her cunt before sliding two fingers into her roughly.

She cried out, her hands latching on to my head and pulling me closer.

My dick was rock hard, but this was all for her. I loved when a woman couldn't control it and did anything to get that orgasm.

"Harder," Tabatha whimpered. "Please."

Slipping a third finger into her, I pushed my hand against her as deep as her body would allow.

A shattered scream exploded from her lips as a gush of liquid sprayed my hand. Taking that as a sign, I began pumping my hand against her, needing another orgasm from her.

My name left her lips. Her knees tried locking around my head, but I didn't let up until she came again for a second time.

Once she calmed down, I pulled my hand from between her legs and wiped my fingers along her stomach and inner thighs. I did it as a reminder to show her how I could make her feel.

"Wow." She sighed, covering her eyes with her arm.

Sliding back up the length of her body, I rested my elbows on either side of her head and placed a peck on her mouth.

She dropped her arm to the side, deepening the kiss.

"Thank you, Kitten," I whispered.

She reached between us and grabbed on to my belt.

"No." I covered her hands and pulled away. "Not tonight."

"But…" She frowned. "Really?"

I grabbed her hand and helped her off the hood. "I can wait for sex, Kitten."

"Huh. And here I assumed you were a selfish bastard." She cupped me over my jeans. "Guess I was wrong."

Wrapping my arm around her waist, I pulled her flush against me. "Trust me, baby, I *can* be a selfish bastard but tonight I just wanted to eat your pussy. You haven't agreed to go on a date with me yet, so we're going to take this slow."

She stared up at me, pulling her hand away from me.

I caught her wrist, putting her hand back against my crotch where it belonged. "This is yours. Whenever you want it. But not tonight. As much as I want your juicy tight as fuck cunt sucking all the cum out of me, something tells me you're not ready."

Her jaw clenched, her eyes looking away. "I want you. I think we both know how much I want you. Even though I know I shouldn't. But…" She sighed, giving me a final squeeze before taking a step away from me. "Thank you."

"Of course." I moved around to the driver's side and slipped into the car as she sat beside me.

Tabatha pulled her shorts back on, going commando. "Figured you could keep my panties as a souvenir."

I chuckled. "You read my mind, baby girl."

She winked, grabbed my hand, and placed it on her inner thigh. "Thank you for wanting to take it slow and for knowing that I need it."

"I haven't been known to be a good guy," I confessed. "Not with women anyway. But I want to be. I'm trying anyway."

"We've all done something we regret, Ashton. We're only human. We make mistakes."

"Yeah, I know." Only when we got back to the city, did I break the comfortable silence between us. "I had fun tonight."

"Me too." Tabatha covered my hand. "A lot actually."

"Oh, I know." I winked at her. "Your pussy gushed fucking hard."

"That's one of my many talents."

My head whipped around.

A sly grin spread on her face.

"Fucking hell, woman."

"I've never been with a guy who thought it was hot though."

"It is hot." I shook my head. "Very fucking hot. It also means that I'm doing something right if I can make a woman squirt like that."

"Thank you for not being weird about it."

"Never." I squeezed her thigh. "You don't have to worry about that when it comes to me, baby. Promise." And I meant what I said. Female ejaculation was one of the hottest things I could get a woman to do. Also made me feel damn proud of myself at the same time.

Tabatha gave me her address and directed me where to go to drop her off at home. Once I had the car outside her building, I frowned when I saw that it didn't look like an apartment building.

"The top floor is a loft that I share with the guys. The ground floor has a gym. My brothers and I work out here from time to time, but we also know the owner. He gave us a good deal on the loft."

I stared at her, mulling over her words and trying to think twice about what I wanted to say before saying it. "You live with the guys? How many guys?"

Tabatha rolled her eyes. "What did I tell you before? I haven't slept with them. I'm not sleeping with them. And I won't sleep with them. Also, whose face was between my legs not even half an hour ago? Yours. Not any of theirs. So enough with this jealousy bullshit, Ashton. Because I won't put up with it."

"Have they hinted for more?" I turned toward her. "You may not want anything from them romantically, but they could."

"No." She laughed. "Trust me, Ashton. Nothing like that will ever happen."

"Are you sure? I mean, are you sure they won't hit on you and..." When my words trailed off, I waited. Because I knew that if I kept on talking, I was bound to say something stupid.

Tabatha opened her mouth to say something but must have thought better of her own words too. "Beck doesn't want a relationship. He's like you that way. Or how you used to be anyway. Jonah is focused on the career they're all trying to build. And Phoenix would probably rather play with you, than me."

I raised an eyebrow. "He's gay?"

She laughed. "If only it were that simple. He's never put a label on it and said it's because he doesn't want to be just one thing. He wants to be many things, whatever that means."

"Maybe he's pansexual." I scratched my jaw. "But whatever he's into, as long as he's safe, that's all that matters."

Tabatha stared at me.

"What?"

"I wasn't expecting you to be so cool about..." She waved her hand in front of her. "Things."

"Trust me, babe." I grunted. "As long as you and I are good, I'm cool about anything."

"We're good," she reassured me. "But I still don't want a relationship, so get that out of your head and maybe I'll let you fuck me like I know you want."

Reaching out, I cupped her jaw. "I think it's you who wants me to fuck you more. Remember what happened tonight, baby? You reached for my pants." I kissed the corner of her mouth. "You were going to do something naughty if I wouldn't have stopped you."

"I guess you'll never know now, will you?" she asked, breathlessly.

With a firm grip, I pulled her toward me, covering her mouth with mine. I didn't want to hear any more of her words because I knew, hell, we both knew, that this was far from being over. No matter how much she pushed and shoved me away, she would end up in my bed.

I swallowed her moans and kissed her like she was the last woman I would ever kiss. Maybe she would be.

One could hope.

SEVEN

Tabatha

ASHTON BROKE THE KISS before I could beg for more. I didn't even need to say the words and he knew. How could he not? He ended up kissing me on the nose, gave me a wink, and told me to have a good night. He waited by his car for me to enter the building. When I did, I looked back at him, expecting him to be gone. But when he stood by his car, watching me the whole time to make sure I got inside safely, my heart fluttered.

Shoving those feelings aside, I headed into the building and made my way down the hall that led to the old elevator. It was one of my favorite pieces of this place, even though I had been trapped a few times because the elevator was old and decided to not work at random times. I always sat on the floor in the corner and read. The guys would call the fire department, who would come and give Sarge, the owner of the building and our foster father, a hard time for not keeping the place up to code and I would go on my merry way until the next time it became stuck.

My phone pinged at that moment, pulling me from my thoughts.

Ashton: I had fun tonight, Kitten. Thank you.

I smiled.

Me: I had fun too. Drive safe.

Ashton: Text me when you're in bed.

Me: Why?

Ashton: Because I want a picture. It'll give me something to think of while I'm sleeping.

I laughed.

Me: Or while you jerk off.

Ashton: That too.

Me: Alright, Ashton. It's a deal.

Ashton: Good girl.

My stomach tumbled at those two single words. I was never *that* girl. I didn't need validation from a guy or approval of any kind. But getting it from Ashton meant something different to me. I didn't know what at the moment, but I knew that I liked whatever *it* was.

As much as I tried fighting these feelings, I enjoyed that Ashton was persistent.

Once I reached the floor the loft I shared with my brothers was on, I heard shouting. I tentatively took a step closer to the door, bracing myself for the wrath of whatever woman was pissed off this time because one of my brothers didn't want to commit. They were bachelors, living the single life and didn't want to settle down. Or so they said. I believed it stemmed from them not finding their person yet.

Pulling my keys from my bag, I unlocked the door at the same time as it swung open. A red-faced woman stood in front of me, glaring down at me.

"Who the fuck are you?" she snapped, her eyes filling with unshed tears.

"I live here." I stood up taller and pushed past her, wondering which brother was in the wrong this time.

"You sleeping with them?" she accused.

I glared at her over my shoulder. "I'm their sister if you must know."

Beck took that moment to come around the corner. "I thought you were leaving."

"I am seeing as you're an asshole and don't want to continue this," she cried, throwing her arms up in the air.

Beck stopped beside me and leaned down to my ear. "You're home late."

"I went for a car ride," I told him.

He chuckled, kissing my cheek. "Right and I'm in a committed relationship and want to have a family of my own."

"You do." I patted his arm. "Just not with her."

"Maybe." He sighed. "Were you out with that guy?"

I stared up at him, searching his face. "You going to give me a hard time about it if I say yes?"

"No. Not this time. I'm tired, so I'll keep my thoughts to myself." He winked, pulling away from me.

"Aren't I lucky?" I expected that woman to jump down my throat again but ended up finding that she'd disappeared. "So, was she a friend of yours?" The guys never introduced me to the women they slept with. They always said they would only introduce me if they thought it was going anywhere.

"She wanted more." Beck leaned against the wall opposite me. "I never want more. I told her this, but I guess she figured she could change me." He shrugged. "It's what they all think."

"Ashton asked me to marry him the first day I met him." I braced myself, waiting for Beck to blow up. "He's been asking me every day since too."

"Huh."

I stared at him. "Huh," I repeated. "Really? That's all I'm getting?"

"What more do you want?"

"For you to say something other than *huh*." I shook my head. "You got in his face when he called me *Kitten*."

"Listen." Beck sighed. "I know you're smart and can handle yourself when it comes to guys. Will we be here to protect you anyway? Yes. Always. But I kind of like the fact that this Ashton stood up to me." He shrugged. "Most of the guys you've been with have been pussies."

"Who are you and what have you done with my brother?" I murmured.

Beck chuckled, pushing away from the wall. He came toward me, wrapped an arm around my shoulders, and led me into the open space of our loft. "I love you, Sis, and I know that we've helped put that good head on your shoulders. But just be safe." He kissed my temple. "It's late." He pulled away from me and walked through the kitchen toward his bedroom. "Sleep well, Tabs."

I stared after him.

Once he reached his door, he opened it and stopped abruptly. "What are you doing in here?"

A muffled voice responded.

Beck only shrugged before entering his room and shutting the door behind him.

I wasn't sure exactly what was going on but I had a feeling that Jonah was in that room with Beck. My brothers were into women but never shied away from doing anything with the same sex either.

But Beck not giving me a hard time, wasn't like him. I wasn't sure if something happened or if the guys talked but the fact that Beck didn't question what I was doing with Ashton, but it seemed almost off to me. Not that I wanted him to give me a hard time about it, but the fact that he hadn't was unexpected and I didn't know what to do.

My phone started to buzz. I fished it out of my purse, my heart jumping when I saw that it was Ashton calling me.

"Hi," I greeted.

"Hey, Kitten. You didn't text me, so I wasn't sure if maybe those orgasms knocked you out and you fell asleep."

I laughed, locking up and making my way to my bedroom. "Nah. I ran into one of Beck's latest conquests and she wasn't happy."

"Oh? You okay?"

My heart warmed that he cared about my well-being. "I am. He ended things, she wanted more, you know…the usual shit."

Ashton grunted. "I know that shit all too well."

My stomach twisted. "I bet you do."

"What's that supposed to mean?" he asked, a bite in his tone.

"You know exactly what it means, Ashton." It was on the tip of my tongue to say that I would make him forget every woman he had ever been with. But with a guy like Ashton, I wasn't sure if that was even possible.

"Fine." He sighed. "That's fair. Doesn't mean I like it when it's pointed out though."

Once I slipped into my room, I tossed my bag on a nearby chair and turned on the speaker phone. "I'm sorry. What we do in our past, should stay there." I should listen to my own words, especially when a part of me felt that Ashton wanted one thing and one thing only.

"It should but sometimes that doesn't always happen, Kitten." Ashton cleared his throat. "But you're right. Was I a player? A womanizer? Whatever the hell you want to refer to it as, yes. I was all of that. But then I head to a bar with my brother, go to leave, and see this flash of pink. I've been obsessed ever since."

My stomach tumbled at his honesty. "Really?"

"Yeah, baby. I also like that you told me no right away."

I slumped onto the edge of my bed and laid down. "I didn't think most guys would like that."

He chuckled.

Sitting up, I grabbed my phone and took him off speaker. "Thank you, Ashton. For tonight. I mean that. But I'm not ready for a relationship or even dating off and on again. I do like hanging out with you. So come over next Wednesday. It's poker night for the guys."

"I don't want to hang out with them, Tabatha," he mumbled, the disappointment clear in his deep voice.

"Well, if you want to date me, Ashton, you'll have to become friends with me first. And that includes my brothers."

"Fine. Wednesday it is," he grumbled. "I'm sure I'll see you at the bar before then though."

"Probably." I thought a moment. "How's your brother?"

"Sleeping. Thank you for asking though, Kitten."

"How are *you* doing?" I asked, sitting on my bed and moving up against the headboard.

"I can still taste your pussy, so I'm good."

A husky laugh left me, my cheeks burning. "We could have had sex tonight, Ashton, and I wouldn't have stopped you."

"I know but…"

"What?"

"It's all I've ever done. Fuck and move on. I don't want that anymore."

"Well, aren't you sweet?" I leaned my head back against the headboard, wondering what we were doing but enjoying this new adventure just the same.

"It's getting late, Tabatha. I'll let you go."

"Not yet." I found I wanted to fall asleep to his voice. Which didn't even make sense when I kept him at arm's length. My reaction to him calling me *Kitten*, wasn't a good one, not in the beginning, but now I craved it.

We spent the next hour talking about anything and everything. I learned that most of his friends were actually married already and had babies of their own. When I mentioned that when I first met him, it had only been a guess. I also found out that he wanted a family of his own too, had for awhile, but he never felt a woman was deserving of it. Not until he met me. I wasn't expecting him to tell me that even though it made sense. Especially when he proposed the first time I met him.

Ashton was refreshing. He told me what he wanted and didn't want. He was honest, never kept things inside. I found that I needed to know more, to learn everything there was to know about him. I wanted all of his truths, his secrets, his fantasies, his hopes, and his dreams.

It hit four in the morning before both of us said our goodbyes. When I disconnected the call, I stared at my phone. My heart felt full. But I realized something then. While Ashton gave me a little insight into himself, I didn't give him much in return. He knew I had three foster brothers. They were my life. I never revealed more than that and I wondered why Ashton never pressed for more information about me. Maybe he would in time. But for now, when he didn't, I took it as a sign. For what, I wasn't overly sure, but I had a feeling that I would find out.

Whether I wanted to or not.

EIGHT

ASHTON

IT HAD BEEN A few days since I had seen Tabatha. I went to Scooters regularly with Aiden and didn't see her working. I tried asking Natalie about her, but she shut that shit down and hit on me instead. My assumptions about them being friends didn't last long whenever she made a pass at me. At times I wondered if it was only to piss Scooter off. Especially when he scowled her way and made her work in the back instead of out front like she usually did.

"What's wrong?" Aiden asked from beside me, pulling me from my thoughts. "You're twitchy tonight."

"How do you figure?" The question left my mouth before I could stop myself. I *was* twitchy and I didn't know why. I hadn't seen Tabatha in a handful of days, and it wasn't sitting well with me. We texted and talked on the phone, but she had a wall up. I needed to show her I wasn't that guy anymore. That I could settle down and be committed. I needed to prove that I could be a one-woman man, but I just didn't know how. Maybe I should talk to some of the girls I knew and had grown up with. I could see if they could give me some sort of advice, any advice at all, and go from there.

"You can't seem to sit still," Aiden pointed out, pulling me from my thoughts. "You've constantly been checking your phone over the past couple of days. Every time your phone rings or chimes, you get this goofy look on your face. But when that doesn't happen, you become even more pissed off than me. And that's saying something, brother."

I stared at my twin, not used to him being so observant. "I…"

He chuckled, which again, was something I wasn't used to. Not anymore.

"What's going on with you?" I asked him, knowing it wasn't the place or time, but the question left my lips before I could stop myself. There was no going back now.

"I'll be fine, Ashton," was all he said, but we both knew that if he kept going down the road he was, he would end up hurting himself, or someone else, or worse.

Before I could ask him anything more, the hairs on the back of my neck tingled. Lifting my head, I found Tabatha standing by a booth filled with three guys I didn't know and had never seen before.

Every nerve in my body told me to go to her. To pull her into my arms and kiss the fuck out of her. To claim her, mark her, do everything I could to let people around us know who she belonged to. But I couldn't. Not with someone like her. Tabatha was strong and fierce as hell. Something was weighing on her shoulders. It had been obvious in the many conversations we had when she never gave any insight into herself. I tried asking without actually asking. I wanted her to *want* to give pieces of herself.

"You really like her," Aiden said from beside me.

"Yeah, I do," I told him, not taking my eyes off of Tabatha and the guys she was talking to.

"If you like her like you say you do, then don't cause a scene, Ashton. I can't imagine she's the type of woman who would go for that sort of thing."

He was right, but it didn't mean I had to listen to him. I probably should have. Especially when I stood and the sound of the stool scraping along the floor made Tabatha's head turn my way.

She raised an eyebrow, daring me to go up to her and introduce myself to the fuckers who had her attention.

Pulling my gaze from hers, I noticed the guys sitting in the booth. Two were larger with tattoos lining the sides of their necks. One appeared to be older with a graying beard, but it was almost a contradiction when he had an eyebrow and a lip ring. His nose could have been done too but I couldn't tell from where I was standing.

I went to take a step toward them when another guy leaned around the side of the booth. His eyes locked with mine, a knowing smirk spreading on his face. He was younger than the other two I could see. Maybe my age or a bit younger. Either way, although he appeared to be young, there was an air about him that made me uncomfortable.

As he continued staring my way, Tabatha suddenly stepped into my line of sight. With her hands on her hips, she raised an eyebrow, challenging me to do or say something that I would definitely regret.

Much to my surprise, she came up to me.

"You need to stop."

"I'm not doing anything." I bit back a growl at how fucking good she smelled. Vanilla and spice, it was like she bathed in chai tea.

"No?" She looked over her shoulder before meeting my gaze. "So, if I went back to talking to those guys, you wouldn't do anything? You wouldn't care, Ashton?"

I opened my mouth to answer but thought about how I should respond. "No. I won't do anything, and I wouldn't care either."

Tabatha tilted her head, staring up at me. "Interesting." She spun around and went back up to the table of men.

Before I could stop myself, I took a step toward them when the young guy slipped out of his side of the booth. His eyes locked with mine and much to my dismay, he pulled Tabatha into a hug. His hands got a little too close to her ass. Any lower and he could have reached under her skirt.

My stomach twisted. If we weren't at her place of work, I would have punched the smug smirk off of his face. But I couldn't, so instead, I watched my new obsession get hugged by a man that wasn't me.

(Tabatha)

I didn't have to look Ashton's way to know that he was pissed. Always assuming he just wanted a piece before moving on, it never even registered how Tike hugging me would affect him.

Before any of us could cause a scene, I pushed out of Tike's hold.

He chuckled, glancing Ashton's way to make sure he saw the whole thing. Which he did.

When Ashton took a step toward us, I slipped between him and Tike. "Stop." I lifted my hand, warding him off.

Ashton raised an eyebrow, daring me to argue with him.

"Ignore him," King muttered from his spot in the booth. "He's just trying to cause shit." I wasn't sure if he was talking about Tike or Ashton but either way, he was right. His dark eyes slid my way. "Calm your boy, sweetheart."

I nodded, blowing out a slow breath before spinning on Ashton. "Come with me." I grabbed his hand and dragged him through the bar and out the back, into the fresh nighttime air.

"Listen." I turned toward him, releasing his hand. "You have nothing to worry—"

Ashton closed the distance between us, cupped the back of my head, and captured my mouth in a hard kiss.

I sighed, melting into his searing touch.

His free hand found my ass, pulling me flush against him. His tongue separated my lips, dipping deep into my mouth and pulling a moan from the back of my throat. Or maybe it was deeper than that. Maybe he had reached a part of me that I had never given to someone before and I just didn't know it yet.

I latched on to his t-shirt, tugging him harder against me. I tried playing it cool and acting like I wasn't attracted to him or didn't want him, but they were lies. All of them. The denial, the sass, it masked how I truly felt. Even though we hadn't known each other for long, if hardly at all, I needed him inside me but at the same time, I wanted to play.

"Fuck." He broke the kiss, his teeth finding the side of my throat and biting there. "I need you."

"Not here." But even though those words left my lips, I only seemed to pull him closer.

"Then spend the night with me." His lips brushed along the shell of my ear. "Please."

I shivered at the desperation seeping from his pores. "No." It wasn't that I didn't want to spend the night with him, but I did need some sort of control. I also wanted to build a friendship with him first. I needed it.

"Kitten." He lifted me into his arms, slamming me up against the nearest brick wall. "I'll fucking crawl on this nasty as fuck ground and beg."

I laughed, tightening my thighs around his waist.

He lifted his head, raising an eyebrow. "You think I'm kidding?"

My laughter faltered. "You're not?"

"No." His hands roamed up my outer thighs until they were beneath my skirt. He pushed his waist further between my legs, grinding against me. "Does it feel like I'm kidding?"

My body burned, my core clenching as his thick erection pushed into me. I knew just by feeling him and by cupping him a few days ago, that he was big. The biggest I'll have ever been with.

"I missed you," he murmured, staring down at me and continuing to grind his hips against me.

I shivered, a soft sigh leaving me as I held onto him. "I…I missed you too."

A small smirk spread on his handsome face. "Where have you been?" he asked, his hips stopping.

"I had a doctor's appointment and took a day off to spend some time by myself." It had been something I did every few months. Self-care was important to me.

"You never told me that you had an appointment." Ashton placed me gently on my feet and released me.

The air around me suddenly turned cold. "I didn't think I had to."

"No, you didn't but we did talk on the phone and texted. I've been here but you haven't. I just assumed you had some days off." He shoved a hand through his hair. "Listen, I know I'm not your keeper and you don't have to report every single thing you do back to me, but I want to get to know you. I want to date you and I will get my ring on your finger one day." He raised his hand. "I'm not done."

My jaw clenched but I only crossed my arms under my chest and waited.

"I like you, Tabatha." He took a step toward me. "I like you a lot. Is this fast? Too soon? Who the fuck knows? It's not like they make a handbook on this sort of thing. If you want me to be your friend first, I will. If you want me to become friends with your brothers, I'll do that too. If you want me on my knees, begging for every inch of you…" He took another step closer. "I will."

I inhaled a sharp breath, staring into his light blue eyes. "I don't want you to hurt me, and I want to become friends. We have to become friends."

"I think we've moved past being friends, baby girl, but if that's what you want," he stuck out his hand, "then you have yourself a deal."

I laughed, slipping my fingers in his.

In a quick move, he tugged me against him.

A gasp escaped me.

"I meant what I said," Ashton whispered, hugging his arms around me.

"I know." Cupping his nape, I let out a soft sigh I wasn't expecting. We stood like that for what felt like a long while, but it was probably only a matter of minutes.

He felt safe. Secure. Everything I had been looking for since my daddy died so many years ago. My brothers helped but it wasn't enough. I wasn't looking for a daddy figure by any means, but I *was* looking for someone who I could call up if I needed something. Anything. The guys meant well but they all had lives of their own.

Voices sounded, interrupting my little moment with Ashton.

He pulled away from me, gave me a small smile, and kissed the side of my head. "I'll drive my brother home later and come back and pick you up. Unless you drove yourself."

"I didn't." My thoughts went back to the last time he picked me up. I could still feel his face between my legs even though it had been days since he had me lying on the hood of his car.

"Good, I'll pick you up then." Ashton started backing away from me, giving me one of his signature smirks. "You better get back to work, Kitten. Don't need your sexy ass getting in trouble."

"Ha. Scooter loves me, so I don't think that'll ever happen." I winked.

"He better love you as family and nothing more," Ashton practically growled.

"Jealous, baby?" I asked, inching my way to the door.

"You're lucky you're working," Ashton called out, disappearing inside the bar.

I laughed, shaking my head then headed through the back door. While he went to join his brother, I went back to work. Even though I was in good with the boss, I also didn't need to push my luck either.

My phone dinged. Fishing it out of my back pocket, I saw a text come into the group chat I had with my brothers.

Jonah: Poker has been postponed to Friday as we have a meeting on Wednesday to get some shit done for this shit.

Me: Lost your words, Jonah?

Phoenix: It's been a long mother fucking day. We've all lost our words.

Me: I gotta get back to work but you guys get some rest. Everything will happen when it's supposed to.

Beck: You sound like a Hallmark card.

I laughed to myself, shaking my head. I shoved my phone back into my pocket and spent the next couple of hours serving customers their drinks and food.

My brothers were working their way towards owning their own brewery. They eventually wanted to turn it into a bar and a restaurant, but making beer was their number one priority. For now, anyway.

While I continued making my rounds, I was vaguely aware of Ashton looking my way. He would still watch me while he hung out with his brother. Especially while I talked to guys. As much as I tried telling myself that I didn't like it, I found that I did. I enjoyed his eyes on me. I wanted more and I wasn't sure how I felt about that.

Closer to the end of my shift, there was something in the air as a fight broke out. Natalie yelled at Scooter for some apparent reason and a second fight broke out shortly after.

"What the hell is going on?" Toya, one of the waitresses, asked as she cashed herself out.

"I have no idea but Scooter's going to fire Natalie if she's not careful." It had been the third time she yelled at him for no reason at all. Or there wasn't a reason that I could tell. Even though I had seen something happen between them, I hadn't seen anything since. Maybe their thing ended before it even began and that was why Natalie snapped at Scooter every chance she got.

Ashton and Aiden were still sitting at the bar but as we got further into the night, the drunker Aiden became. Ashton kept looking between him and me, probably trying to make sure both of us were safe. But he didn't have to worry about me. Scooter looked out for his staff and King, Tike, and Bishop were still around too. The three guys had been coming to Scooters for as long as I had been working there. Maybe even longer. They knew Scooter and made sure to stop by every time they were in town. I didn't know anything about them really, but they were always nice to me whenever they showed up. Tike never got handsy before tonight and I knew that it was only to piss Ashton off.

As I was putting the clean glasses away and getting ready to leave, a sudden thump sounded, startling me.

"Shit, Aiden."

My head snapped up, finding Ashton standing and his brother nowhere in sight. I rushed around the bar. Aiden was sitting on the floor, pinching the bridge of his nose.

Laughter sounded around the bar, but no one offered to help. I looked around, not seeing Scooter anywhere, so I joined Ashton to do what I could to assist him.

When he took a step toward his brother, Aiden glared up at him. "Stop."

"Let me help you up," Ashton insisted, reaching out for him.

I stepped around him and crouched beside Aiden.

Ashton's gaze burned into me, but I ignored him.

"Let's get you up," I said gently.

Aiden swatted Ashton's hand away. "I'm fine."

"You are *not* fine. You're sitting on the fucking floor because you fell off the stool," Ashton growled.

I placed a hand on his arm. "Let me help."

Ashton's jaw clenched but he nodded. "Fine." He shoved to his feet and took a step back.

I stood, holding out my hand. "You need to get up. I don't think Scooter would want you spending the rest of the night here."

Aiden looked between us, slurred some words I didn't quite hear or understand, and finally slid his hand in mine.

Ashton came up behind me, reaching out to take hold of Aiden's wrist before he could protest. Both of us were able to pull him to his feet, but to my surprise, Aiden shoved me back into Ashton.

I gasped, falling back when Ashton caught me and steadied me on my feet.

"Outside," he growled, after making sure I was okay and stomping toward his brother. "*Now.*"

Aiden's eyes widened a bit, clearly only just realizing that he shoved me instead of Ashton like I had assumed he intended in the first place.

When Aiden didn't move, Ashton stepped around me but not before he grazed his hand along my hip. "I won't say it again."

Instead of waiting for him to respond, Ashton grabbed Aiden by the scruff of his neck and turned him roughly toward the front door.

They exited the bar, sucking all the air in my lungs along with them.

"Well, that was fun." Natalie laughed.

"You know what, Natalie?" I spun on her. "Instead of standing there and fucking judging Aiden, you could have helped, or you could have gotten Scooter and *he* could have helped. But no, you had to stand back and watch the damn show." I made sure to make a point of looking around the room. "All of you did. Did you take pictures? A video? You all should be ashamed of yourselves." I shouldered past her and made my way to the back of the bar. "All of you need to stop overserving him. Period," I yelled out.

"What's going on?" Scooter asked, coming toward me. "I heard yelling."

"People are stupid," I grumbled, stomping past him and down the hall. Once I was outside and into the fresh air, I took a breath and then another. I wasn't one to blow up like that and I was sure Natalie was going to go to Scooter about it, but at the moment I didn't care. I could get a job elsewhere if he was going to fire me for it.

My phone started to buzz then. Fishing it out of my back pocket, I saw that it was Ashton calling me.

"Hey," I answered, stepping from out behind the club.

"Hey, Kitten. Listen, I can't pick you up, but can you come here when you're done work?"

I frowned, rounding the corner and saw that he wasn't anywhere in the parking lot with his brother. "I didn't think you left already." My heart skipped a beat that he wanted me to come over, even after what had happened with Aiden.

"I thought Aiden was going to pass out on me, so I dragged him to my car and drove his ass home. But I..." Ashton sighed. "I don't want to leave him alone."

Even though we were on the phone, I could feel the weight of his emotion. I wished there was something I could do for him, but for now I would take him up on his offer.

"Text me your address and I'll take a cab over when my shift ends."

"Thank fuck."

"Did you think I was going to argue?" I asked gently, knowing that right now he was too emotionally raw for my sass.

"I don't know, Tabatha. Maybe. But just finish your shift and come here because Lord knows I need a distraction." When he disconnected the call, my heart gave a start. Would we have sex tonight? Did he want something else? Most guys always wanted sex, but did I? I did. I practically begged for it the one and only time we messed around. Maybe I could give him something in return. But whatever he wanted and however he needed it, I would give it to him.

NINE

Tabatha

WHEN MY SHIFT WAS over, I called a cab and headed over to Ashton's place. Once the car pulled up in front of the apartment building the brothers lived in, my stomach started fluttering. It felt like tiny butterflies were trying to escape the closer I got to Ashton.

I tried fighting these feelings, but I wasn't stupid. He affected me in ways no one else ever had. Maybe he could be good for me. I had closed my heart off for so long that I wasn't sure how it would feel when you find someone you want to spend time with.

After paying for the cab, I muttered a thanks and made my way to Ashton's floor. I wasn't overly sure what I was doing. Was I going to spend the night? Is that what he wanted? Or did he just want some company for a little bit and then I would leave before the morning came? It was already pushing three. Maybe he wasn't even awake, and I was there for nothing.

When I stood inside the lobby, I pressed the button beside his last name and waited. The door buzzed but no response came from him or his brother. Not that I expected Aiden to even be awake with how drunk he was when they left the bar, but I thought Ashton would have at least given some sort of greeting.

Once I reached their floor, I took a deep breath and made my way to their apartment. The door opened as I neared.

Before I even had a chance to greet Ashton, he pulled me into his arms and wrapped them around me.

My heart stuttered, my body stiffening at the unexpected gentleness coming from him.

He pushed his face into the crook of my neck, letting out a soft sigh.

Getting the hint, I returned the embrace, figuring maybe he needed a hug.

A low purr left him, the sound easing the nerves rushing through me.

Turning my head, my mouth brushed along his.

Before I could even catch a breath, he deepened the kiss and pushed me back against the door. It shut behind me, the lock clicking into place. The sound jarred through me, making me realize that Ashton wanted a little more than just a hug.

With my arm around his shoulders, I pulled him even harder against me.

"Baby," he whispered, kissing and licking his way to the side of my throat. "I need inside you." His hands roamed down my back, cupping my ass and lifting me into his arms.

I shivered, wrapping myself around him and crushing my mouth to his. I didn't want words sliding between us. I didn't want anything. I just wanted to feel. Both of us were desperate for that physical touch for very different reasons. But my own reasons were ones I couldn't explore yet. They were there, in the back of my mind.

Ashton lifted me away from the door and carried me down the hall to where, I could only assume, was his room. I didn't get a chance to look around me as I was focused on the man between my legs.

"Tabatha," he murmured against my jaw.

"Shhh…" I kissed his neck, sucking and licking my way to his ear. "Introduce me to your bed, Ashton."

His breath hitched at my words.

Before I could hint or suggest even more, I was tossed on a soft bed. He released me and went to his door, pushing it closed.

"Aiden's sleeping. He'll be passed out for hours." Ashton clicked the lock into place, the sound sending a shiver down my spine. "That means I can make you scream as loud as I fucking want, and he won't hear."

I swallowed hard at the desperation rolling off him. "What if I say I don't want to have sex tonight?"

Ashton's light blue eyes slid to mine. "Then I'll just hold you for the rest of the night, but I need you here. With me. I don't give a shit what we do. I need you. Here."

Leaning back on my elbows, I bent my knees and let them fall open.

His gaze dropped to my center, a low grown leaving him.

"Come here," I demanded gently, thankful I chose to wear a skirt today.

Ashton pushed away from the door, reached behind his back and pulled the t-shirt he was wearing up and over his head.

My mouth dried at the sight before me. He was hard, his chest and shoulders wide, his waist dipping into strong powerful thighs that I needed to feel between mine.

I waited for the cocky smirk and comment about the fact that I was staring at him but when neither came and he only knelt at the edge of the bed, it bothered me. I didn't get a chance to dwell on it when he grabbed my hips, pulled me closer, and dove his head under my skirt.

(Ashton)

I was beyond desperate for her. For that connection. For that little something that we shared between us. If we had sex, great, but if we didn't, that was fine too. I just didn't want to be alone.

The mess with my brother was a shitshow to say the least and I didn't know how to help him. But for now, I could at least help myself.

With my mouth against Tabatha's panty covered center, I breathed against her.

She trembled under me, her hands latching on to my hair.

Lifting my head, I placed pecks and bites along her inner thighs, my dick lengthening at the sudden redness of her pale skin.

Rising to my feet, I towered over her and pulled her red panties over her hips and down her legs before tossing them to the floor.

Tabatha sat up and removed her black t-shirt, throwing the fabric to the floor.

My gaze fell to the red satin bra pushing up her full tits.

She unclasped the bra, and slid the straps down her arms before tossing it over the edge of the bed. She was now sitting in only her skirt.

I let my eyes roam over her, soaking in every inch of her tattooed and pierced flesh. Gold barbells pierced both nipples, those three diamonds in her hip taunted and teased me.

She reached out a hand, brushing her fingers down my abs before turning over and rising to all fours.

My dick hardened at the sight before me. Her back was covered in a full tattoo of a phoenix rising out of flames and ashes.

Kneeling on the bed behind her, I grabbed a fistful of her pink hair and brushed my mouth along her ear. "I didn't have any intention of fucking you tonight, but it seems my little Kitten wants something. Doesn't she?"

"Yes," she whispered, fisting the blankets beneath us.

The bows sitting at the backs of her thighs, teased me, begging for my mouth. Releasing her hair, I kissed her shoulder and let my mouth linger down the length of her spine. She shivered, pushing back into me, her body greedy for whatever I had to offer it.

Unzipping her skirt, I watched as the fabric fell away from her body, leaving her completely naked and bare to my feasting eyes.

"How long has it been?" I asked, my voice low as I pressed my lips against her hot flesh.

"Since I had an orgasm? When you went down on me against your car. Before that, it was by my own hand."

My dick leaked at the thought of her touching herself.

"When was that?" I asked, sinking my teeth into the flesh of her ass.

She gasped, arching her back like the fierce and feisty kitten she was. "Before I met you."

"Did you come hard?" I rained tiny bites along the curves of her rear, dipping my tongue between the cheeks of her ass.

"God, Ashton. Yes, I came hard but not as hard as I'm about to if you keep that up."

I chuckled, grabbed fistfuls of her ass, and spread her open. "I haven't been with anyone since I met you." I wasn't sure why I told her that. Maybe it was because when we first met, she accused me of being a player and a womanizer. Which I was. Until I met her. But even before that, there was a time where I just didn't want easy sex anymore. I just never told anyone that because I knew they wouldn't believe me.

"I don't care what you did before me, Ashton." Tabatha pushed her ass back against my tongue. "But whatever you do, just please don't stop."

"You like that, baby?" I asked, licking along the tight little rim I would eventually fuck.

"Yes," she moaned. "God, yes."

Running two fingers along the seam of her hot pussy, I slowly thrust them into her as I flicked my tongue back and forth. My fingers pumped in and out of her, working her up to that edge I wanted to shove her off of and right into my arms.

(Tabatha)

The pleasure was almost too much. As Ashton pumped his fingers in and out of me, he licked at a spot I had never given to anyone before. Most of the guys I had been with thought it was gross after I asked them about it. They were tame when it came to sex and made me feel dirty for even suggesting such a thing.

Ashton's fingers picked up speed, pulling me from my thoughts.

A loud moan left me. Resting the side of my face against the mattress beneath me, I fisted the blankets and silently begged for Ashton to give me that orgasm we both wanted me to have.

"Fuck, baby." Ashton shoved his fingers into me as deep as my body would allow and pumped his hand hard against me. "You hear that?"

I whimpered, the sound of my wet pussy the only thing I could hear besides the erratic thumping of my heart.

"That's what I can do to your body." Ashton placed a peck on my tailbone before towering over me. "You want to come?"

"Yes."

"Good." He pulled his hand from between my legs, running his wet fingers along the side of my body. "You on the pill?" he asked, a zipper lowering a moment later.

"I have an IUD," I told him.

"Even better." He kissed my cheek, his hot breath fanning along the side of my head. "I need to feel you." He covered my hands, pushing his waist into the seat of my ass.

My eyes widened as the tip of him bumped against my center. He wasn't even inside me yet, but the crown of his cock stretched me just enough that I knew that this was going to hurt and feel so damn good all at the same time.

"Fuck, Kitten." Ashton's teeth sunk into my shoulder. "Take a deep breath."

I inhaled at the same time he slammed into me. A scream lodged its way in my throat.

"Fuck me, Tabatha." He shook above me, his teeth biting down hard.

"P-Please." My thighs trembled, my pussy burning around the thick length of him. I had never felt something so damn big inside of me. "Please move."

"Just give me…fuck, I can't…so good." His words were jumbled, his teeth scraping along my shoulder. The area stung and I knew that he left a mark but at the moment, I didn't care. I just needed him to move.

"Ashton," I whined, arching my hips to take him even deeper.

"Fucking hell." His mouth found my ear, his moan sending a hot shiver racing down my spine. He pulled his hips back, his cock sliding most of the way out of me, pulling a gasp from the back of my throat. He thrust back into me, filling me to the hilt. He kept up the movements, rolling his hips and giving us both what we wanted.

It only took a couple of thrusts from him before that familiar tingle started in my toes. My breathing picked up, spots danced in my vision, his name leaving my lips repeatedly.

"Already, baby? Fuck yes, give me that orgasm."

"God," I sobbed, the release slamming into me and taking my breath away. "Harder, Ashton," I finally pleaded.

"Fuck, fuck, fuck." He squeezed my hands, picked up speed with his hips, and slammed his pelvis into the seat of my ass. "I can't. Fuck, I can't control…"

"Don't control," I cried out. "Just fuck me. God, I can't either…I just…" Another release exploded through me, making my eyes roll into the back of my head.

Before I could calm down, Ashton pulled out of me and had me in his arms and straddling his lap.

He cupped the back of my head, pulling my mouth down to meet his and kissed me as he fucked another orgasm out of my body.

I whimpered, shaking against him. The pleasure was almost too much but his hold wouldn't loosen. It only tightened as he thrust up and up. The movements were fast and deliberate, almost like he was chasing that release but could never quite catch it.

"Come, Ashton," I whispered against his lips.

He growled, deepening the kiss and tightening his arm around my waist.

Pushing him onto his back, I broke the kiss and placed my hands on his chest. Moving my hips back and forth, up and down, I rode him and watched as he fell.

It didn't take long but when he yelled out my name, my own release followed. Something switched in that moment between us. I could feel a piece of my wall shattering and I wasn't sure how I felt about it.

TEN

Tabatha

WHEN I WOKE A few hours later, Ashton was sleeping beside me. His hand was cupping my breast while his leg was thrown over mine. I never thought I would feel safe and secure in someone's arms. Especially someone who wasn't my father. Sure, I hugged my brothers from time to time, but it had never felt right. It felt like I *had* to more than I wanted to.

But now, lying beside Ashton, feeling his big heavy body half covering mine, set a flutter of something I didn't want to think about at the moment. If ever at all.

When he shifted beside me, I stiffened, expecting him to say or do something. But when he just sighed and finally settled once again, I let out a breath of relief.

Rolling onto my back, I closed my eyes as Ashton pushed my legs apart with his knee.

His hand moved from my breast to the spot he had spent hours in the night before.

I swallowed a moan as his fingers lightly brushed over my center.

Rolling back onto my side, I pushed my ass into his waist.

His teeth found the side of my neck, a low growl leaving him. God that sound. That deep vibrating sound.

I wasn't sure if he was still sleeping. Should I stop? Should I keep going? I didn't know. I needed to leave and go home before it became awkward. Before it became something I wasn't ready for. These feelings I had weren't normal for me, especially when it came to a guy like Ashton.

In a quick move, Ashton had me on my stomach. "You thought I was sleeping, Kitten," he purred in my ear, sliding his beautiful cock back into me.

I whimpered, trying to lift my lips when he rested most of his body weight on me.

"You were trying to take control." He nipped my shoulder. "Weren't you?"

I swallowed hard, not responding and deciding to let him hurry up and do his thing so I could leave.

"Were you wanting to fuck and then leave?" Ashton brushed my hair off the back of my neck, breathing heavily into my ear. "Is that it? You wanted a piece, so you could go home?"

"Yes," I blurted.

He stiffened. "Why?"

Because in the short time I knew him, he was digging his way into my heart, and I didn't like it.

"Tell me," he demanded.

"Because."

Much to my surprise, he pulled away from me and left the bed. The light turned on, blinding me for a half a second when something soft hit my face.

I jumped, looked down and found my clothes sitting in a pile on the bed in front of me.

"Leave."

My eyes snapped to Ashton. "Excuse me?"

"You wanted to fuck and leave." He pointed to my clothes. "Why don't we skip the fucking part since I have two hands anyway, and you can just go home like you so desperately want to do."

"Ashton." I left the bed and went up to him. Yes, I wanted to leave but not like this. If I would have left while he was still sleeping, I was sure he would still be pissed. "I don't want you to be mad." God, I sounded dumb. How did I think he was going to feel?

"Mad." He laughed. "Oh, I'm not mad, Tabatha. Surprised maybe. But not mad."

I turned away from him and grabbed my clothes when a hand covered mine.

"I deserve this," he told me. "I can't tell you how many hearts I've broken by leaving the next morning without a single goodbye. Maybe this is karma punishing me for the shit I've done."

"I don't want to punish you. I just...there are some things I can't talk about yet and I feel..." I chewed my bottom lip, bracing myself. "This was a mistake," I said before I could stop myself.

"A mistake?" He spun me around. "You think us making love was a fucking mistake?"

I winced at the bite in his tone. "We didn't make love, Ashton."

"Well, we sure as hell didn't just fuck, Tabatha."

"Yes, we did." I pushed away from him. "We hardly know each other for it to be considered making love." He wasn't making sense. None of this was making any sense at all.

"What have I ever done to you?" He grabbed my upper arm and pulled me against him.

"Stop." I pushed him. "Just let me leave."

Instead of releasing me, he crushed his mouth to mine.

I moaned, melting into him.

"That's why it was more than us just fucking." He leaned back, staring into my eyes.

He looked at me like he was reaching into my soul.

Ashton kissed the corner of my mouth, sliding his lips to my ear. "I'll let you leave now, Kitten. But the next time we fuck, and we will fuck again, you will spend the night with me. The full night." Ashton pulled away from me and grabbed my clothes from his bed. "Here." He shoved them into my arms and went to his dresser.

I didn't know what to do or even say. He wanted me to come over and I did. He never even hinted for sex, but he did tell me he needed inside me. So, I complied. Willingly. Spending the few hours with him had been the best night of my life but there was no way that we could take this further than we already had.

My thoughts traveled back to my last doctor's appointment. Everything was fine, for the most part. But I often wondered if my doctors were wrong at times. I felt okay, so that was all that mattered. Or that was what I tried telling myself anyway.

The sound of a drawer slamming shut made me jump and pulled me from my thoughts. Ashton met my gaze in the mirror on his dresser.

I was still naked and holding my clothes in my arms. It had been a long time since I had a one-night stand. Back in the beginning, I had accused Ashton of using women for his own personal gain when I had done the same thing to the guys I had been with.

"I thought it would be different with you." Ashton pulled on gray sweatpants, but the loose fabric did nothing to hide the beast beneath them. The part of him I had felt and nearly fell apart for within a matter of seconds. "I thought it would be easier."

"I don't know what you're trying to tell me." I quickly got dressed when I realized that I didn't have my panties.

"Looking for these?" Ashton asked, my panties dangling off his finger.

I stomped up to him and went to grab them when he snatched his hand back. "Ashton."

"You're leaving, so I'm going to keep these as a souvenir."

"Why the hell are you upset by me leaving? It's almost seven in the morning anyway. So technically, I did spend the night with you."

His brows narrowed, that familiar muscle in his jaw ticking. "I was going to cook you breakfast. I was going to ask if you wanted to spend the day together." He pushed away from his dresser and took a step toward me, forcing me back. "I was going to ask if you wanted to go on a date tonight. Or do you still not want to date and fuck only? Are you fucking other guys too? Is that it, Tabatha? You don't want just me? Am I not enough to satisfy that hunger in you?"

"Fuck you, Ashton. I'm not the one who has slept with anyone that walks. That's you. You said so yourself."

"Why the sudden change?" He shoved my panties in his pocket before closing that final distance between us.

With nowhere for me to go, I was trapped between the door and him. But I found that I liked this side of him. He was unhinged, unraveled and pissed off. And I was ashamed to say it, but it turned me on.

"Why the sudden need to be a bitch and shut me out?"

I winced, looking away.

Ashton placed his hands on the door at either side of my head, lowering his mouth to my ear. "Tell me, Kitten."

"No."

"Tell. Me." He pulled me away from the door and into his arms. "Say it, Tabatha. Tell me the reasons why you're so fucking scared."

"Stop." I tried pushing out of his hold, but he was too strong for me.

"Baby." His mouth found the soft spot under my ear, his hands roaming up my back before capturing my hair in their firm grip. He held my head in place, staring intently into my eyes. "Tell me."

"You shouldn't want me," I whispered, reaching up to brush my fingers along the scruff on his strong jaw.

"You can't stop me from wanting you, baby girl." His voice was low, gentle, nothing like the man holding me.

I knew he wouldn't hurt me. Not physically. But I was concerned for my heart. And for his. If my health took a turn for the worse, what then? I could never forgive myself for hurting him that way. Add to the fact that everyone eventually left anyway, he was better off without me.

"Spend the day with me." Ashton's other hand cupped my ass, his fingers grazing beneath the fabric of my skirt. "Please."

I melted into him before I could stop myself.

He lifted his head, lightly brushing his mouth along mine.

I let him kiss me before I could push him away. Before I could run and never look back. But just the thought of never seeing Ashton again, forced a sob from my lips.

Ashton growled, nipped at my lips, and deepened the kiss.

I whimpered, my mouth tingling as he attacked it with his.

Sliding his hands beneath my skirt, he cupped my ass and lifted me. In a rough move, he dropped me onto his dresser, the items falling off of it and to the floor at our feet.

Not letting him get a chance to stop kissing me, I blindly reached between us and grabbed onto his waist. Pulling him closer but not close enough, I dipped my hands into his sweatpants.

The kiss picked up speed, our chests rising and falling. I wasn't sure where he began and I ended but I knew, for the first time in my life, I didn't want this to end. And that scared the shit out of me.

(Ashton)

Something was wrong. I hadn't known Tabatha for long, but I knew women. When they wanted to fuck instead of talk, it wasn't good. For the most part anyway. I didn't want it to be like this but when she decided to leave instead of spending the day with me like I had assumed she would, it pissed me off. Words left my lips before I could stop them.

I knew going in that she had baggage, but I didn't realize it was that bad. Did she have a crazy ex? Had she been abused? Something else? Something worse? Those questions were on the tip of my tongue to ask but when her hands reached into my pants, I pushed them aside and would deal with her issues later. For now, I would give her what she wanted. Everything she wanted and more. I would be the only thing she needed. She could push and shove me away, but I refused to give up. There was no way in hell I was letting her go when she had been the first woman who affected me like this. None of my exes, not even the couple of friends I had slept with to try and fill a void, had left me feeling this…want…this need and drive for more and a better life.

Latching on to her hair, I deepened the kiss and let her control us. Whatever she needed.

When her hands wrapped around me, she pulled my cock free from my pants and lined the tip up with her center. I didn't need to see to know where she was. Thrusting into her, I stopped and breathed.

She moaned, shaking around me.

Breaking the kiss, I stared down into her beautiful gray eyes and mentally patted my own back at the flush in her cheeks I had put there. "I'm going to say this only once, Kitten," I murmured, my voice low. I brushed the tips of my fingers along her swollen lips. "If you need space, I'll give it to you. If you need to fuck, I'll give you my dick and more. If you need company but you just want to sit there and do nothing, I'll be there. Every day. Every hour. I will be there."

"Ashton," she whispered, her eyes welling. "You can't promise me something like that. No one can."

"I can and I am. I mean every single word, Kitten. I've waited this long for you, I can wait a little longer."

"But we just met," she reminded me, slipping her hands around my waist to my ass.

"That may be true." I pushed into her, earning me a sharp gasp. "But I've been looking for you this whole time. I just didn't know it until now."

Instead of waiting for more of her words, I crushed my mouth to hers and lifted her off the dresser. With her in my arms, I carried her to the bathroom across the hall from my room.

We stripped and took a shower. While I knew she had wanted to leave, there was no way I was letting that happen until I was damn sure she would remember how I felt.

ELEVEN

Tabatha

A FEW DAYS LATER and I could still feel Ashton all over and inside of me. His words, dirty and vulgar, whispered into my ear. His rough hands roaming over my wet naked skin. His body filling me and making me move and experience things I never thought possible.

Ashton cupped my breasts, pounding into me from behind and lifting me up onto my tiptoes with each hard thrust.

I whimpered, my head falling back against his shoulder. "Please," I heard myself beg.

"Take it, Kitten." He wrapped a hand around my throat, kissing my forehead. "Take it all."

I shivered at the memory, blew out a slow breath, and continued cleaning up the kitchen. I did take it. Every inch of him. It had been like he was staking his claim with each thrust of his cock. He was stamping ownership on my soul and there wasn't a damn thing I could do about it.

"You're so hard." I moaned. "God, you feel good."

Ashton wrapped both hands around my throat that time. "So do you, Kitten. So do you."

It was now Friday and poker night. I had told Ashton to join my brothers, but I wasn't sure if he would. The thought of seeing him again sent a shiver throughout every inch of me.

We still hadn't talked about what was said between us, but I knew that we would. In time. But for now, he left me alone and hadn't brought it up.

While I was cleaning and preparing the snacks the guys liked to have for their game, the door to the loft banged open.

"Fucker, you could at least help me with this shit."

"You look like you're doing just fine on your own."

"How old are you? You're so damn immature."

I laughed to myself as the guys rolled in, the peace and quiet popping like a bubble, but I embraced the noise with open arms.

"Tabs, we found you a friend," Phoenix called out, coming around the corner and carrying a case of beer. He brought it over to the counter, nodding behind him. "Someone was waiting at the door."

"What do you—" Ashton waltzed into the kitchen like he owned the place. His light blue eyes found mine. "Ashton, I…what are you doing here?"

He came toward me. Just when I thought he was going to keep his distance while my brothers were around, he slipped his arm around my waist and leaned down to my ear. "You said to come over for poker. To become friends with your brothers, so I can become friends with you. Well, here I am, Kitten."

"I didn't think you'd actually come over." The scent of him was overwhelming. He smelled like spice and everything that made up Ashton.

He pulled away from me, gave me a wink, and started putting beer in the fridge.

"How's your brother doing?" I asked, figuring it was a safe topic and one that my brothers wouldn't give us shit for having.

Ashton's gaze flicked to mine. "Fine I guess."

"You guess?" I went up to him. "Did something happen?"

I was vaguely aware that we were now being watched but I didn't care. I liked him and needed to make sure that his brother was okay too.

"Nothing big," Ashton said, pulling a couple of bottles from the case and starting to put them in the fridge. "Natalie hit on him."

"She's always a problem," Phoenix added, carrying a tray of sandwiches over to the counter.

"She really is." Jonah joined us and started helping Ashton. "I remember when she hit on Beck while he was dating that chick. I thought she was going to lose her shit."

While they talked, I caught a flash of metal in Phoenix's face.

"What's that?" I caught his jaw before he could pull away. He was sporting a new piercing in his eyebrow.

"Leave it alone, Tabs," Beck called out, joining our little party.

"It's an anniversary," I said to Phoenix, my voice low.

"It's nothing." He licked along the gold ring in his lip. "I'm fine."

"Phoenix." I stared up into his dark eyes. "Are you?"

His jaw clenched but he only nodded and pulled away.

"What was that about?" Ashton asked gently, coming up to my side.

"Every year around this time, Phoenix does something drastic like getting a piercing or a tattoo," I explained, backing into the corner of the kitchen, so my brothers wouldn't hear me. "For most people, it's fine and normal but for Phoenix…"

"It's not," Ashton answered.

I nodded.

"What do you think happened?" he asked, looking out at my three brothers who were poking fun, talking shit about each other and being just that. Brothers.

"It's the anniversary of when his parents gave him up and he was thrown into the system," I explained, staring at the guys I had lived with since I was a small girl.

"Wow. That's…" Ashton followed my gaze. "Shitty."

"Yeah, it is. All of them came from bad childhoods. I'm the only one lucky enough to have had a good upbringing before I was put in the system." Before I could say any more on the matter, the guys called Ashton over to join them for their poker game.

He leaned over and kissed my cheek. "Until later, Kitten."

I nodded, watching him head to the table and join in on the fun. I couldn't help but notice how he seemed to fit in. Sitting at the table with three guys who were my whole world, it appeared as if he just belonged. I was the youngest but I still worried for them. I worried that they would never truly be happy when they had come from nothing. They were working on starting up their own business but having a good steady job wasn't everything. Happiness and love were needed too. As that thought crossed my mind, my stomach twisted, knowing I never allowed myself to have such things. So how could I expect my brothers to have it?

"How come you don't play?"

My gaze snapped to Ashton's.

The guys chuckled.

"She's too good, that's why," Beck told him.

"I remember when I first played with her. It was the fastest I ever lost a grand. I could have burned that shit up and it would have taken longer." Phoenix shook his head. "But I was impressed."

Something flashed in Ashton's gaze.

My cheeks burned. Looking away, I cleared my throat and grabbed a beer from the fridge. "I grew up around the game. Not a big deal." But for some, it was a very big deal. Having that kind of power and knowing how good I was at poker, didn't sit well with some people. So, it was a secret that we usually didn't talk about. Until now apparently.

While the guys continued playing, I couldn't help but notice how right it felt to have Ashton there.

Shoving those thoughts aside, I grabbed my beer and headed to the living room. Even though Ashton should have been paying attention to the game, I could feel his eyes burning into me. They followed my every move.

"Focus on the game, buddy," Beck bit out.

I smiled to myself, knowing that Ashton got caught.

Sitting on the sectional, I pulled my knees up to my chest and allowed myself to look at him.

He caught my gaze, giving me a wink.

I laughed softly, suddenly wishing I could introduce him to my bed much like he did for me with his own.

"Stop staring at our sister and focus." Phoenix threw a poker chip at Ashton.

"How old are you?" Ashton threw one back at him. "Five?"

"Now, now, children." I stood. "Play nice." I headed to the hall that led to my bedroom.

"Where are you going?" Ashton called out.

"I'm going to read in bed." I stopped, looking at him over my shoulder. "You can join me."

When Ashton went to stand, my brothers did the same.

"Sit the fuck down," Beck snapped.

A laugh bubbled through me.

Giving the guys a wave, I continued down the hall until I reached my room. Once I was inside the four walls, I let out a slow breath. I never had a guy here that I was even remotely interested in and definitely not one that constantly tried pissing the guys off. It was highly amusing the way Ashton got under their skin. Especially Beck's.

Changing into a tank top and little shorts, I grabbed a book I had been reading for a while and curled up in bed.

The sound of the door closing and a lock clicking into place, made me jump.

Ashton stood inside the room, leaning against the door. "Sorry, I didn't mean to scare you."

I sat up, rubbing the grit out of my eyes. "I must have fallen asleep."

He flicked off the light and came toward my bed. "Mind if I join you?"

My body heated. "You spending the night?"

Ashton pulled his t-shirt up and over his head before slipping out of his jeans. Even in the dim lighting from the moon, I could still see that he had gone commando. He was all Ashton beneath those jeans, and it set my blood on fire.

"Did you want me to?" he asked, crawling onto the bed.

"God." I cupped his cheek. "Yes."

Before he could say anything more, I covered his mouth with mine and showed him just how much I wanted him to spend the night with me.

I woke sometime during the night to a heavy body half on top of mine. Ashton had his arm curled around me, his hand cupping my breast and his deep breaths fanning over the back of my neck.

As much as I tried pushing him away, I couldn't help but wanting to keep him close at the same time. These feelings that I was slowly catching for him, scared me. I didn't want to hurt him. Because of my health concerns, I had never allowed any guy to get close. Even I knew that I had attachment issues. It was why I had been alone for so long. It also didn't help the fact that the first man I ever loved left me. I stared into the dark room, wondering what life would be like now if my father hadn't been murdered. If he hadn't made those wrong choices and end up in jail. I also wondered what would have happened if my mom never left. My brothers had been the only people I could ever count on. But even then, a part of me feared that they would leave me too.

"You awake, Kitten?" Ashton asked, his voice a low purr.

"Kind of," I murmured.

His hold on me tightened, pulling me even closer into his side.

Turning my head toward him, I was met by his hot mouth covering mine. The kiss was soft and gentle, nothing like the man who had invaded my body a couple of hours before.

"Do you work today?" he asked against my lips.

"No." I spent most of my time working because it was distracting but every once in a while, Scooter forced me to take a day off. And today was one of those days.

"Spend the day with me?" Ashton asked, hope filling his voice.

It was on the tip of my tongue to tell him no but who the hell was I kidding? I needed it and I needed him. "Okay."

"Good, because I wasn't taking no for an answer."

I laughed lightly, resting my head back on my pillow.

"How was the game?" I asked, realizing that instead of asking him how it went with the guys, I had jumped him instead.

"Good. They took all my money but it's fine. It meant the faster I lost, the faster I could get to you. Which is what happened."

I rolled onto my back, his hand moving to my hip and back up again. "What are we doing, Ashton?" I didn't want to ruin the moment because of my insecurities and asking stupid questions but I needed to know. I needed to know that he wasn't just using me to get his fill and then once he was good and satisfied, he would leave.

"Having fun, Kitten." He curled his arm under the pillow, keeping his other wrapped around me. His eyes burned into the side of my head.

I shifted, pulling the blanket up to my chin but wouldn't meet his gaze.

"What are you scared of?" he murmured, running his thumb back and forth along the piercings in my hip.

Nothing. Everything. That you'll hurt me. That you'll rip my heart out of my chest and laugh in my face and tell me what a stupid little girl I am for trusting you. That you'll leave me like my mom did. That you'll be taken away from me like my dad was.

But I never said those things. I had never let myself think them before either.

"Nothing," I whispered.

Ashton flicked on the lamp sitting on my nightstand before reaching out for me. He cupped my cheek and turned my head to face him. "I'm not going to hurt you."

"That's what they always say."

"Have I given you any reason not to trust me? Have I been unkind to you? Have I been too rough when we fuck? You gotta tell me something here, baby, because I thought what we were doing was fun and that everything was good between us."

I pulled away from him and sat up. Swinging my legs over the edge of the bed, I took a few deep breaths, but they didn't ease the anxiety resting in my body.

"Hey." He moved to the spot behind me and kissed my shoulder. "Talk to me. You don't have to tell me all of your dark and dirty secrets, but you have to give me something."

"You have my body, Ashton," I mumbled. "What more do you need?"

"I don't have a lot of friends."

I looked at him then, wondering what he was getting at and why he would suddenly blurt that out.

"I've grown up around the same people my whole life, but I wouldn't consider them friends. Not really anyway. I also tried coming between some of the relationships that were forming." He shoved a hand through his hair. "I don't know what I'm trying to say. Before you..." He dropped his arm to his side, looking down at it. "I didn't overly give a shit about...well...anything really. My career path was set out for me, so I never had to worry about that. I guess I'm trying to right my wrongs in a way and before you say anything." His eyes snapped to mine. "I'm not using you to make things right. But I like you, Tabatha. I like you a fucking lot. What you accused me of when we first met...you were right. All of it was right."

My stomach twisted. "I shouldn't have said those things. I shouldn't have assumed."

"Yes, you should have, and you did. I'm not mad about that." He stared at me, a small smirk spreading on his face. "Can't say I've ever had a woman call me out on my shit like you have though. And I know some women who tried knocking me down a peg or two but you..."

"What?" I breathed.

"You succeeded."

The conversation was suddenly getting too heavy for me. I left the bed, which earned me a soft growl, and went up to the window. Our loft overlooked the top of another building, so the only way to see me standing there naked was if you were standing on the other roof. I would sometimes stand there, staring out as the sun set, wishing I could be a bird and just fly away.

Heavy arms wrapped around my middle, Ashton's front to my back. Both of us were naked, very naked I might add, but he never took it further. Never even hinted.

"What would you be doing today if I wasn't around?"

"I would probably go to the gym or maybe a bookstore or two. Or help Sarge with some paperwork."

"Sarge?"

I turned, leaning against the windowsill and placing my hand on Ashton's chest. "Sarge was our foster father. Even when we lived with him, we always referred to him as Sarge. He was a cop but got mixed up with the wrong people and was forced into an early retirement. He had some issues with some bikers, so I'm actually surprised they let him live." I ran my fingers down Ashton's torso, brushing them lightly over his abs. I counted eight, how was that even possible? I remembered back to when I asked my brothers about it and they just laughed it off like they always did.

"Was he good to you?" Ashton asked. "Sarge I mean. I know you said that the guys had hard lives."

"They did. Before they were put in the system." Dipping my hand lower, I trailed my fingers lightly over his hip. It had the muscle that made most women damn near faint just by looking at it. "Has anyone ever told you that you're beautiful?" I asked softly.

"Not really." Ashton shrugged. "I guess my shitty personality changed people's minds about my looks."

"Well…" I placed both hands against his chest and pushed him back. "Then I'm the lucky one."

"Oh?" Ashton sat on the edge of my bed, pulling me onto his lap. He laid down, keeping his hands on my thighs. "Is that so, Kitten?"

"Yeah." I ran a finger up the length of his cock, reveling in the way it twitched beneath my touch. "As much as I don't want a relationship, no other guy has made me feel this way."

"Good." In a quick move, he cupped my ass and lifted me until my knees were locked around his head.

A gasp escaped me, my eyes wide as I stared down at him.

He winked, dropping my body onto his mouth.

I sighed, throwing my head back as the sounds of his humming and my moaning slid throughout every inch of me.

TWELVE

ASHTON

I WAS FALLING FOR her. It was the only thing that explained these feelings rushing through me. They were new and they came on fast. I wasn't used to it. Was this how it was for the people I had grown up with? When you found your person, did you just know?

Tabatha and I had been spending as much time together as she would allow. I wanted to ask her to move in with me and never leave my bed but apparently, when you knew a person for only a short time, that was frowned upon.

We had become closer over the past few weeks, but she still wouldn't let me into her heart. I tried hinting at her secrets and why she was so damn closed off, but she would change the subject or kiss me. She would do anything to distract me from finding out her deepest and darkest worries and fears and while I appreciated the extra attention, I found that I still didn't know her as well as I should have. Especially when we had been spending all of our free time together.

One night, I was sitting at home since Tabatha was working. I had just gotten back from having dinner at my parents' place and there had been no sign of my brother anywhere.

"Have you talked to him?" Mom asked, hopeful.

"I have, Mama," but not in the way she wanted to know about.

"Is he…" Her breath caught.

"Hummingbird," Dad said gently, kissing her temple and wrapping his arm around her shoulders. "He'll come around when he's ready."

"But he needs us." Mom curled into Dad and started crying softly.

My chest tightened. If I could and if I knew that it would make a difference, I would force Aiden to watch this shit, but he was never around. One day. One day I was going to force him to his fucking knees and make him beg for our mom's forgiveness.

As soon as I left their place, after spending the better part of an hour trying to convince Mom that it wasn't her fault, I texted Tabatha, telling her that I needed her tonight. But I hadn't heard from her. The silence only seemed to increase this rage inside of me.

When it started pushing midnight and I still hadn't heard from Tabatha, I grabbed my keys and headed over to Scooter's. She was nowhere to be found but my brother sure as hell was. He was hunched over at the bar, nursing a beer. A few empty shot glasses sat in front of him.

"Who the fuck gave him alcohol?" I bellowed, not giving a shit in the least who heard.

Natalie rolled her eyes, pouring a pint and placing it in front of Aiden.

When he reached for it with a shaky hand, I stopped him. "You don't need anymore," I told him softly. "Does he look like he's in any condition to have more alcohol?" I asked anyone who would listen.

"It's none of my business," Natalie said, shrugging and going back to putting dishes away.

"It's none of your business," I repeated through clenched teeth. "It's not your business why he's drinking so much, but it is your business when he's clearly on the verge of passing out. He should be cut off. Scooter could lose his license."

"He's right," Scooter said, heading behind the bar. He leaned down to Natalie's ear, muttering something to her.

Her eyes widened, her cheeks going red. Her gaze met mine. "Sorry," she muttered, threw the cloth on the counter, and quickly left the bar area.

"I'm sorry for this," Scooter said, coming from around the bar to join Aiden and me. "I'll help you."

"He should have been cut off," I told him. "He shouldn't even be here." But that was a different story for another day.

"I know. I was doing paperwork, but I told the girls two hours ago not to serve him anymore drinks. Coffee and water only and food if he wanted, but they obviously didn't listen to me."

"I think it was Natalie who didn't listen to you."

He grunted. "Yeah, I'll deal with her later."

I looked at him then. I went to ask what he meant by that exactly even though it was none of my business, when Aiden swayed on the stool. He damn near toppled over but I was able to catch him just in time.

With Scooter helping me, we all but dragged my brother to my car.

"He needs help," Scooter bit out.

"Yeah, tell me something I don't already know." Once we had him in the passenger seat, I closed the door behind him and let out a slow breath. "I don't know how to help him when he clearly doesn't want it."

"Maybe he does want help but doesn't know how to ask. He knows he has a problem, Ashton."

"How do you know that?"

"Because he looks at his drinks for a while before actually drinking them." Scooter shrugged. "I don't know exactly but I can only guess that he's trying to figure out a way to stop. But sometimes it takes something big happening before they'll change." He clapped my shoulder. "Trust me. From someone who lives with an addiction every damn day, you can't force him to change. He has to want to do it himself and even if he does get the help he needs, it'll be a battle he'll face for the rest of his life."

I looked at Scooter then, wondering what his story was.

He only winked, gave my shoulder a squeeze, and left the parking lot.

"Thank you," I called out.

He gave me a wave over his shoulder and headed back into the bar.

Once I was sitting in the driver's side of my car, I glanced at my brother. Surprisingly, his eyes were still open and he was looking out the window. They were glassy and unfocused. The fact that he hadn't passed out yet after all he drank, didn't sit well with me. It meant that he could keep going.

"I saw my crew die," Aiden muttered, slurring over his words.

My eyes widened, never hearing him talk about his time in the Navy. Even though it was short-lived, he did what he had to, to move up the ranks pretty quickly. Dad and his Navy brothers were impressed.

I waited for him to continue, but when he didn't and only closed his eyes, I thanked whoever was listening up above. Maybe this was a start. I wouldn't press but Aiden needed to know that I was there. Whenever he was ready to talk, I would be ready to listen. But at the same time, I wasn't sure how much help I could be. It was worth a shot. Maybe he needed a woman, a guy, or a friend. Someone outside of our group that we had grown up with.

When we arrived at home, I helped him up to our apartment. I kept him close, holding him tight so he wouldn't fall over.

"I got you, Aiden," I told him. I wasn't sure if he could hear me, but I hoped he could. I hoped my words registered even a little bit. He needed to know that no matter what he was going through, he wasn't alone. I just wished he would talk to me about it.

Once I had Aiden in his bed, I made him drink some water and take some Tylenol as well. He tried fighting me like he always did but when I threatened to shove the pills down his throat, he complied and took them. Less than a minute later, he was passed out on his stomach.

"I wish you would tell me what's going on," I told him, even though he couldn't hear me. His deep snores grated on every nerve in my body. Sitting on the edge of his bed, I dropped my head in my hands and mentally begged to whomever would listen that Aiden would get through this. If I couldn't help him, I prayed that there was someone out there who could. No matter how long it took.

Kicking off my shoes, I stood and helped him out of his before lying down beside him. As much as I wanted to go see Tabatha, I couldn't leave Aiden. Every time he got like this; it was hard for me to fall asleep because a part of me feared that he would stop breathing throughout the night. So, my sleep was always restless.

My phone started vibrating. I fished it out of my jeans, a growl lodging its way in my throat that it was Tabatha who was texting me.

Instead of texting her back, I dialed up her number and waited.

"Hey," came her soft greeting.

"Hey, yourself. Where the fuck have you been and why haven't you responded to my texts?"

"Wow, Ashton."

"Woman." Alright, so it was rude of me to demand answers from her, but I wasn't in the right frame of mind for niceties.

"If you must know, I had some appointments and Phoenix was in a mood."

"Fine." I sighed, pinching the bridge of my nose. "I'm sorry."

"Everything okay?" she asked gently.

"No. Aiden drank tonight. I know it's normal, but Natalie kept feeding him alcohol even after Scooter told her not to."

"I'm sorry. Maybe he needs to stay away from the bar or any bar and alcohol."

I grunted. "Sure, try telling him that."

"I know. Well, if there's anything I can do to help, just let me know."

"There is but that needs to wait." As much as I needed her wrapped around me, this was more important at the moment.

"Oh." She paused. "What do you need?"

"Sex, Kitten." I sat up, careful not to disturb Aiden, and leaned back against the wall.

"Come over in the morning. We can have breakfast after."

"Fuck." My dick stirred. "That sounds damn near perfect."

A husky laugh left her. "Would it help, Ashton?"

"Yes." I imagined how it would go. I made plans mentally and hoped she would be down for whatever it was that I took from her.

We continued talking for the next hour or two. It was late before we said our goodbyes and turned in for the night.

When I laid down beside my brother, I faced him and watched. His features mirrored my own but as we got older, I found that people could easily tell us apart. Especially when he had lost so much weight from drinking rather than eating and fueling his body with the nutrients he needed.

Reaching out, I brushed his bangs off his forehead.

He inhaled and let out a heavy sigh.

Relief flooded through me that he was still breathing. I feared the day would come that he wouldn't wake up and I had to tell our parents that he drank himself to death. I just prayed that it never came to that, and that he was able to get the help he needed.

Before it was too late.

THIRTEEN

Tabatha

"HOW'S HE DOING?" I asked Scooter over the phone as I poured myself a cup of coffee.

"He's resting." He sighed. "I know I wanted him to fight but not like this. He got the shit kicked out of him and if I hadn't stopped it, it could have been a whole hell of a lot worse, Tabs. A whole lot worse."

When a higher pitched voice sounded in the background, I frowned. "Who's with you?"

"Uh…Natalie." Scooter coughed. "She was there last night and helped me with Phoenix."

"Oh okay." I was reminded that I wanted to ask Natalie about that little scene I saw one night between her and Scooter. Not that it was any of my business, but it was hot as hell, and I was curious about it.

"Listen, Tabby. Don't worry about your brother. I know that's easier said than done but I promise, we're both taking care of him." In more ways than one I imagined.

"Thank you, Scooter. I appreciate it."

"Of course. Also…" Scooter coughed again, which I had come to learn over the years that he did that whenever he was nervous about something.

"What is it?" I gripped the phone tight in my hand, my stomach clenching at what he could possibly tell me about my brother. All of the guys came from shitty pasts, and they all coped with it differently. Phoenix fought and he fought hard. I had only been to one of his fights and after watching him almost get killed, I stopped going.

"Something triggered him. It wasn't good. That's why the fight was nasty as fuck last night." Scooter paused, letting his words soak in. "I'm going to keep him here for a few days but will bring him home as soon as I'm able."

"Thank you. And please thank Natalie for me too."

"I will."

We said our goodbyes and disconnected the call. I placed the phone on the counter in front of me and drank my coffee, watching my cell. I wasn't sure what I was expecting. Phoenix had issues. Serious issues. We were usually able to talk him down off the ledge most times but obviously in this case, he needed a little more help than me and our brothers could provide.

"Tabs."

I jumped, spun around, and found Beck coming toward me. He poured himself a cup of coffee and leaned against the counter. He nodded toward my phone. "You talk to Scooter?"

"Yeah, just got off the phone with him. Phoenix is doing better. These fights bother me though," I told him, voicing my worry out loud.

"They're getting bad again, huh?"

"Yeah." I sighed. "I'm just glad Scooter was there to help him. I guess Natalie is there too." I shrugged, not sure what was going on between the three of them but would support my brother in any way that I could.

"He'll get through this. We all will." Beck blew the steam off his coffee before taking a sip. "We have you to help us."

"You will always have me. No matter what." Before I could say any more on it, the screen on my phone lit up with an incoming text from Ashton. My eyes widened as I read what he wrote.

Beck's eyes dropped to the phone but before he could read the text or sext in this case, I snatched the cell off the counter.

"What was that?" he asked, frowning.

I laughed, dumped my coffee in the sink, and went to leave the kitchen when his next words stopped me.

"You think he's not using you?"

"Have you ever thought that maybe I was using him or that we were using each other?" Before Beck could comment any more on it, I quickly made my way to the door of the loft.

Ashton's text burned into my memory, sending a hot shiver down my spine.

Ashton: I'm outside your door. I need your pussy. I need it fucking dripping…

That had been all I read before I shoved my phone back in my pocket.

Reaching the door, I looked behind me to see if Beck had followed. When he hadn't, I unlocked the door and opened it.

Ashton grabbed my hand, pulling me into his arms.

"Wait, I—"

His mouth came down hard on mine, silencing every word I was going to say.

Ashton snaked his arm around my waist and pulled me even closer.

"Ashton." I broke the kiss, taking a step back. "Beck's still here."

"Don't give a shit." He came into the apartment and shut the door behind him. In a rough move, he threw me over his shoulder and stomped to my room. Luckily my room was close, so you wouldn't be able to see us from the kitchen.

When we were inside my room, Ashton kicked the door closed, clicked the lock into place, and tossed me onto the bed.

"Ashton," I breathed, watching him. He was unhinged in the way his hands roamed over every inch of me. He gripped the hem of my tank top, shoved it up to my neck, and covered one of my pierced nipples with his mouth.

I arched into him, a breathless gasp leaving me.

He repeated the movement with the other one, releasing it seconds later with a wet pop. His mouth roamed down the length of me, licking and sucking, biting and nipping a path to where we both wanted him most.

He hooked his fingers into the waist of my pajama shorts and pulled them down my body. In a rough move, he spread my legs, keeping his palms pressed firmly against my inner thighs. He leaned down toward my center, taking a deep inhale.

"Fuck, you smell good."

I whimpered, shaking and watching him with wide eyes. "Please."

Our eyes locked.

He smirked before lowering his mouth to my pussy.

I sighed, my eyes rolling into the back of my head.

Ashton hummed, happy noises left him as he lapped and sucked at my center. A tingle spread in my toes, indicating the impending orgasm but as my breathing picked up, he released me with a wet smack.

"Ashton," I whined.

He grabbed my thighs, pulled me under him, and leaned his mouth down to my ear. "I need you to come on my cock."

My heart jumped.

Wrapping my arms around his shoulders, I spread my legs even more. While both of us were still partially dressed, it almost made it seem that much better. Like we couldn't get completely naked because we needed that connection so damn badly.

Ashton reached between us, the sound of a zipper lowering sent a shiver throughout every inch of me.

Lifting my leg, I wrapped it around his waist at the same time as he sank into me.

I whimpered, a slight tinge of pain erupting through me at him stretching me wide.

He cupped my thigh, pulling my leg from around his waist and pushing my knee against the bed. The movement kept me spread open for him as he partially held me down.

Holding onto him, I couldn't control the moans and whimpers leaving my lips as he slowly gave us both what we wanted. His thrusts were deliberate, torturous even, as he pumped in and out of me.

"Ashton," I whispered, licking along the length of his neck.

He leaned back, ripping his shirt up and over his head.

Before I even had a chance to touch him, he was back on me. With his mouth fused to mine, he linked his fingers between my own and pulled my arms up and over my head.

His hips picked up speed, forcing the pleasure higher and higher.

Ashton broke the kiss and lifted his head. He stared down at me and if I didn't know any better, I would say that he was searching for something. Anything at all that would give him a hint that I wanted this to either end or continue. I hoped he didn't ask, because I wasn't sure. All I knew was that I just wanted to enjoy this moment with him. The rest could wait.

(Ashton)

A couple of hours later and Tabatha was passed out beside me. She gave as good as she got. When I started fucking her, she came rather quickly. Her soft words had begged me to stop because she couldn't take any more but it only made me go harder and deeper. My dick felt like it was going to fall off with how hard her pussy squeezed me, but the pain was worth it. Everything with her was worth it.

It was later in the morning. The curtains were partially closed, the sun streaming into her bedroom. It cast a glow around her, shining down on her pale skin.

"I can feel you staring, creeper," she teased, her voice rough with lack of sleep.

"Careful, Kitten." I reached between us and brushed my fingers over her center before running them higher to the tight little spot at her ass. "Not sure your body could handle me fucking you here yet but keep up the sass and I'll see if I'm right or not."

A husky laugh left her. She rolled onto her side away from me, pushing her ass into my waist.

Hooking one arm under her head, I kissed the spot by her ear. Wrapping my other arm around her chest, I pulled her back against me and continued running my fingers along the spot I would one day fuck.

Dipping my fingers lower, I found that she was once again soaked. "Is this from my cum, Kitten, or do you really like that?"

"Both." She moaned.

"Open for me," I said, tapping her pussy lightly.

Tabatha ripped off the covers and threw her leg over my hip.

"Good girl." I lowered my mouth to her shoulder and bit down at the same time I ran my fingers up and down her swollen clit.

She cried out, her thighs trembling.

She was beautiful in the way she let herself go. Her cheeks were rosy, her pink hair was a mess of curls around her head. Dark makeup was smudged around her eyes. But she was fucking stunning.

"Ashton," she whined, reaching behind her and grabbing onto my dick.

My hips bucked into her touch. A low growl escaped me.

Tabatha lined the tip of me up with her ass.

My eyes widened. "What are you doing?"

"I want you to come on me," she whispered, her cheeks turning even darker.

"Don't be embarrassed by something you want, baby." I kissed her softly on the mouth. "I got you." Turning her onto her stomach, I brushed the hair off the back of her neck. "I do suggest biting the pillow though."

"What? Why?"

I chuckled, lifting her hips and pushing a pillow under her waist. Reaching above her, I pulled her pillow closer. "Bite it," I growled.

She did as she was told, her breathing coming out in short bursts of air.

Leaning back, I ran my hand down her spine. Cupping the cheeks of her ass, I spread her open. Her juicy pussy glistened. Running my thumb along her slit, I brushed the juices from her body up to the spot at her ass.

"Do you have any toys?"

She pulled the pillow from between her teeth, nodding to her nightstand. "In the top drawer."

Towering over her, I quickly looked through her collection until I found something that would work. It was about eight inches, not overly thick but she would still feel it. "This will do."

"What are you going to do with that?"

"Trust me, Kitten." I kissed the side of her head. "You'll enjoy this."

Kneeling back between her spread legs, I ran the tip of the dildo along her center. Pushing it into her body, it forced a low moan from somewhere deep inside her. I pumped it a few times to get it nice and wet before pulling it from her pussy.

"God," she breathed.

Brushing the dildo up to the tight spot at her ass, I gently pushed it against her. Her hips bucked, pushing back into me.

I chuckled. "Patience, greedy girl." I ran the toy over her soaked center and back up to the tight little rim. Repeating the movements, I got the area nice and wet before slowly pushing it against her.

She moaned, fisting the blankets in front of her.

"I think you'll love my cock in your ass," I told her, slipping two fingers into her pussy at the same time I pushed the dildo into her ass.

She gasped, throwing her head back. "Probably," she whined.

Hooking my fingers, I rubbed them against her G-spot while I pumped the dildo gently into her ass. The sounds of pleasure leaving her made my cock leak and become even harder.

"Ashton, please."

"You're lucky I'm in a good mood." I pulled my fingers from her and lined the tip of my cock up with her pussy. "Deep breaths, baby. I don't want to hurt you but you're going to feel quite full."

"I don't care." She shook her head. "I need you inside me."

"Damn right you do." Sinking into her in one smooth move, I shoved the dildo into her even deeper.

She cried out, biting down hard on the pillow. It muffled her cries but it did nothing for the sounds of her pussy sucking me even deeper inside her body.

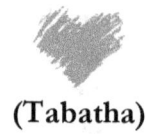

(Tabatha)

It had been on the tip of my tongue to tell him to stop. The pleasure burned through me but I craved it. God, it felt good. He felt good.

Ashton pulled me to all fours, fucking his cock into me in slow torturous moves as he pumped that toy into my ass.

"Harder," I heard myself cry out.

He grunted, pulled out of me, and gently removed the toy from my body.

I was about to ask what he was doing when I felt the crown of his cock rubbing against my ass. My eyes widened.

Ashton towered over me, leaning his arms on the bed at either side of my head. "Let me in, Kitten," he whispered, kissing the corner of my mouth. "Let me in every inch of you."

I whimpered, knowing he wasn't just talking about my body but my heart too.

He pushed against me; a part of my body that had definitely never been used for pleasure before no matter how many times I had hinted at it with previous guys I had been with.

Leaning my chest on the bed, I pulled my knees under me. Biting down hard on a part of the pillow, I reached around and cupped the cheeks of my ass, spreading myself open for him.

"Fuck, baby," he groaned. "Now that's a sight."

Ashton ran the tip of his cock over my center and up to my ass. He repeated the movements a few times before keeping it at the tight rim.

He pushed.

I moaned.

He pushed some more.

I damn near exploded out of my skin.

"That's a good girl," he murmured, linking his fingers between mine and holding my hand by my head. "Take me, Kitten. Take all of me."

"Do it," I demanded. "Please. I need you." Before I could beg some more, he thrust forward, breaking past the barrier of my body and filling me to the hilt.

A sharp gasp left me, the hairs on my body tingling at the new foreign feeling.

"Fuck, you're so damn tight." Ashton released my hand and grabbed my hips, pumping his cock in and out of my ass.

Every nerve in my body came alive as his movements picked up speed. His fingers dug into my hips, no doubt leaving a mark.

He was big and it stretched me to the point it burned. I rose onto shaky arms and began meeting him thrust for thrust.

"Fuck yeah, that's it, Tabatha."

I reached under me and began running my fingers along my swollen clit. A whimper left me, my eyes rolling into the back of my head.

"Make yourself come, baby." His hips powered forward and back, rolling in circles, damn near fucking my very soul. "Do it," he growled.

"God, Ashton." I cried out, rubbing frantically at my clit. "Harder, fuck my ass harder."

He grunted, grabbed me around the waist, and pulled me upright until I was leaning back against him. Wrapping his hand around my throat, he reached between my legs, both of us rubbing at my clit.

A tingle started in my toes, my breathing picked up. Before I could prepare myself for the orgasm, it slammed into me, knocking the breath out of me.

"Yes, yes, yes, fuck, Kitten, come all over me." He shoved two fingers into my pussy, slamming his hand hard against my center.

I gasped, a scream about to break free when his hand moved from my throat to my mouth.

"Your screams are mine, Tabatha," he growled, sinking his teeth into the side of my throat.

I whimpered, shaking against him.

Ashton gently pulled out of me and bent me over. He kissed the spot between my shoulder blades. My muscles hurt, my eyes heavy, and when a warm liquid hit the cheeks of my ass and tailbone, I couldn't help the moan leaving my lips.

"Fuck," he breathed. "I'll never get used to what your body does to me."

I laughed lightly, falling onto my stomach. "Can't say I've ever experienced that before."

"You mean you don't let every guy you're with fuck you in the ass, baby?" he asked, a teasing lilt to his voice.

"I've asked but they always turned me down."

"Good." He slipped off the bed and pulled me into his arms. "Means it was meant for me and only me."

"Hmm…" I wrapped my legs around his waist and ran a hand through his hair. "Maybe."

We stood like that for what felt like a while, staring at each other. Holding the other. I didn't want to think about these feelings I had for him because they scared me. He could break my heart. It had already been through so much, I didn't need to cause it any more pain.

"Let's get cleaned up," Ashton suggested, his voice lowering.

I nodded.

While we took a quick shower together, I couldn't help but watch him. The way he looked at me. The way he touched me. The way he made me feel alive. His hands roaming over every inch of me were soon replaced with his mouth. As much as I hurt, I couldn't help but want him again. My heart would have to wait because my body was the one talking at the moment.

FOURTEEN

ASHTON

TABATHA AND I HAD spent every chance we could, together. While she still had walls up, I could feel her letting me in. Even if it was slowly.

So much time had passed for us that the next thing I knew, we had already been sleeping together for just over three months. But even though that had been the case, she still wouldn't let me refer to what we were doing as a relationship.

We were fucking. Her words.

Most days I could let it go but sometimes, it pissed me off. Like the other night.

"Tell me again that we're just fucking." My hand around her throat, squeezed.

Tabatha gasped, her pupils dilating. "We're just fucking."

A wicked grin spread on my face. "You're a naughty girl, Kitten."

My back still hurt from her nails scratching it.

When I had first met her and proposed, my feelings then were more of the fact that she turned me down and called me an asshole. But now that my bed constantly smelled like her and I hung out with her as much as I could, I couldn't help but feel...more.

Aiden had been off lately. More so than usual. I didn't see him at the bar anymore, thankfully, and he would come to work, do his job, go home, and hide in his bedroom until the next day. It was on the tip of my tongue to ask him what his deal was but I didn't know how to broach the subject.

"I think I want to dye my hair light blue," Tabatha said one morning after I woke her up with my face between her legs. She was lying naked beside me with no covers on her, so I could stare at her beauty. My hand was currently on her hip, and it took everything in me not to dip it back between her milky white thighs.

"I think you could dye your hair neon orange and you would still look hot as fuck," I told her, watching my hand on her body.

She laughed. "Thank you but I think I'll stick with blue. Although a Creamsicle shade of orange would be cute."

My hand moved from her hip to the bow tattoo on the back of her thigh. "I can't get enough of you."

"Why did that sound like a bad thing?"

My eyes snapped to hers. "What do you mean?"

"I mean just what I said." Her gray eyes moved back and forth over my face.

"I don't know, Tabatha." I pulled my hand away from her and laid back, staring up at the ceiling. "Maybe it's because I still hardly know anything about you. We've been fucking for months. I know your name, your job, and the guys you live with. But I don't know where you're from. I don't know anything about your parents or family. I don't know *you*."

She looked down at the pillow. The pillow she had bitten because I didn't want anyone in her loft to hear her scream out my name. Her brothers knew we were sleeping together, they weren't stupid. Especially after the last time when I had left her room early in the morning to grab us both a bottle of water. Beck sat at the table, watching me the whole time, but didn't say a single word about it. I often wondered why but hadn't seen him much since to question him on it.

"I don't know much about you either, Ashton," she threw at me.

"Are you fucking serious right now?" I stared at her. "Remember all the conversations we've had on the phone? I told you about my brother. My family. My friends who are getting married, having kids and all that shit. I've told you about my job and how stressful it can be running the business on my own because my brother is having issues dealing with his PTSD that he won't admit to having." I sat up, swinging my legs over the side of the bed. I didn't want to fight with her but having sex was one thing. This wasn't what I wanted. I wanted it all. Every piece of her.

"Ashton." She came up behind me, her naked chest pressing against my bare back. "Why do we have to put a label on what we're doing?"

"Because as much as I like just fucking you, there's more that I want." I looked at her over my shoulder when she didn't respond. Instead, she pulled away and slid off the bed. A bed that I had spent countless hours in. A bed that was messy because of me. A bed that smelled like *us*.

It was almost like I could physically see her putting up another wall between us and as much as it pissed me off, I couldn't help the way my body reacted to hers. She was flawless. Curved to perfection. Marked by my touch. Kissed by my mouth.

"God, Ashton." Tabatha shivered beneath me as I trailed my tongue along every black line on her back. It had been something I wanted to do ever since I first met her. Now that I had, I wasn't stopping until she begged for more.

"I have to help Sarge with some paperwork," Tabatha said, pulling clothes from her dresser.

"Fine." I slipped off the bed and got dressed. "I'll get a workout in and then maybe, you'll want to talk to me. Or go out for dinner. Or something." We still hadn't gone on a proper date. No matter how many times I tried asking her, she always shot me down.

Her eyes snapped to mine in the reflection of her mirror. "I said no."

Before I could stop myself, I was standing directly behind her with my hand in her hair. I ripped her head back, probably a little too hard, but the whimper that left her full lips, made my dick twitch.

"You didn't say no when I had my cock deep in your cunt." I moved my hand to her throat, held her head back against my shoulder, and leaned down to her ear. "You didn't say no when your ass was filled with my dick." I could feel her throat move behind my hand. "You didn't say no whenever I called you, texted you, told you I needed you."

"Why can't we just keep fucking and that's it?" she asked, her eyes holding so many emotions that she wouldn't reveal to me.

"Why can't we have more?" I growled, staring directly into her eyes in the reflection of the mirror.

"Because you..." When she looked away, I tightened my hold on her throat.

"No, tell me, Tabatha. Tell me what the fuck you were just about to say."

Her gaze snapped back to mine.

"Tell me." I pushed my fingers against her jugular. "Say it."

"Because you deserve better," she whispered.

My heart jumped at her confession.

I released her and took a step back before turning her around. "What do you mean by that?" I asked her gently.

She only shrugged.

"Are you suggesting that you're going to end up hurting me? Do you have an ex I need to worry about? The guys say shit to you?" I pinched her chin, tilting her head back. "You gotta give me something here, Kitten, because I don't know what the fuck I've done or what you think you're going to do but I need something..."

Her eyes welled, her teeth grazing over her pierced bottom lip.

"Hey." I wrapped her up in my arms, lifting her onto her dresser and stepping between her knees. "Talk to me."

"I like you, Ashton," she finally said, her chin wobbling. "I really like you. I like what we're doing. But I can't have more.

Not now. Maybe not ever. So, if you want to end this, I get it."
Her gray eyes met mine. "It'll hurt but I understand."

"Are you fucking anyone else?"

Her eyes widened. "What? No." She shook her head. "Of course not."

"Good. Neither am I." I kissed her softly on the mouth. "We can keep doing what we're doing. Just fucking if that's all you can handle. But just know that I will make you fall in love with me. I will get my ring on your finger. And I will take you on that damn date. Even if it's fifty years from now. I don't give a fuck how long it takes." I pinched her chin, forcing her head back to meet my stare. "You are mine. You hear me?"

She opened her mouth to respond but she only nodded instead.

"Good girl." I stepped away from her and finished getting dressed. "I have a family thing tonight, but I'll text you after."

"Maybe you shouldn't."

My back stiffened. "Seriously?"

Tabatha got dressed and even though she was now fully clothed, my body still burned. For her. For this woman who was my undoing and who drove me fucking crazy at the same time.

"I think I need some time," she mumbled.

"Fine." I grabbed my wallet and keys off her nightstand. I was going to just leave but changed my mind. Stomping up to her, I wrapped my arm around her middle and pulled her flush against my body.

"Ashton." She tried struggling against me, but I only tightened my hold on her small body.

Before she could wiggle her way out of my grip, I grabbed a handful of her ass and slammed my mouth down hard on hers.

She sighed, slipping her tongue between my lips.

I pushed my waist into her, rubbing my growing erection against the apex between her thighs.

Tabatha moaned, snaking her arms around my neck.

Before the kiss could turn into more, I gave her bottom lip a gentle bite. "I'll see you later tonight."

She nodded, licking her kiss swollen lips.

"Have a good day, Kitten." I kissed her one last time, gave her ass a light swat, and left her room instead of doing what I really wanted to do.

Consume her completely.

(Tabatha)

It took everything in me not to go after him. Not to run into Ashton's arms and bring him back to my bed. I could feel him getting close. Too close. And then my mouth got away from me and said things I didn't mean. I liked him. I liked what we were doing. He wanted to actually date and I wanted that too, but words left my lips before I could stop myself.

Ashton was determined, I gave him that much. But I also knew that one of these days, he was going to have enough and leave. For good. I wouldn't blame him though. I was a difficult person to be with and I had no idea why he was even remotely interested in me.

When I was finished getting ready for the day, I grabbed my bag and left my bedroom. I couldn't hear anything coming from the kitchen, so I hoped Ashton slipped out quietly. Not that my brothers didn't already know I was sleeping with him. It was just easier if they pretended that I was still that little girl they used to tease and pick on.

Bracing myself, I headed out to the kitchen and found Beck sitting at the table.

"I saw Ashton," Beck said, taking a sip of his coffee. "He looked pissed."

Pouring myself a cup of coffee, I joined him. "He's getting too close."

"Ah yes, it seems we all have commitment issues." He stood from the table and went to the fridge. He came back with a pint of chocolate chip ice cream and two spoons.

It was on the tip of my tongue to say that it was too early for ice cream, but I found that I suddenly needed the cold sugary substance.

"You don't have to be like the rest of us, Tabs," Beck said, sitting back at the table beside me.

"I know." I popped the lid off the pint and shoved my spoon into the ice cream. "I like him, but I'm not used to having a guy tell me exactly how he feels. Is that even normal?"

Beck chuckled. "It depends on the guy. But I've been known to say what's on my mind from time to time."

"I'm sure most women would appreciate the honesty, but I'm just not used to it. I don't know. I just don't want to…what if my health…" I sighed, not really knowing how to voice out loud what I was feeling.

"Hey." Beck moved to the empty chair beside me. "You can't live like that." He pulled me in for a hug. "You know you can't."

"I know." My chin wobbled, my eyes welling. As much as Beck never approved of whichever guy I dated, he was always there when I needed to talk. I pulled away from him and took another spoonful of ice cream. "I don't want to hurt him."

"You must care for him if you're concerned about this."

"I do but even if this had nothing to do with my health, what if he leaves me like…" God, I couldn't even finish the question.

"I like him for you. I think he's actually what you need but I understand your hesitation. I don't have time for a relationship but if I did, I'd want what you have."

I looked at him then. "Ashton and I aren't in a relationship."

"You can say you're not in a relationship all you want, but you're in denial. That is a relationship, Tabs. Maybe an unconventional one, but it is. No matter how much you push him away, he's still there." Beck paused. "But just remember that a person can only take so much. Don't push him away too hard or it might end up being for good. I also know that you're wanting to protect your heart. Your parents…that shit was fucked up."

A shaky sigh left me. My mom leaving when I was just a little girl and my dad dying far too soon, was never something I wanted to dwell on. Before I could let those thoughts take control completely, I left the table to grab another coffee.

"You working at Sarge's today?" Beck asked, joining me in the kitchen.

"Yeah, he's helping a few guys train for some fights, so I told him that I would work on the books for him. Gotta keep that man on the straight and narrow."

"Good." Beck pulled me in for a tight hug. "I love you, Tabs, and I only want the best for you. If that means being with Ashton, then I support you. If you don't want to be with him, I support that too. But just make sure you think long and hard before you push him away for good." He released me and left the kitchen. "I'll see you later," he called out, the door shutting sounding a moment later.

After cleaning up the kitchen, I finished getting ready and made my way down to the gym on the main floor. It had been convenient when Sarge decided to open up a gym. He had wanted to do something now that he was no longer a cop. So, he bought the gym and let my brothers and I stay in the loft for cheap. It worked out for us all.

When I entered the gym, I saw a couple of guys sparring and working out. One guy looked my way, nodded once, and went back to punching his fists into the pads another man was holding.

Tucking my head, I quickly made my way to the back of the gym.

Beck's words rang in my head. Should I give Ashton a chance? Could he make me happy and not hurt me in the process? So many questions bounced around in my head but at the moment, I would just enjoy what I currently had with him and hope for the best that he wouldn't end things before I had a chance to let my guard down.

FIFTEEN

ASHTON

PULLING UP IN FRONT of Angel and Jay Rodriguez's place, I killed the engine and stared out at the big house sitting to my right. They were friends of my parents and while I had known them my whole life, a part of me felt like I didn't belong. Much like my brother, both of us struggled with our own…issues. His involved drinking and mine involved a woman who wanted nothing to do with me, but at the same time never told me no.

Checking my phone, I didn't see any new calls or texts from Tabatha, so I decided to call her up instead. Not expecting her to answer, the sound of her voice mail picking up instead, grated on my nerves. When it indicated that it was time for me to leave a message, I left the car. "I was going to text you but decided that you deserve to hear my voice instead. I don't know what the fuck is going on with you, but I refuse to let you push me away. So, get ready, Kitten, because every inch of your body is mine. Every. Single. Fucking. Inch. Oh and, Tabatha?" I chuckled for added effect. "I'm not going to be nice." I disconnected the call, blew out a slow breath, and shoved the phone back in my pocket.

I could hear voices coming from the backyard. Cars lined the street and driveway. I recognized one of the vehicles as my parents', along with the people I had grown up with.

My phone took that moment to start ringing as another car pulled down the road and parked in front of the house.

Without checking to see who was calling me, I answered my phone. "Hello?"

"You can't send me voice mails like that, Ashton," Tabatha said instead of greeting me back.

I chuckled, holding the phone up to my ear. "No? Is there a problem with what I promised you?"

"Yes."

"And what problem is that?" I asked her when I saw an old fling leave the passenger side of the car that just drove by me. Her husband left the driver's side and they both helped their two children out of the back. It felt like not too long ago, where I had caused issues for Jaron and Piper. I acted like she had hurt me when she ended things when really, my feelings weren't actually hurt. I was jealous. Of what they had. Their happiness. That she was smart enough to break it off with whatever my brother and I were doing with her before it became too weird. Aiden had never been overly into it anyway, but I always used the excuse that she ripped his heart out.

"You're not here to do anything about it, Ashton," Tabatha grumbled.

"Aww, is someone missing my cock?" I teased.

"Asshole," she muttered. "Just come here when you're done with your family thing."

"Trust me, baby. I was going to come over even if you told me not to." I disconnected the call and shoved the phone back in my pocket. Taking a deep breath, I braced myself for Jaron to say something like he always did.

"Hey, Ashton." Piper gave me a small wave, holding her daughter, Brynlee, in her arms. "How are you?"

"Not too bad. You?"

"Good." She looked behind her as Jaron came up beside her with a car seat in one hand. Their son was sleeping and even from where I stood, I could see the tanned complexion that was all his father.

"We going to behave tonight?" Jaron threw at me, hooking his free arm around his wife.

I grunted. "I haven't given you shit in months."

"Yeah." Jaron's gray eyes met mine. "Let's keep it that way."

"Be nice," Piper scolded him. "You sure you're good?" she asked me.

"Yeah, I am." I would be better if my girl stopped trying to keep me at arm's length but in time, I knew I would get through to her.

"Where's your brother?" As soon as the question left Jaron's mouth, a cab pulled up in front of the house.

Aiden exited the back and stumbled toward us.

My stomach twisted. I went near him before he could cause a scene, or our father ended up killing him on the spot.

"You couldn't have waited until after to drink, Aiden?" I bit out, stepping in front of him.

He grunted, swaying on his feet. "I'm fine."

"Ashton."

I wasn't sure who said my name but at that point, I didn't give a shit. My brother was my main focus at the moment. "You have to stop this, Aiden," I mumbled, low enough for only him to hear.

His brows narrowed, eyes that mirrored my own, locked on me. "Yeah, and because you're so fucking perfect, Ashton."

"I'm not perfect. No one is. But alcohol is taking over your life. You have to—"

"I don't have to do shit." He shoved me back, forcing me to stumble and almost land on my ass.

"No?" I grabbed him by the collar of his shirt and pulled him closer. "You keep showing up drunk off your ass. Dad is going to kill you. You remember what happened last time?"

Aiden's jaw clenched. "Let go of me."

I released him roughly and began walking away from him. "Fine. I'm done." I went around the side of the house and to the back, no longer giving a shit if Dad did something or not. I had spent the last couple of years trying to protect my brother. Our father was an amazing man but when it came to his wife and her being hurt or upset, he became evil very quickly. Though we were his sons, and even now that we were adults, he didn't give a shit what our relation was to him. If mom was involved, he would do what he could to make things right. No matter the cost. Aiden was going to have to learn the hard way it seemed.

"Ashton." Meadow Allen came toward me, holding her son Andrew in her arms.

"Hey, buddy." I messed up his hair. "Treating your mama well?"

"Always." Meadow laughed. "How are you doing?"

"Aiden's here and drunk off his ass." I shrugged, looking around the backyard. My parents were nowhere to be found.

"I feel bad for him." Meadow sighed. "Other than that, you good?"

It was the same question she had asked ever since we stopped sleeping together so many years ago. But now that Aiden was an alcoholic, she asked it more. I appreciated her being nice, but she didn't have to worry about me.

"Don't worry about me, Meadow." I kissed the side of her head and walked away, joining some of the guys I had grown up with in the backyard.

Before I could say hi or any sort of greeting for that matter, a commotion sounded at the front of the house.

"Shit," I mumbled.

"Ashton." Piper rushed to me. "Aiden got in your dad's face."

"Fuck." I ran from the backyard to the front of the house, finding Aiden on the ground with my dad clutching his shirt.

Mom was off to the side with Jay and a few of the other parents.

"Asher, get off of your son," Mom cried, pleading with her husband to not damage my brother more than he already had.

I rushed to the bundled heap on the ground and grabbed my dad around the shoulders. Pulling him back, I tore him away from Aiden but not before I heard his muttered words.

"You're a disappointment."

Aiden stared at him and for the very first time in years, I saw a hint of emotion in his eyes.

"What the hell's going on?"

"Asher."

Aiden rose to his full height and swayed on his feet. He would have fallen over if not for Jaron catching him. "Let's take a walk."

Much to my surprise, Aiden didn't put up a fight and let Jaron push him away.

"Fuck." Dad pulled out of my arms and went up to Mom. "I'm sorry, Hummingbird."

She clutched his shirt and pushed her face against his chest.

"Ashton." Dad met my gaze, years of worrying about his other son written in the lines on his face.

I nodded. "I'll take him out of here."

I quickly said bye to everyone and rushed to where Jaron stood with Aiden. They were by my car with Aiden sitting on the back bumper and Jaron standing in front of him.

"I'm going to take him home," I said more to myself than to Jaron or even my brother.

Aiden stood, wobbling toward me. "I'm sorry."

"You have a real funny way of showing it, Aiden," I threw at him, opening the passenger side door for him.

"I am," he muttered, slipping into the car.

Once he was safe in the car, I let out a hard sigh.

"Did he say anything to you?" I asked Jaron.

"Nope." Jaron clapped my shoulder. "I know we've never really gotten along but if you need anything, I'm only a phone call away." He gave my shoulder a final squeeze before walking past me to join Piper and the rest of the group I had known my whole life.

I wasn't exactly sure what that was about, seeing as Jaron never offered his help before, but I couldn't focus on that at the moment.

Checking on Aiden to make sure he wasn't going to leave the car and do something stupid, a breath of relief left me when I saw he was sleeping.

"Ashton."

I turned, finding Mom and Dad coming toward me. "Listen, it's obvious that something happened to him while he was in the Navy. We all know that. But we need to be patient with him," I told them before either of them could say something about Aiden's current condition.

"Yeah, but he won't talk about it," Dad pointed out.

"I know but he will talk about it when he's ready. Maybe not to us but to someone." I glanced back at Aiden sleeping in my car. "I think something happened to his squad."

"Shit." Dad hugged Mom into his side. "I'll try and talk to him again. Maybe if we keep pressing, he'll unload."

"Let me try again," I insisted gently.

"Please try." Mom pulled away from Dad and came toward me. "I need your brother back. I need him happy. I don't care if any of you get drunk and have a good time but he's going overboard. I need…" Her eyes welled.

I hugged her to me, kissing the top of her head. "I know, Mama. I'll see what I can do."

"Take care of him." She leaned back. "I know he's struggling, and you may not think he needs you or that he's pushing people away, but he does need you. Both of you," she said to my dad and me.

"I know, Meeka." Dad grabbed her hand and kissed her knuckles. "Take care of your brother, Ashton." He pulled me into a one-armed hug. "Please take care of him."

"I will." My chest tightened. Returning the hug, I gave him a quick squeeze and released him to head back to my brother. He was still passed out thankfully, so I would drive him home and go over to Tabatha's at some point. Maybe she could come to my place. I didn't know. I didn't overly care. I just needed to see her. I needed her to tell me that everything would be alright.

Sending her a quick text, I told her what I was doing and asked if she would be willing to come over or if she would rather I go to her place. When her response came back with that she would come over to my apartment, I breathed out a sigh of relief that I didn't even know I had been holding.

Slipping into the car, I reached over without even thinking and checked Aiden's pulse. When I felt his heart beating beneath my fingers, another breath left me. "We'll get you sorted, Aiden. Somehow." I was determined to do what I could to help him, even if it meant just sitting there and doing fuck all.

Once we arrived at the apartment we shared together, I helped him into the building. I struggled a bit since he was practically dead weight, but we managed.

When I finally had him in his bed, I started taking off his shoes when the buzzer sounded indicating someone's arrival.

Rushing out of his room and down the hall, I smacked a hand against the control panel, without even answering. I could only assume it was Tabatha.

I unlocked the door and then went back to check on Aiden. He was still passed out on his stomach.

Rolling him onto his back, I moved the pillow under his head, so he would be comfortable.

"Thank you," he whispered.

My heart jumped. "You're welcome, brother." Kissing his head, I gave him a second look, making sure he was, in fact, fine. He was breathing and that was all I cared about.

Stepping out into the hall, I saw Tabatha coming toward me.

My body stirred at seeing her. Stomping toward her, I cupped the back of her neck and crushed my mouth to hers.

"Naked. Bed. *Now*." I pushed away from her and went to the bathroom but not before I caught the shiver trembling through her.

(Tabatha)

Something was wrong. It was in the air. I could sense it. I could practically feel it coating my skin and tickling every hair on my body.

When Ashton had texted me asking if I wanted to come over instead of him coming to my place, I figured something had gone down that involved his brother.

Once I entered Ashton's room, I slipped out of my clothes like he instructed. Usually, I would have given him a smart remark or been a brat about it, but truth was, I needed him just as much as he needed me. I would never tell him that. Not yet anyway. But I wanted to hurt. I wanted to ache as he gave us both the pleasure we so greatly desired.

Turning away from the door, I had just pulled off the last bit of clothing when the door shut behind me. The soft thump made my heart skip a beat and when the lock clicked into place, a hot shiver raced down the length of my spine.

"It's been a shitty night," Ashton said, his voice low and guttural. He came up behind me, brushing my hair off the back of my neck.

"Is your brother okay?" I asked softly.

"He's sleeping." Ashton's hand moved to my hair, fisting it and pulling my head back in a rough move. "But we're not here to talk about him. Now are we?"

I swallowed hard. "No, I guess we aren't."

"Turn around and kneel, Kitten."

I did as I was told, staring up at him.

"You're fucking beautiful," he whispered.

My cheeks heated, a slow grin spreading on my face at the compliment. Reaching for his jeans, I pulled him closer and pressed my mouth against his growing erection. Blowing out slowly, my hot breath forced a growl from somewhere deep inside of him.

I repeated the movement, unbuckling his belt and pulling down his zipper at the same time. Pushing my hand beneath his shirt, I grazed my fingers over his hard stomach and took him in my mouth.

"Fuck." Ashton's fingers latched on to the side of my head, pushing his cock deeper between my lips.

I gagged around him, taking a deep breath through my nose and letting him take the control he currently needed.

"So good," he panted, a moan following shortly after.

That single sound made the ache between my thighs more pronounced. Hearing him lose it and take what he wanted from me, knowing I was the only one who could give it to him, made me feel powerful.

Ashton pushed his cock deeper into my mouth, forcing me back against the edge of his bed.

Spreading my knees, I inched a hand between my thighs, needing to please that ache. Even if it was just for a moment, knowing that he was truly the only one who could make it better, I needed something to hold me over.

His eyes darkened, a knowing smirk spreading on his face.

Rubbing my fingers against my pierced clit, I moaned around his dick that was currently fucking my throat.

"Yes, baby, just like that." He leaned his head back, his hold on me tightening. "Fucking hell. So damn good."

My fingers rubbed harder, my body trying to find that release but, much to my dismay, it wouldn't come. A frustrated whine left me as I rubbed harder and faster.

Ashton pulled from my lips, gripping my jaw. "Stand."

I swallowed hard at the rough demand, never seeing him unhinged like this before. I rose to my full height as he kept his hand locked firm around my jaw. He pushed me back onto his bed, our eyes remaining locked with each other. He released me, stripped completely and crawled between my spread knees.

I went to turn over when he stopped me.

"No." He pushed my legs apart, lining the tip of him up with my center. "I want to watch you fall apart for me."

My jaw clenched and, even though he still had a hold of me, I tried turning my head away from his heated stare anyway.

"No," he repeated, his voice firm. When he thrust into me, he released my jaw, a shiver trembling through him.

I bit back a whimper at how good he felt to be back inside me once again. I couldn't get enough of him. His body. His words. His heated looks. His persistence. His need for me in a way I had never experienced before.

"Look at me," he growled, thrusting slow and deep.

Squeezing my eyes shut, I gripped the blankets beneath me.

"I said," he leaned down and bit the side of my throat, "look at me."

"No," I threw back at him.

His hand moved to my throat, squeezing just enough to force my eyes open. "You seem to like my fat dick deep inside your cunt. So why the fuck don't you want to look at me?"

Because you could possibly see my truths.

"It doesn't matter why." I reached around him and scratched my nails down his back. "Just fuck me."

He pushed into me as deep as my body would allow him.

I gasped, trying to reach for the air my lungs needed.

"I will ask you again." He tilted my head back. "Why won't you look at me?"

I looked at him then, knowing I was being a bitch but not caring at the moment. My feelings for him were growing. As much as I tried fighting it, I couldn't help it. Ashton had wormed his way into my life and my heart, and I wasn't sure how I felt about it.

"We're fucking, Ashton. That's all we're doing. Why do we need to talk when you're inside me?"

"Because something's wrong." He released my throat and cupped his hands under my knees before pushing them to my chest. "Hold your knees," he demanded gently, resting his hands on the bed at either side of my head. "Tell me why you don't want to look at me." He pulled most of the way out of me before lowering back into my body in one smooth rough thrust.

"I don't want you to look at *me*, Ashton," I cried, holding my knees to my chest.

Ashton's hips slowed, pumping hard and giving me what I needed. He lowered his mouth to my throat, his hot breath fanning the side of my head. "I see you, Kitten. Whether you want me to or not. *I see you.*"

"I...just...please don't stop." I latched on to him, sinking my teeth into his shoulder. "Please don't ever stop."

"I won't," he whispered. "I can promise you that."

SIXTEEN

Tabatha

ASHTON FUCKED ME TWO more times before he left me alone. But he still kept me close. He passed out with half his body on top of mine, his hand cupping my breast, his dirty words and whispered truths in my ears.

Glancing over at his still form, the sound of his deep breathing mixed with some soft snores, settled the anxiety that had rushed through me earlier.

When he made me look at him, it was unsettling. They say that eyes are windows to the soul. I didn't want him to see into mine. I didn't want him to see how jealous I was of random couples I didn't know but envied nonetheless. I didn't want Ashton to see that I was lonely but scared of being loved. Because once I opened myself up for those feelings, it would backfire. I knew it would because it always did.

Leaving the bed and Ashton's warmth, I quickly got dressed and grabbed my bag. As I stepped out into the hall, I looked back into the room. He hadn't moved and a part of me wished he had. That same part wished he would jump out of bed and demand to know why I was so damn scared. Why I fought this when clearly I had feelings for him.

Swallowing a sigh, I quietly closed the door.

"Sneaking off so soon?"

I jumped, finding Aiden standing behind me. "I just...I don't..."

"You don't have to explain anything to me." He walked by me. "I'm not the one you're fucking. But I do know that if Ashton doesn't find you beside him, he's not going to be happy about that." He stopped at the entrance to the hallway. "Coffee?"

"Yeah. Sure." I followed him, knowing I should leave if I didn't want to face Ashton's wrath, but there was something stopping me. I just couldn't figure out what it was.

Heading to the dining room table, I dropped my bag on the floor and sat at one of the chairs.

"How do you take your coffee?" Aiden asked from the kitchen.

"Just milk please." I kept glancing at the hall that led to Ashton's room, expecting him to come barreling out at any moment and ask me questions I wasn't ready to answer.

Aiden finally left the kitchen carrying two mugs. He placed one in front of me before sitting on the other side of the table.

"How are you feeling?" I asked him, taking a sip of the much-needed sustenance.

He shrugged. "Same old." He drank from his mug and looked my way every so often.

Every time he glanced at me, I fidgeted in my chair. It got to the point where I was ready to just up and leave but that would be rude, and I wouldn't do that.

"What?" I finally demanded. I wasn't sure what it was about these brothers, but it was like as soon as they looked at you, they could reach into your soul and find out all of your secrets.

"We haven't officially met," Aiden said, placing the mug on the table in front of him. He ran the tip of his index finger along the rim, looking at it longingly.

"We have actually. The first night I met both of you, Ashton ended up leaving and had me call a cab for you. You introduced yourself and I did the same." I leaned forward. "You don't remember?"

"Nope, but I don't remember a lot of things. And things I do remember, I wish I didn't." His eyes lifted, looking straight ahead.

I followed his gaze, finding Ashton standing at the entrance to the hallway. His gaze was locked on me, his jaw as hard as granite. He was pissed. At me. And for once, I didn't blame him.

"You were going to leave," Ashton said, nodding toward my bag on the floor at my feet.

"On that note." Aiden stood, grabbed his coffee, and left the dining room. He went up to his brother, muttered something to him, and headed down the hall.

Once Ashton and I were alone, I looked away.

"I was expecting to wake up to a fight with you, but I never expected you to be gone."

"I didn't leave." I rose from the chair, grabbed my coffee, and went to the kitchen to dump it out. It was good but my mouth had suddenly gone dry and I wasn't overly in the mood for it anymore.

"You didn't leave," Ashton repeated, following me. "I text you last night, tell you I need you, you come over, we fuck. A lot. And then this happens. Why? Why the hell are you keeping me at arm's length?"

Grinding my teeth together, I inhaled deep, sharp breaths. I couldn't tell him. Hell, I didn't even know the answer to his question anymore. I had feelings for him. I knew I did. But it wasn't enough. He would leave me. Just like my parents did.

"I have commitment issues," I heard myself say.

"Yeah, no shit."

My head whipped around. I glared at him, wishing he could go back to being the womanizer he said he used to be. Why the hell did he have to choose me to fall for?

"Keep the dirty looks to yourself, baby." He closed the distance between us, overcrowding me and making me wish I could give him more.

"What do you want with me? Is it because I keep telling you no?" I threw at him. "Is it because you're not used to the fact that a woman doesn't want more from you?"

"Oh, but that's where you're wrong, Kitten." He pushed a loose strand of hair behind my ear. "You do want more. You're just scared. And before you bite my head off and tell me I'm wrong, just think about it. You know I'm right. I don't know why you're scared but you are." He paused. "I won't hurt you."

"I never said that I was scared that you would hurt me." I placed my hands against his chest, feeling the beating of his heart beneath my palm.

"Are you scared that you'll hurt me?" He covered my hand, bringing it up to his mouth.

"I don't know. Maybe. I've never been one to talk about my feelings. I like you, Ashton. I like you a lot. But that's all I can give you right now." Maybe ever.

Ashton's beautiful blue eyes searched my face. His jaw clenched and I knew he was ready to demand for more. But what more could I give him?

"I'm falling in love with you," he murmured.

All breath left me at his confession.

When I went to pull away from him, his hold on my hand only tightened.

"No. You don't want to talk to me? Fine. But you're sure as fuck going to listen to me talk to *you*." He pushed me back until I hit the edge of the counter. Closing that final space between us, he pressed his hard body up against mine, closing me in. "I'm in love with you. I don't expect you to say it back because I know you won't. Maybe you never will. But I need you to know how I feel since you're giving me shit all."

Ashton reached around me, cupped my ass, and lifted me onto the counter in a rough move. He shoved his waist between my legs, caging me in to the point I had nowhere to go but directly into his arms.

"I remember the first time a woman told me they were falling in love with me. I didn't take it well. I was an asshole and broke up with her. But to be fair, I was also only in high school. I don't know who hurt you but I'm not him. I won't leave you even though you push me away." He kissed my jaw. "I'm here. I'm always here. I see you, Tabatha, even though you don't want me to. I see your pain. Your fear of getting too close. You have the strongest fucking walls I have ever dealt with before, but I promise you, no matter how much you drive me fucking crazy or we piss each other off, I won't leave you."

My chest tightened, my eyes welling at his words. "How come?"

He tilted his head, his bright blue eyes searing into my soul. "How come I won't leave you? Have you learned nothing about me at all? All this time we've been hanging out and sleeping together, you haven't learned one single thing about me?"

"They always leave. Always. People are not dependable."

"No. Some people aren't. But I am not them. I am just me. Ashton. A man who finally found a woman he wants to be with only for her to want nothing to do with him. Karma is a fucking bitch, but I guess I deserve this." Ashton leaned his forehead against mine. "Give me something, Kitten."

My breath hitched.

"You have to give me something." His voice was thick with desperation, and I knew. Even though he told me he wouldn't leave, Beck was right. A person could only handle so much before they had to move on.

"I can't," I whispered, wrapping my arms around Ashton's thick shoulders.

"What the hell are you so damn scared of?" he demanded, his mouth finding the side of my throat.

"That you'll leave me just like my parents did. That you'll get sick of me. That you will move on to something better. I'm a mess. I have a temper. I can be a bitch just for the sake of being a bitch. I'd rather deal with animals than people. My brothers are the only ones who have never hurt me but even they don't know me. Not completely. I just... I'm scared..." Tears streamed down my cheeks. "I'm scared that I'll get cancer again and won't be able to beat it and then you'll be left alone. I'm scared that I'm too much for you." A sob left me, my emotions ripping through me.

"Fuck, baby." Ashton hugged me to him, murmuring words in my ear I couldn't make out but could feel just the same.

My sobs wracked through me. They were so damn hard; I couldn't control my breathing.

"Shhh…I'm here." Ashton lifted me off of the counter, cradling me against his chest.

Next thing I knew, we were on his bed. He sat on the edge with me on his lap.

Even though I never expected to get my truths out, I did feel a little better that I finally told him what my issues were. Besides the cancer, my parents leaving fucked me up. Even though my dad dying wasn't his fault, a part of me still blamed him because it was his choices that had gotten him killed.

Wiping my face, I was met by beautiful blue eyes.

"You good?" Ashton asked gently, running his hands up and down my back.

"Yeah. Who knew that crying like that could make you feel better?" I tried making light of the situation, but we needed to talk about what I told him.

"Is that what the recent doctor's visits have been for?"

Okay, so we were going to start with that.

I took a breath, nodding. "I have to go regularly to make sure the cancer hasn't come back. They were able to catch it early because I wasn't feeling well. I know my body, so I went to my doctor's and thankfully, he actually listens to what the patients say, and he set me up with a whole bunch of tests. They came back with early signs of cancer in my right kidney. I had surgery." I lifted my top, grabbed his hand and ran his fingers over the light scar in my side. "They were able to remove it but if the cancer comes back, I'll need a transplant."

His face softened. "I never noticed this scar before." He ran his thumb along the bumpy ridge. It was covered by a tattoo of a flower, so he wouldn't notice it unless he knew what to look for.

"That's why I got the tattoo."

"Did you have your brothers there with you?"

I nodded, thankful for the guys who had been put in my life at a time I didn't know I needed them.

"I remember when I met them as a girl. We were all put in the same foster home around the same time. I was the only girl and I've heard stories about other foster homes being awful, but I was blessed. Even though none of us are related by blood, the guys took me under their wing right away. They promised to protect me, and they have ever since." I laughed to myself at a memory. "Once we got older and other guys started noticing me, it was hard to date. Beck was the worst of them all and would fight any boy who showed even a little bit of interest in me."

Ashton gave me a small smile. "I imagine it was hard to form any relationships with the opposite sex with those guys involved."

"Yeah." I ran my fingers over the light scruff on his strong jaw. "But maybe it was for a reason. Maybe they were unintentionally letting me know that those random guys in high school, weren't who I was meant to be with. Maybe they were helping me wait for you."

"Tabatha," Ashton murmured, his voice low.

"I have trust issues. Which I'm sure you figured out already. My mom…" I took a deep breath, never telling anyone other than my brothers this. "I was six when my mom left. She gave me a kiss one day, told me to be a good girl for my dad, and I never saw her again."

"Shit," Ashton mumbled.

"I remember crying and screaming for her for days. My dad couldn't console me. But I guess the silver lining in that shit was that it brought my father and me closer." My chest ached. "I miss him. He was shady as hell, but he treated me well enough. He would bring me to his poker games. I would sit on his knee, he would teach me and eventually it got to the point that his friends treated me like their own kid. They all taught me how to play and they also taught me how to cheat without getting caught."

"What happened to your dad?" Ashton asked, running his hands up and down my back.

I pulled away from him, sliding off his lap. Taking a deep breath, I began pacing. "My dad ended up cheating at the wrong game and he was killed for the money he stole."

"I'm so fucking sorry, Kitten."

I stopped, looking at him. "One of the guys put me in the closet, told me to be quiet, and took my dad out. So I never saw it. But I heard it. I heard him die." My eyes welled, all of these emotions coming on strong. I had pushed them away for so long, it was like the fact they had built up over the years, I could no longer control them.

Ashton left the bed and closed the distance between us, wrapping me up in his warm embrace. "I can't imagine. But I'm here. I'm here, baby."

I grabbed his shirt, pulling him even closer, needing to get under his skin. As much as I tried denying it, he was my safe place. He was what I had needed this whole time. "I'm in love with you, Ashton."

His breath caught, his body stiffening in my touch.

"But I'm scared, and I need you to be patient with me."

He cupped the back of my head and crouched until we were at eye level. "You ever feel like you're backed into a corner or that fear becomes so much, you feel like pushing me away, come to me and at least tell me. Tell me and we'll talk it out. I've been a shithead for most of my adult life when it comes to women, but I've changed. You have changed me."

I stared at him, searching his face for any sign that he didn't mean what he said. That he was only saying it because he wanted to get laid. But the sincerity rolling off of him took my breath away.

"This..." I touched his lips. "This is intense."

"I know." He kissed my fingertips as they passed over his mouth. "I thought I was cursed to never find what my friends have. I thought maybe because I wasn't always good to women, that I would be doomed to be alone forever. It's dramatic but it's how I felt. And then with the shit my brother's going through, a lot of women wouldn't want to deal with that anyway."

"My own brothers have their baggage. It's not our fault."

"I know." Ashton placed a soft peck on my forehead before leaning his against mine. "I told you I'd make you fall in love with me."

A light laugh left me. "It's not like I had any choice."

He chuckled. "Spend the day with me."

I only nodded and watched him pull away from me.

"I'll grab your bag." He left the room, coming back a moment later with my bag in hand. I was still standing in the same spot, waiting for him like I had been doing my whole entire life.

Instead of saying anything, he placed the bag by the foot of his dresser. His gaze met mine in the reflection of his mirror. "If you end up needing a kidney, I'll give you one of mine if I can."

My stomach tumbled. "What?"

"I'm serious." He turned toward me. "We only need one, right?"

"Yeah, but that's…you can't be serious." That was a lot to ask of him. To ask of anyone.

"Of course, I'm serious." He came toward me, taking my hands in his. "Lots of people donate kidneys to absolute strangers. We aren't strangers. I'd be honored to give you a kidney, if it came down to it."

My eyes welled, tears dripping down my cheeks. Pulling my hands from his, I threw myself around him, unable to form the words.

"Thank you for putting up with my shit."

A laugh rumbled through him. "I'm not any easier to deal with."

Lifting my head, I wiped my cheeks and stared at the man who had been persistent from the very beginning. The man I had fallen in love with. The man I had become stripped bare for.

"Keep looking at me like that, Kitten, and we won't be talking for much longer," Ashton murmured, his mouth finding my jaw.

"I don't want to talk anymore." A yawn trembled through me. "But I don't want to go back to bed, just yet."

Instead of answering, he pushed me off of his lap and stood. Grabbing the hem of my shirt, he lifted it up and over my head before lowering to his knees in front of me.

"Marry me," he finally said.

"No." I gave him a small smile.

He smiled in return.

My breath caught at seeing the love in his eyes. Unsure as to what he was about to do, I found that I couldn't stop him. Whether this turned into sex or him just kissing and touching me, I wanted it. I wanted it all. And I didn't care what or who I had to go through to get it.

(Ashton)

She was in love with me, and it was the greatest mother fucking feeling in the world. But it would still take some time for her to lower her guard down completely and I had to say that I didn't blame her for that.

When Tabatha finally revealed her truths and her fears, it all made sense. I didn't like it, but I understood it.

I meant what I told her. I was there and I wasn't going anywhere. Not when I just found her. Not when I realized that I was, in fact, in love with her. Sure, I had joked around and proposed to her the first night I met her, but now it all made sense.

She was who I needed. This whole time.

When she yawned, I was going to put her back in my bed, so we could get some more sleep. Until she told me she didn't want to go back to bed just yet. Another idea came to mind, and I hoped that it would help her pass out in my arms and lower another of her walls.

Kneeling in front of her, I pressed my mouth against the tiny scar. I never noticed it before but now that she told me about it and why it was there, I couldn't stop seeing it. It showcased her strength and her vulnerability.

I had also meant what I said. If she needed a kidney transplant, as long as I was a match, I would give her one of mine. If it meant saving her life, I would give her a piece of me.

Tabatha ran her fingers through my hair, pulling me from my thoughts.

I looked up at her and began unbuttoning her jeans. Keeping my gaze locked with hers, I brought the fabric down over her ass.

She kicked them off her feet, standing in just her bra and panties. Without even having to ask, she reached around her back and unclasped the bra before letting it fall off her arms and to the floor.

Running my tongue along the piercings in her hip, I lowered her panties, exposing all of her.

"I never wanted to settle down," I told her, revealing one of my truths. "It wasn't until I started seeing everyone I had grown up with settle down and have kids of their own, that I thought maybe I should do the same." I ran my fingers over the beautiful black lines on her torso. The tattoos were classy, with flowers, a skull, and a snake, staring back at me, I had a moment of jealousy that someone else had touched her before I ever could.

"I think I fell in love with you the first night I met you." I tapped her inner thigh lightly, hinting for her to spread her feet a little more. "When you called me an asshole, when you called me out on my shit, when you had accused me of being a womanizer and pointing out things that no other woman ever would. You saw me, Kitten. You saw every inch of me."

"I shouldn't have said those things," she whispered.

"But you did, and I thank you for it." We had this conversation already, but I needed her to know that I meant what I said. That I meant every single fucking thing that left my mouth. "I promise to never hurt you. To never leave you. I will erase those doubts in your mind, baby.'

"Ashton."

I looked up at her.

Her eyes welled. "God, I just…"

I placed a soft kiss just under her belly button. "I promise to tell you that I love you every single day and to not go to bed angry. Even if it pisses you off more, we will talk our shit out before going to sleep."

She laughed, wiping under her eyes.

"I also promise to take care of you, love you, and just be with you." I pushed to my feet, suddenly needing her body against mine. "I promise to see you."

Tabatha reached for my shirt, pulling me close. "I promise to tell you when I need something, when I'm scared and when I just need a moment."

I pushed a hand through her hair before cupping the back of her head. "I promise to be patient," I finished, crushing my mouth to hers.

In a quick move, she had my jeans undone and her hand shoved inside the fabric. When her fingers came into contact with my dick, a low groan left me.

"Make love to me," she whispered.

All breath left me, knowing it was the first time she had ever said it that way. It was usually just referred to us as fucking, but this, this was a whole new level.

Pushing her back onto the bed, I cupped her ass and pulled her to the edge. I had every intention of taking this slow but right now, I needed inside her like I needed air to fucking breathe.

Tabatha ripped open my jeans, pulling my cock out and wrapping her leg around my hip. "Please."

As soon as that single word left her mouth, I thrust forward, filling her with every inch of me.

We sighed, connected once again.

SEVENTEEN

Tabatha

ASHTON AND I DECIDED to take things slow. A few weeks had passed since we both revealed our love for each other but even though that was the case, I still had walls up. I tried. God, did I try to break them down. But I couldn't. Even though I wanted to.

One night I was at Sarge's, sitting in his office and researching local therapy sessions online. I thought maybe speaking to someone about everything I was scared of might help Ashton and me on a deeper level.

"Hey, Tabs."

I looked up, finding Sarge himself standing in the doorway. "Hey, I thought you went home."

"I did but had to go out again to grab dinner, so thought I'd pop in."

"And check up on me?" I was the only one at the gym, the guys were off doing their own thing and Ashton was working.

"Nah, sweetheart." Sarge smiled, the wrinkles on his older face softening at the movement. "I would never even consider doing such a thing."

I laughed. "Right," I said, drawing out the word slowly.

He chuckled. "I'm about to head back out but just wanted to say hi."

"Hi." I rose from my spot at the floor and went up to him, suddenly needing one of his hugs. When I wrapped myself around him, he stiffened for a moment before relaxing into my touch.

"You good?"

"Yeah." I held him for a second longer before releasing him, then went back to the couch. "Just needed a hug."

"That's something we could all use every so often."

I agreed even though I tried ignoring that sentiment from time to time. Especially in the beginning when it came to Ashton.

"Looks like you have a visitor," Sarge told me, leaving his spot at the doorway.

I looked up, the sound of mumbled voices sliding through me. Just when I was about to get up to make sure Sarge didn't say or do anything to Ashton, he appeared in the doorway.

My breath caught in my throat at the sight of Ashton smiling down at me. "He say anything to you?"

He joined me on the floor, kissed my cheek and then my mouth. "Introduced himself and threatened me a little. Nothing big."

I laughed, shaking my head. "Of course, he would."

"I'm glad you have protection when I'm not around." Ashton hooked his arm around my shoulders, pulling me close and leaning his forehead against the side of my head. "I missed you," he whispered.

My stomach tumbled. "Did something happen?" I asked him, finally noticing the bags under his eyes.

"Had another moment with Aiden last night." He kissed my temple. "Nothing to worry about."

I remembered him coming over and waking me up in the middle of the night. But I had been too focused on what he was doing between my legs to ask him what was wrong.

"I should have asked you earlier about your brother." I turned my body toward Ashton. "I'm sorry I didn't."

Ashton shrugged. "Not a big deal, babe." He nodded toward the paperwork I had on the table in front of us. "Need any help?"

"No, thank you. I'm done. Just being lazy and didn't feel like packing up yet." I yawned, which was followed by a cough.

"You good?" Ashton frowned, his eyes searching my face.

"Yeah, someone decided to wake me up and not leave me alone," I teased, yawning again.

"I've woken you up before." His frown deepened. "You sure you're good?"

There was an underlying meaning beneath his question. He didn't have to actually voice it out loud. He was concerned after what I had told him about my health but my last check up was fine. I was a normal twenty-five-year-old woman now. I drank way too much coffee, probably had a little more wine than I should but other than that, my doctor told me I had a clean bill of health. It still wasn't reassuring though but that wasn't something I would tell Ashton. I had to be strong for the both of us.

"You'll tell me if something's up, right?" Ashton asked me, pinching my chin and turning my head to meet the soft impact of his mouth. "Right?"

"Of course." I cupped his cheek, licking along his bottom lip.

"Careful." His mouth moved to my ear. "I don't need any of the other men in your life coming in here and finding you in an awkward position."

"Oh?" My body heated. "And what kind of position would that be?"

"You bent over with my big dick filling that tight little ass."

I shivered at the image he put in my head. "Sounds like a promise for later."

He chuckled, the deep sound vibrating over every inch of me. "You want that? Me filling every inch of you. Making you scream, beg, and cry for more."

"God, when you put it that way." I winked.

Ashton grinned, pulling me closer into his side. He kissed my temple, cheek, and then the spot by my ear. "I love you, Kitten," he whispered.

I sighed, my heart jumping at hearing those words. I wasn't sure if I would ever be able to get used to them. "I love you too, baby."

I could feel his lips pull into a small smile.

"Are the guys here?" I asked him, needing to change the subject a bit for fear that I would get caught doing something my brothers wouldn't want to see.

"Beck and Jonah are." Ashton leaned back, dropping his hand to my waist and slipping it under my shirt. "They're getting a workout in." His hand moved beneath the cup of my bra. "That's what I overheard them say anyway."

"Phoenix isn't here?"

"No." Ashton's thumb brushed over my pierced nipple, pulling a sigh from my lips. His eyes caught mine. "Relaxing?"

I nodded, gathering up the paperwork that was strewn about on the table in front of us. "It's like you know when the right moment to touch me is."

Ashton lifted my bra up and over my other breast. "Every moment is the right moment, Kitten."

"True but it's just...I could be in a bad mood or tired or worrying about Phoenix or something else entirely and the moment you touch me, I feel..."

His deep blue eyes burned into mine. "You feel what?"

"Better."

Ashton smirked, leaning his forehead against the side of my head. "Anything you ever need, I'm here. I know this is new for both of us but everything I've ever said to you, has been the truth, Kitten." His free hand cupped the back of my head, turning it to meet his intense stare. While his other hand massaged and kneaded my breast, his eyes seared into my soul. "One good thing about you wearing my hoodie, is anyone could come in and won't know that I'm playing with your tits."

A laugh boomed through me. He had forgotten his hoodie at my place a few nights ago and I kept it ever since. It was worn in and smelled like him. It was my favorite.

"I like it when you play with my tits." I reached under the hoodie and unclasped my bra, letting it fall open.

"Oh, I know you do." He pinched my pierced nipple, the tinge of pain shooting right to my clit. "Is something wrong with Phoenix?"

"I don't know. But I think he has a thing with Scooter and Natalie."

Ashton leaned back, staring at me. "What do you mean?"

I explained to him what I saw in the hallway and how it was quite obvious that Natalie and Scooter at least had a thing. And then I told him about talking to Scooter on the phone and how both he and Natalie were taking care of my brother.

"That could mean many things but yeah, I'm sure what you're thinking is probably right." Ashton paused. "I actually think that Natalie only hit on me and other guys, just to piss Scooter off. I mean, after I ended things with her."

"Maybe. As long as my brother is happy, that's all I care about." I lifted the hoodie, revealing my naked breasts. "But enough about that. You need to continue doing what you were doing."

"Hmm…" Ashton lifted the hoodie even more, his eyes dropping to my chest. He took a handful of my breast, lowering his mouth to the budding peak. "Always fucking delicious."

"God, if we get caught, I won't be able to stop the guys from killing you." I shivered, pushing my chest into his face.

"It'll be worth it, baby girl." His mouth latched on to the other nipple, twirling the other between his finger and thumb.

"Ashton," I breathed, liquid heat rushing through every inch of me.

"I wish I could take you out of here and fuck you. Baby, I'd fuck you so damn hard, the earth would shake."

"Tell me more," I whispered.

Ashton cupped my breasts, pushing them together and closing his teeth around one of my nipples.

A hard yelp left me as he bit me.

"I'd fuck you to the point you'd beg me not to stop. It would be hard, deep, and I'd get you pregnant."

My skin erupted into goosebumps. "More."

"I'd fill your cunt with so much cum, you'd taste it on your tongue," he murmured against my hot skin.

His words made something inside of me snap.

Pushing away from him, I jumped to my feet and grabbed his hand. "Come with me." I lowered the hoodie, covering myself. "*Now*."

"We can wait," he said, rising to his full height.

"No." I spun on him. "We are not waiting. You come to me when you need me. Well, now I need *you*."

The smile fell from his face, lust flashing behind his eyes. "Your move, Kitten."

There was a storage closet outside the office. We would have to be quiet, but I didn't care. I didn't care at all.

Leading Ashton to the door, I opened it and looked down both ends of the hall. When I didn't see anyone, I practically dragged him to the storage closet at the end of the hallway.

Opening the door, I shoved him inside and joined him.

"Something you want, Tabatha?" he asked, his voice low.

"I want you to bend me over and fuck me." I pushed him out of the way and went up to the door, clicking the lock into place and placing my hands against the door. "Do it. Now. Please, Ashton."

"Fuck." He came up behind me, flicking on the dim light in the small room. He ripped my sweatpants down and over my ass but instead of thrusting into me, like I thought he was going to do, he slipped his cock between my legs instead. He wasn't inside me but the tip of him bumped against my swollen clit.

A moan left me, my hips moving back and forth as I slid along the length of him.

"That's it, Kitten. Coat my cock with your juices. You're so fucking wet."

"I need you." I leaned my head against his shoulder, pushing into him.

"Marry me," he demanded, his voice rough. "Marry me so I can fucking breed you."

My pussy clenched at what he was suggesting. "God I never thought something like that would sound so hot."

"Sorry, it slipped out." He chuckled.

"No, don't be sorry." I looked at him over my shoulder. "I like it."

A wicked smirk spread on his face. "Good because I did mean it."

"You want to marry me still, Ashton?" I asked, my hips moving back and forth over him.

"Yes," he breathed, digging his fingers into my waist. "I want you wearing my ring. I want you swollen with my baby. Maybe not all in that order but I want it all."

"Ask me again," I whispered, standing on tiptoes and shivering as he slipped inside me. "Ask me," I said louder that time. "Ask me to marry you, so you can breed me."

His fingers tightened, no doubt leaving bruises. "Marry me, so I can fucking breed you, Tabatha." He pulled me back, the angle forcing him deeper inside of me.

"Yes," I whimpered, my body shaking through a hard release.

"Fuck, fuck, fuck." He pumped into me. "I'm going to paint the walls of your pussy with my cum, baby."

"Do it." I had never been opposed to dirty talk, but this was on a whole other level. It had never been something I thought I would be into, but I was. I was into it a lot.

"Say it again," he demanded, his hips stopping until his thighs were pressed up against the backs of mine.

"Yes, I'll marry you." As soon as the words left my mouth, his release poured into me.

"Jesus, Kitten." He pushed deeper into me, wrapping his arm around my shoulders. "I knew I could make you say yes."

I laughed, shoving my elbow back into his stomach.

He grunted, chuckling behind me.

Ashton slowly pulled out of me.

When I went to pull up my pants, Ashton stopped me. "What's wrong?"

"Place your hands back against the door," he demanded, his voice low.

I swallowed hard but did as I was told.

He came up behind me, pressing his chest up against my back. "If you get pregnant or even if you don't..." He slipped his fingers between my legs, slowly inserting two into me. "Just remember where I've been and where my cum belongs." He continued fingering me, pushing his release deeper and deeper into me.

"I'm…" I shivered. "I'm going to come if you keep doing that."

"Good." Ashton kissed the side of my throat. "Suck up all that baby gravy, Kitten."

"That is so dirty." I laughed breathlessly.

Ashton's laughter eased some of the tension I had been feeling for weeks but before I could dwell on that, a fast and hard release erupted through me. My knees almost gave out at how powerful it was.

"Always beautiful." He helped me fix my pants that time before making himself presentable. "You meant what you said?"

"That you telling me you wanted to breed me, turned me on?"

His laugh deepened. "That's not what I meant."

"Yes." I kissed his cheek. "I love you, Ashton." As much as I fought him in the beginning, I realized now that I did actually want to spend my life with him. "Even though you drive me crazy." I winked.

A sharp swat landed on my ass. "Careful."

I laughed, opening the door and turning off the light in the storage room. "I do expect a ring soon though."

"Of course." He closed the door behind us. "Only the best for my girl."

My smile widened and I realized then that I had smiled more in the time I had been with him, than I had in years. For that, I could never thank him enough.

"Stop checking me out and let's go back to your place or mine or a hotel. I don't give a shit. But we do need to celebrate."

I took a step toward him and went to say something naughty when a commotion sounded from the main gym area of the building.

"Tabby."

I jumped, spinning around and finding Beck rushing toward us. "What's wrong?"

"I..." He shook his head. "Fuck, it's Phoenix. It's bad, Tabs. It's really bad."

Ashton and I glanced at each other.

"Go," he insisted. "Family first. Always."

I nodded, kissing his cheek. "You're my family now too, Ashton," I whispered, before following Beck to what I could only hope was an exaggeration and that Phoenix was in fact fine. But knowing the guys I had grown up with, he was anything but fine.

EIGHTEEN

ASHTON

I FOLLOWED TABATHA AND Beck down the long hallway, my little moment with her long forgotten as she prepared to console their brother.

"Did you call Scooter?" Tabatha asked Beck as we neared the main area of the gym. The man I had met earlier, known as Sarge, was standing with an unraveled Phoenix. He was walking back and forth, ripping at what little hair he had on his head.

"Why would we call him?" Beck asked, frowning.

"Well…he told me that after Phoenix's last fight, both he and Natalie were helping him." Tabatha shrugged. "I don't know exactly what that means but if it worked, we need to make a call."

"Yes, I called him," Jonah answered. "He's on his way. I haven't seen it this bad. Ever."

"I've seen worse."

All of us turned as Scooter walked into the gym.

"What happened?" he asked, going up to Tabatha.

"He was training with me, left for about fifteen minutes to take a break and then came back and was like this," Sarge answered, running a hand through his graying hair. I almost forgot he was there, he had been so quiet.

"Scooter," Beck said gently. "It's bad."

Scooter took a breath and went up to Phoenix. He stopped pacing once he realized who was approaching him. It was like all of us had held our collective breaths as we watched the display before us.

"We should give them some privacy," I blurted, keeping my voice low.

"Good call," Beck responded but none of us budged.

I didn't know Phoenix but watching him break, tore at a piece of me. It reminded me of my brother, and I made a mental note to check up on him.

Before any of us could utter another word, Phoenix threw himself around Scooter. His lithe frame folded into Scooter's muscular arms, his brown hair unkempt from running his fingers through it.

A collective sigh of relief filled the room.

"It's okay, pet," I heard Scooter tell him. "I'm here." The rest of his words trailed off as he tried his best to console him.

Sarge went up to them, clapping Phoenix's shoulder but Phoenix never reacted and just continued holding onto the large man wrapped around him.

I reached for Tabatha's hand. "Let's give them some privacy," I murmured in her ear.

She nodded, spun on her heel, and led me back up to the apartment she shared with her brothers. Thankfully, Beck and Jonah also followed us.

I didn't know Phoenix's story but clearly, he still had issues he was trying to work his way through. It made me feel even more sorry for my brother. Phoenix obviously had someone besides his sister and brothers to help him, but Aiden didn't have anyone. Not like that anyway. I wasn't even sure if there was someone he was even remotely interested in.

Can I ask you a question?" I asked my brother, my twin, my best friend. My heart started racing as soon as the words fell from my mouth.

Like most times, I could never control the things that left my lips. I always said what was on my mind. Had been that way ever since I was a kid and I almost lost some friends over it.

"Hold that thought." He went to the kitchen and came back a moment later with two beers. He sat on the couch beside me and handed me one. "Okay, now you can ask me."

I took the beer, twisted off the cap and watched my brother as he drank half the bottle. A sour taste filled my mouth. He had been drinking more lately and I wasn't sure if it was because he missed being in the Navy or if something had happened. He had been discharged a few months ago but you would never know because Aiden didn't talk about it. The only way we knew was because my dad told us. Not Aiden and I often wondered why.

"Are you..." I cleared my throat. "Are you gay?"

Aiden's head whipped around at my question.

"I mean, I don't give a shit if you are. I don't give a shit if you're not. Or what you're into. I couldn't give a flying fuck what you like. But..."

"But what?" he asked, finishing off his beer before placing the bottle on the table in front of us."

"I don't know. I don't even know why I'm asking really but the last few times that I tried bringing someone home for us, you weren't into it. Hell, even with Piper, you weren't really into it." We had been drinking with a mutual friend and things got out of hand. One thing led to another and we ended up having a threesome. But it lasted for more than just one night.

"I'm not gay," Aiden finally said. "But I'm not straight either. I don't really know what to label myself as but I do know that I haven't been into it, because it didn't feel right. I guess I'm ready to settle down or at least find someone outside of our circle. Someone I can relate to on a deeper level than just sex."

"You'll find someone. If that's what you want. But either way, they will have to go through me first."

Aiden gave me a small smile.

"Are you okay though?" I asked, figuring that would be a safer question and knowing he would tell me more whenever he was ready.

Aiden ran a hand through his hair. "I don't know, Ashton. I really don't know."

"Okay." I took a swig of my beer then. "Just know that I'm here. For whatever you need. If you want to talk, break some shit, whatever, I'm here."

He sighed, his shoulders slumping. Almost like he was relieved that he had my support. "Thank you."

That conversation had been so long ago, I almost forgot it ever happened in the first place. I needed to do as my mom asked, and try and talk to my brother. I didn't need to know everything that had happened to him and why he suddenly started drinking heavily but I did need to make sure that he was okay. Because I knew that he wasn't.

"Ashton?"

I jumped, finding Tabatha staring at me with a deep frown between her brows. "Sorry, what?"

"You okay?"

I nodded, taking her hand and pulling her down beside me. We were sitting on the couch in her living room, some shitty show on the TV, but I couldn't even remember coming into the apartment.

"Are you sure?" she asked, snuggling into my side.

I went to nod again when I hesitated that time. "I don't know. I'm okay. I really am. But I'm still worried about my brother. I don't think he'll be able to get through his issues unless he gets counseling or..." I shrugged then. "I don't know. I just want him to be okay."

"He has you." Tabatha turned onto her side, wrapping herself around my arm.

I reached a hand down the collar of her shirt, cupping her breast and letting out a slow breath. "He does and I'll always be here for him, just like you are for your brothers."

"I had no idea that Phoenix, and Scooter, and I guess Natalie now too, were a thing."

"I didn't know that either but I'm not surprised. I've seen Natalie not only hit on men. Maybe she finally found her person. Or people in this case." What I had with Natalie had been fun at the time but I was thankful that she finally moved on.

Tabatha's soft snores suddenly erupted through me, settling some of the anxiety resting on my shoulders.

We had come back to her apartment after the moment with Phoenix. Her other brothers had gone their own separate ways. I wasn't sure what was going on but something felt off. I just hoped we were ready. For whatever it was.

NINETEEN

Tabatha

"*I WANT YOU TO* meet my parents."

Ashton had told me that a few nights ago and now, it was Friday evening, and we were driving to his childhood home.

My knee wouldn't stop bouncing, my palms were sweaty. My heart was damn near beating out of my chest.

"Hey." Ashton reached over and cupped my knee, giving it a light squeeze. "They'll love you, Kitten. You have nothing to worry about."

I swallowed hard, covering his hand with mine and pulling it onto my lap. "Have you ever brought a girl home before?"

"No," he grunted. "So, they'll be more shocked to meet you than you are nervous to meet them. Trust me."

"I do." I linked my fingers between his. "God, I trust you, but...I've never met the parents before. Hell, I've never been in a relationship before. I just..." I chewed my bottom lip. "I don't want to screw it up. A lot of people take one look at me and assume I'm like some junky because I have pink hair, piercings, and tattoos."

"My parents are not judgemental. They would never assume any of that shit." Ashton pulled his hand from mine and cupped my inner thigh.

I appreciated his words but they didn't help. At all.

I pulled at the collar of my cardigan, fidgeting in my seat and wishing the earth would swallow me up somehow.

"Breathe, baby," Ashton demanded gently.

"I just want them to like me because if they don't, it could ruin what you and I have and I don't want to lose you," I said all in one breath.

The car came to a stop, and I realized that we were now sitting outside a home. Before I could ask if we had finally arrived at his parents' place, Ashton cupped my cheek. He turned my head to meet the hard impact of his mouth.

I sighed, welcoming him in.

His tongue peeked out, licking along mine before delving deep between my lips. The kiss pulled a moan from the back of my throat. He chuckled, giving me one final peck before leaning his forehead against mine.

"I love you, Kitten. And it feels so good each and every time I say that." His hand moved to my throat, cupping my jaw and tilting my head back. "My parents will love you. You've helped me with my brother. You know things about me no one else does or ever will. You called me out on my shit right away and made me fall in love with you instantly. But this…" He fingered the collar of my cardigan. "This isn't you. This isn't the woman I want to spend the rest of my life with. I need you to show my parents, you. The Tabatha I know."

"I don't think they would want to know that Tabatha," I teased, giving him a wink.

"You know what I mean. You're dressed too prim and proper. It's not you."

I sighed, looking down at myself. I had thrown on a knee length skirt and a light blue cardigan with a white blouse underneath. But he was right. The outfit wasn't me.

"Good thing I packed you something to change into."

My head whipped around. "You did what?"

"When I saw you come out of the bathroom in this, I realized that you were nervous. Maybe even scared. My parents are good people. But I get it. I've never met the parents of the woman I'm fucking either. So, I understand. After I kissed you and messed up your makeup a bit, I waited for you to go back to the bathroom and I grabbed you some things." He handed me a bag. "These items weren't at the back of your closet, so I'm assuming they would be a better choice."

"God, I love you." I kissed his cheek, left the SUV, and slid into the back seat. "Thank goodness for tinted windows and thank you for this."

"Just want you comfortable. No point in showing my parents a version of you that's non-existent. It'll just make things more awkward. It's going to be weird enough for them since…"

"What?" I asked when his voice trailed off.

"It's going to be weird for them to meet you, given my history and all."

That made sense.

"If tonight goes well and I imagine it will, I want you to come to a family thing tomorrow with me."

My head snapped up. "You're just laying it all out there now for me, aren't you?"

Ashton chuckled. "I've spent countless hours playing poker with your brothers. You owe me."

I stuck my tongue out at him. "I've let you fuck my ass. That should be reward enough."

"Nah." He ran his fingers along his mouth. A mouth I had felt on every inch of me. "You're a dirty girl and would have let me fuck your ass no matter what."

"How dare you know me so well?" I grumbled, while I finished getting changed. Ashton had grabbed me high waisted black jeans with several rips in them, a white short sleeved crop top, and an oversized forest green sweater. It was much too big for me, but it was a favorite, so I would never get rid of it.

I went to put the clothes I had been wearing, back in the bag, when I came across deodorant. "You thought of everything, didn't you?" I asked him.

"I tried to. Now hurry your sexy ass up. The sooner we get done here, the sooner I can get you back in my bed."

"So romantic." I laughed, shaking my head.

Ashton left the vehicle, his deep chuckle sliding through every inch of me. As he walked around to my door, I took a deep breath and prayed that this would go well. I didn't want to lose him when he finally succeeded in breaking down my walls.

The door suddenly opened, revealing the man who had consumed every inch of me, but most of all my heart and soul.

Ashton leaned in, placing a soft peck on my mouth. "Come. It'll be fine. I'll be with you."

"You're lucky you're hot." I pushed him back and slipped out of the SUV.

"Is that so?" He slammed the door shut and came up behind me, wrapping his arms around my middle from behind. "So, if I was a mutt, you wouldn't come meet my parents?"

I snorted. "Looks aren't everything, baby."

"Nope. They aren't." He spun me around, hugging me to him. "But you're hot. I'm hot. So, it works."

I laughed, leaned my cheek against his chest, and took a deep inhale. Spice and everything that made up Ashton, wafted into my nose. It sent a shiver down my spine, because I could also smell me on him. It was faint but it was there.

"Stop smelling me."

I grabbed his shirt, leaning my head back. "You smell good."

"I'll smell even better later when your cum's all over my face." He waggled his eyebrows.

"God." I pushed out of his hold. "You're so nasty." But I couldn't help the way my body heated over his words.

"You enjoy it, babe." He wrapped his arm around my waist and pulled me into his side. "I know you really enjoy it." He kissed my temple, taking a deep inhale.

"Yeah, I do." I smiled up at him and took his hand. "Think they'll like me?"

"No." He winked. "I *know* they'll like you."

I laughed, shaking my head. "Ass."

Ashton kissed the side of my head before leading me up the driveway to his childhood home. A part of me was a little envious that he always had a place to come home to. While I had my brothers, I didn't have a childhood home. Sure, I had Sarge's place but as soon as we all moved out, he moved as well and got himself a smaller house. It wasn't the same.

"Are you going to tell your parents that you proposed and that I said yes?"

Ashton stopped, looking back at me over his shoulder. "Do you want me to tell them?"

"Well...I'm not sure. I mean, it's not like I've met them at all and now suddenly we're engaged. I just don't want them to think any less of me or..." I sighed. "I'm rambling."

He gave me a small smile. "It's all on me, Kitten, and I'll be sure to tell them that. I did propose to you the first night we met. Remember?"

I laughed. "I do. What would you have done if I'd said yes?"

A cheeky grin spread on his face. "We'd already be married and you'd have a baby in your belly."

A shiver raced down my spine. "I have no idea why that's hot but it is."

A laugh boomed through him. "Come on, my dirty girl. Let's meet the fam."

(Ashton)

She was nervous but in fact, so was I. I had never brought a woman home before. Any of the ladies that my parents had met, they already knew since we all grew up together. But this was different. Tabatha wasn't part of our circle. She wasn't someone I had known as a kid. She was someone I knew as a man. A man who had grown so much since meeting her.

Before we made it to the door, it opened, revealing my mom. My chest tightened at seeing the dark circles under her eyes and the wrinkles lining her face from the added stress my brother caused. A sour taste filled my mouth, wishing there was something I could do to make him stop drinking but I wasn't stupid. Something bad would have to happen for him to stop. If that even worked.

"Ashton?"

I looked down at Tabatha. "Sorry." I gave her a smile for reassurance even though I didn't feel it one bit.

"You okay?" she asked, tightening her hold on my hand.

"Yeah." I looked back at my mom. "Mom, this is Tabatha. Tabatha, this is my mom, Meeka."

"I've heard many things about you," Mom told her, giving her a wide smile.

"It's so nice to meet you," Tabatha said, holding out her hand.

"Put that away." Mom laughed. "I want a hug."

I grinned, giving Tabatha a gentle nudge with my shoulder. "Told you she'd love you," I whispered in her ear.

She let out a slow breath, released my hand, and went up to my mom.

Mom was small but Tabatha was smaller. It wasn't often I saw someone Mom could wrap herself around. "You're a tiny thing." She leaned back, cupping Tabatha's cheek. "You good?"

I heard Tabatha's breath catch, the sound hitting me square in the chest. I never once thought how this interaction would be. It was stupid of me to even think that Tabatha wouldn't get emotional, especially since she never grew up with a mother and definitely not one as amazing as mine.

"I am," Tabatha whispered.

"Oh, sweet girl, I'm sorry." Mom smiled. "Ashton, go see your father. We need a girl moment."

My back stiffened. "Mom, I—"

"Ashton." Tabatha looked up at me over her shoulder. "It's fine."

I nodded, doing as I was told and went into the house, but not before I saw the tears falling down her cheeks.

TWENTY

Tabatha

I COULD SENSE THE concern rolling off of Ashton, but I couldn't dwell on that. Not yet anyway. I was fine. Really. I just never had a motherly type figure before and apparently, meeting Ashton's mom, brought up these emotions in me I never knew were there.

"Talk to me." Meeka grabbed my hand, leading me to the patio couch on the long porch. "I don't expect you to tell me all of your secrets, you can leave those for my son, but I want to know why you're crying right now."

"My mom left when I was six," I blurted, shocked that she could get something like that out of me after only just meeting her when it had taken Ashton months to get that information from me.

"Oh, Honey." Meeka sighed, pulling my hands on her lap and patting them. "I'm so sorry. I know that doesn't help but I truly am."

"Thank you," I whispered, slipping my hand from hers and wiping my cheeks. "I wish I could say that I grew up with a father and that we got through it. We almost did but he was taken from me too. It's just...I never realized how much I miss him until meeting you, I guess. And even though my mom left, a part of me misses her too. And I really can't believe that I'm telling you all of this." I laughed, the sound almost tinny in my ears.

"It must be a mom thing." Meeka turned toward me, the lines on her face softening. "Having children is hard. It's the hardest thing I've ever done. And they like to put you through hell too. There's not a day that doesn't go by where I don't worry about them. Especially Aiden." A dark shadow passed over her face before she shook her head, ridding herself of whatever thoughts that threatened to take over. "What I'm saying is, and I'm in no way sticking up for your mom, but just remember that something could have happened that you don't know about. Not that it's an excuse, because it definitely isn't, but you were a child. And if your dad is no longer in the picture, I imagine you'll never get the answers you're looking for."

"I didn't know I was looking for them until just now. I always knew I had abandonment issues. It's why I had a hard time trusting Ashton in the beginning. I still have issues but he's patient with me."

Meeka's smile widened. "I'm glad. I was beginning to worry that I would never have grandkids."

My mouth fell open, a cough sputtering free. "What? No. We haven't...that's not...he only just proposed. I—"

"He proposed?" She grabbed my left hand. "There's no ring."

"Um..." My cheeks burned, remembering exactly how and when he proposed. We were still looking for a ring, but I was really in no rush. That was him. He wanted to show the world that someone with his past could actually settle down. But I had a feeling that he wanted to show the people he had grown up with instead. "We're working on that," I told her.

"You said yes?"

"I did. This time anyway." My thoughts traveled to when he was inside me, begging to breed me and make me his wife. My body burned. God I was going to hell just thinking these thoughts around Ashton's mother.

"He asked you more than once?" Meeka laughed. "Okay, now you have to tell me what happened."

I told her about when Ashton and I first met and how he proposed that very night. The look of utter shock on her face made me laugh. Looked like his friends wouldn't be the only ones surprised that he found his person.

"I'm just…" Her eyes welled and before I knew what was happening, she threw her arms around me. "Thank you. Thank you for making him happy. Thank you, thank you." She muttered those words over and over when really, I should be the one thanking her.

"No, thank *you* for him." I squeezed her harder, reveling in the feel of being hugged by a mom.

Meeka leaned back, holding me at arm's length. "Let's go inside before my husband sends a search party."

"Thank you for talking with me," I said, following her into the house.

"Thank you for feeling like you *could* talk to me." She stopped in the entranceway. "Do you feel better?"

"I do actually," I told her just as Ashton came down the hall toward us. "Much better."

Without even saying anything to his mom, he walked right up to me and cupped the back of my head before lowering his mouth to mine. "You good?" he asked against my lips.

"I am." It was a quick kiss, seeing as we were at his parents' place, but it still left me yearning for more.

"You sure?" His eyes moved back and forth over my face, almost like they were searching for something. Whatever they were looking for, they wouldn't find it because he already knew.

Everything.

"I am." I hugged my arms around his middle, leaned the side of my head against his chest, and took a deep breath. He smelled like his aftershave and cologne. Spice and everything that made up him.

"Sorry to interrupt, you two, but dinner is almost ready," Meeka called out from the kitchen.

Ashton stepped out of my hold, linking his fingers with mine and bringing my hand up to his mouth. "I love you, Kitten."

"I love you," I breathed.

A cheeky grin spread on his face. "I know you do."

I laughed, playfully smacking his chest and walking by him with his hand still in mine. He fell in line behind me, but I could feel his eyes searing into the back of my head. Glancing over my shoulder, I caught him staring at my ass. "Seriously?"

His gaze snapped to mine. "I can't help it." He shrugged. "Your ass—"

"Alright, I don't need you to finish that sentence," Meeka said, stepping out into the hall. "Ashton, set the table. Tabatha, please help me gather the food."

"Of course." I gave Ashton a quick peck on the cheek and went to help his mom.

"So, Tabby. Can I call you that?" Ashton's dad, Asher, asked me.

"Of course. I tried getting your son to call me that but he refused and started full naming me right away." As soon as the words left my mouth, Ashton's hand landed on my inner thigh. His fingers were inappropriately close to the apex between my thighs. I looked up at him. "Problem?"

"Nope," he said, popping the P.

I laughed, covering his hand with mine and pulling it higher up my thigh. Two could play this game.

"Alright, Tabby." Asher looked between us both before continuing. "What line of work are you in?"

"Oh. I work at Scooters. It's a bar downtown. I also help the owner with paperwork from time to time and I do the same for my foster father. He owns a boxing gym." After helping Meeka set the table, I had quickly met Ashton's dad after he had come out of his office. He had kissed his wife and began complaining how his friends were retired but didn't want to go fishing like they used to. As he talked to his wife, I couldn't help but notice how much Ashton and Aiden looked like him. They were smaller in comparison but the three of them could almost pass for siblings, instead of father and sons.

"Do you like it?" Asher asked, taking a sip of his water.

"I do. It's not the career path I had really chosen for myself, of course, but it helps pay the bills." Even though my brothers told me time and time again that they could pay my way while I paid back my medical expenses, I would never take them up on their offers. It just wasn't how I was wired. I didn't like owing people anything. Especially after my dad had lost his life because of it.

"It's hard finding a career path that you actually enjoy. I was lucky and loved being in the Navy." A dark shadow crossed his face. "I wish I could say the same for Aiden."

Ashton shifted in his seat beside me, while Meeka placed a hand on her husband's arm. Her bottom lip quivered, sending a sharp pain through my chest.

The air in the room suddenly become thick with tension and unease. I quickly thought of something to change the subject but I also didn't want to be rude, so I secretly hoped that Ashton would come up with something instead.

"I don't want to wait to get married," he blurted.

My head whipped around. Okay, I was not expecting that to come out of his mouth.

His parents looked our way.

"I…" Ashton glanced down at me. "I don't. I should have told you sooner but I really don't want to wait."

"Buy me a ring first and then we can get married whenever you want." Who would have thought that I would agree to marrying him. Especially this fast.

Meeka laughed, wiping under her eyes. "I like her."

"Me too." Ashton grinned. "A lot."

While he went back to talking to his parents about his brother, work, and the family get- together that was happening the next evening, I couldn't help but be thankful for Ashton's persistence in the beginning. It paid off and while I still had some trust issues to work through, along with my fear of getting sick again, I couldn't ask for a better man to be at my side.

TWENTY-ONE

Tabatha

AFTER HAVING DINNER WITH Ashton's parents, we spent another hour with them. It was nice seeing Ashton in a family dynamic. I knew he was a good guy. Even when he drove me crazy with his persistence back in the beginning. But seeing it play out before me was something else. We had joked about him getting me pregnant right away, but I realized that I wouldn't overly mind if that happened. Even if it happened before we got married, I would be okay with it.

While Ashton drove us back to his apartment, I couldn't help but place my hand on my stomach. What would it feel like to have a life growing inside of me? I imagined that it would feel pretty amazing. Knowing that I had a hand in creating a human life would be my greatest accomplishment.

"Thinking about the future baby I'm going to put in your belly, Kitten?"

A laugh boomed through me. "You know, I've read a lot of romance books and I've read where the hero loves when their women get pregnant, but I never thought…"

"What?" he asked, his deep blue eyes flicking my way before glancing back out at the road in front of us.

"I never thought I would experience it or like it." I covered his hand that was on my inner thigh, wishing that we could get married now. My stomach tumbled, not expecting that thought to cross my mind. He had said that he didn't want to wait to get married, but I never knew that I didn't want to wait either. It all made sense now though.

"I never thought I would like it either. Before I met you, the thought of getting a woman pregnant scared the shit out of me but now, it's all I can think about."

When we pulled into the parking lot of his apartment building, I unbuckled my seat belt and turned toward him. "I don't want to wait. I want a ring and then I want to get married." I raised a hand when he went to speak. "It's not just because I want to marry you. But I…with my health and battling cancer, it's at the back of my mind that it could come back. So, I want as much time with you as I can. I want to live the rest of my days, married to you, Ashton."

"You're not leaving anytime soon, Kitten, so get that thought out of your head." He left the car and went around to my side at the same time I opened the door.

"We have to talk about this before we get married, Ashton, because you know it's a possibility. You're not stupid. You have to know."

"Tabatha."

"No." I latched on to his shirt, pulling him closer. "I love you and I want to marry you. I want to have your babies if it's meant to be. But most of all, I just want you. But I want you to remember that the cancer could come back."

His jaw clenched, his beautiful eyes burning into me. "I told you I'll give you a kidney."

"I know, baby, and I appreciate that, and I can't thank you enough." My breath caught when he crouched so he was at eye level with me. Running my fingers through his hair, I stared at him. "I can't control my health."

"I know." He took a deep breath, shutting his eyes like he was in pain, before letting the air out slowly.

"I don't plan on leaving anytime soon," I reassured him. "But I do want to live each day to the fullest." I fisted his shirt, pulling him toward me. "And I'd like to start with you."

Ashton took the hint, thankfully, and crushed his mouth to mine. He cupped my ass, lifting me to my tiptoes and tugging me hard against him.

Wrapping my arms around his shoulders, I deepened the kiss, pulling a moan from somewhere deep inside of him. I nipped and sucked at his lips, taking his tongue deep into my mouth. But it wasn't enough. I needed more. I needed him. All of him.

Breaking the kiss, Ashton grabbed my hand and headed to the elevator. He all but dragged me along with him and I knew that once he had me in his bed, I was going to be left feeling sore in the morning. It was something I looked forward to. He had been the only guy I'd ever been with who didn't judge me for my wants and desires. For the semi-kinks I was into. I wasn't overly submissive when it came to sex, but I did enjoy giving up some of my control when it came to Ashton. I trusted him and I knew that he wouldn't hurt me. Even back in the beginning, I knew that he would do everything he could to make sure I felt good and worry about his needs later. My pleasure came first. Always.

Once we stood inside the elevator, Ashton's jaw was hard as granite. I knew that look. That look meant that every inch of me would end up being used by him. My body heated at the mere idea of him fucking every piece of my soul.

"Ashton?" But I still needed to make sure he was okay.

His deep blue eyes dropped to mine.

"You okay?"

The hard lines on his face softened. He cupped my cheek, placing a soft peck on my mouth. "As long as I'm with you, I'll always be okay."

My breath caught. I had never been one to be into hearts and flowers or anything even remotely romantic but this...his sweet words...yeah, I could get used to this.

(Ashton)

I wasn't stupid. I knew that the cancer could come back. It wasn't like once it was gone, it was gone for good. As much as we all wanted that to be the case. But hearing Tabatha talk about it and the possibility of her getting it again, it set me on edge. It made me want to grab her and take her to the nearest courthouse and marry her on the spot.

Once the elevator dinged, I grabbed her hand and pulled her out into the hallway. I had a mission. That mission was to fuck her, every single inch of her, and then take her in the morning to get an engagement ring.

When we stood outside the door leading to my apartment, I quickly unlocked it, shoved her inside, and had her back in my arms before she could take her next breath. Crushing my mouth to hers, I cupped her ass and pulled her flush against my body.

She sighed, a little moan leaving her.

I kicked the door closed, blindly fumbled for the lock until it clicked into place, and lifted her into my arms.

Tabatha wrapped her legs around my waist, deepening the kiss.

Carrying her to my bedroom, I quietly closed the door behind me and gently placed her on my bed. I had every intention of making this fast but at the moment, I needed to savor her. Every inch.

Pushing my waist between her legs, I smirked against her lips as her breath caught. I was hard. For her. I couldn't help it. She could say my name and my dick would twitch. She could just be there and I would want to pull her into my arms and kiss the very breath from her.

Resting my arms on the bed at either side of her head, I nipped and sucked at her lips. Her hips lifted. Up and down. Side to side. A hot shiver raced down my spine, my dick lengthening the longer it wasn't inside her. But as much as I wanted that to happen, I couldn't stop her. Even though we were both fully clothed, it felt good. So damn good. Feeling her rub herself against me, taking what she wanted and giving me everything in return.

Her breathing picked up, her hips moving faster. She went to pull her mouth from mine but I only deepened the kiss. If she was going to come, she was going to do it with my tongue deep in her mouth.

Trailing her hands down my back, she cupped my ass and pulled me even closer. She whimpered, a sharp gasp leaving her as her thighs shook around me.

"Keep coming," I whispered, rubbing my pelvis against hers. "I want your panties fucking soaked."

Tabatha reached between us, unbuckling my jeans. As much as I liked being in control, right now at this very moment, I wanted to see what she would do and just how far she was willing to go to get me back inside her.

Lifting my head, I stared down at her. Her mouth was swollen from my rough kiss, her cheeks were flushed, and her hair was a mess around her head, but she was absolutely breathtaking. Her tongue peaked out, licking along the piercing in her bottom lip.

With some maneuvering, she had her jeans and panties off and my cock in her hand before I could take my next breath.

"I want you to stop taking birth control," I blurted.

A sly grin spread on her face. "Way ahead of you. I had my IUD removed after we had sex in that storage closet at Sarge's gym."

"I knew I fucking loved you for a reason." It was like we shared the same brain.

She laughed, her eyes dropping before meeting mine. "I want to feel all of you against me."

I took the hint and left the bed, slipping out of my clothes.

Tabatha did the same, leaving herself bare and naked for my hungry eyes.

Once I joined her back on the bed, she grabbed onto me. "As much as I like it when you're fast, I need slow right now."

"I got you, Kitten," I murmured, slipping into her tight body where I belonged.

TWENTY-TWO

ASHTON

AFTER SPENDING THE NIGHT wrapped up in Tabatha, I realized that I hadn't heard from Aiden in over twenty-four hours. For most, it would be normal, but when I had lived with my brother my whole entire life, it didn't sit well with me when I didn't know where he was. Not that I was his keeper or anything but with his drinking problem, I often feared that I would see him on the news after being found in a ditch somewhere.

Pulling myself from Tabatha's warmth, my stomach clenched, a wave of nausea coming over me. My heart jumped. I only ever became nauseous if something was wrong with my brother. It brought me back to a time when Aiden had developed a high fever when we were seven, or the time we had gotten lost in the woods because we were playing hide-and-seek and he ended up breaking an ankle.

Something was wrong.

The twin sense came on strong, hitting me square in the chest and it took my damn breath away.

I left my bed and slipped into sweatpants before grabbing my phone.

Dialing up Aiden, I went out to the kitchen to get the coffee started. His voicemail came up and that set my nerves on edge even more. I called him again and again but still got his voicemail and I didn't know why. He always answered his phone. Even when he was shitfaced, he would still answer.

"Ashton?"

I let out a sigh, turned around and was met by my beautiful fiancée wearing my t-shirt. It went down to her knees, so if Aiden actually did come home, he wouldn't see anything he shouldn't see.

"Everything alright?"

"I can't find my brother," I blurted, not liking how desperate I sounded.

"What?" Her eyes widened. "What do you mean you can't find him?"

"He always checks in. Even if he doesn't come home and holes up somewhere, he always calls me or at least texts me. I haven't gotten anything from him in over twenty-four hours and I don't like it." It wasn't like Aiden. Something was wrong. It was like a lead weight was deep in the pit of my gut.

"Okay, let me get dressed and then we can see if we can try and find him." As soon as those words left Tabatha's mouth, the door to the apartment opened.

Every cell in my body was on high alert and before she could see me kick my brother's ass, I stomped up to her and kissed her hard on the mouth. "Go to my bedroom. This isn't going to be nice."

She nodded, quickly heading down the hall and closing herself into my room. A room I had spent years in. A room that I had spent the night before, making love to every inch of her body. I hadn't been concerned for Aiden's well-being then. Maybe I should have. Maybe I should have done a lot of things but now, as I stood there waiting to face my twin, I took a few deep cleansing breaths or else I was going to kick his ass.

But as the door opened even more, it revealed someone I did not expect to see. "Dad?"

"Ashton." Dad came into the apartment, the door remaining open behind him.

"What's wrong?" He never used his key. Even though we insisted that our parents could come and go as they pleased, they never did. They gave us our independence but always kept hold of that key just in case.

"It's…" A shuddered breath left him. Our father. A man who hardly ever became unhinged. Mom grounded him, kept him sane. His words. She calmed him. But now she wasn't here, and he was losing it.

"What happened? Where's Aiden?" My words came out in a rush but I didn't like this air coming off of Dad.

When his crystal blue eyes met mine, my knees almost buckled beneath me.

"Your brother…" He swallowed hard.

My stomach sunk.

"He…he was in an accident." Dad came toward me. "Ashton."

"He's fine though, right? He has to be fine." Yeah, he was being a shithead lately but that didn't mean anything. He would still be fine. He had to be.

"I don't know much yet but it doesn't look good." Dad's eyes welled.

"No." I took a step back, lifting my hands to ward him off. "Don't you fucking say it."

"Ashton." Dad came toward me, pulling me into his arms before I could get away. "They don't know if he'll make it."

As soon as those words left him, I collapsed.

(Tabatha)

The sound that came from the living room was something I had never heard before. I could feel the pain and sorrow down to the marrow of my bones. Something was happening and I didn't know what. Ashton told me to stay in his room, but this was different. He needed me.

After quickly getting dressed, I rushed to the door and stepped foot in the hallway. I could hear deep voices, Ashton's and another man's. The closer I got to them, the scene in front of me was not what I had expected.

Ashton was kneeling on the floor with an older man cupping his shoulders. I realized then that it was his dad.

"Ashton?" I didn't want to interrupt but I needed to make sure everything was okay.

His head snapped up, his deep blue eyes finding mine. Just when I thought he was going to tell me to go back to his room, he jumped to his feet and closed the distance between us. He threw himself around me, pulling and tugging at my clothes. Almost like he was trying to burrow himself under my skin, but still couldn't get close enough.

"What's going on?" I asked, wrapping myself around him. He was shaking.

"Aiden's in the hospital," Asher explained. "We really need to go. I stopped here after I made sure your mother was okay. She's with the girls and I left them in the waiting room."

"I can't lose him." Ashton lifted his head, pain etched in every line on his handsome face.

"He's strong and stubborn as fuck." Asher cupped his son's nape. "We have to go."

Ashton nodded, grabbing my hand.

"I can stay here," I offered, not wanting to overstep.

"Not fucking happening," Ashton practically growled. "Where I go, you go. End of."

If things were different, I would have been a brat and said something sarcastic but it wasn't the time or place. So, I just nodded, complying willingly and following them out of the apartment.

Once we were seated in Asher's car with Ashton in the front beside him and me in the back, Ashton reached behind.

I linked my fingers in his, trying with everything in me to give him the strength he needed to make it through whatever this was.

"Tell me what happened," he said, breaking the unnerving silence.

Asher inhaled a sharp breath, blowing it out slowly a moment later. "Your mom and I were about to sit down for breakfast. We got a visit from two police officers. Thankfully our city is still small enough that we know some of the cops. Even though there's a process, they made it a point to come to our house personally. They said that your brother was nearly four times the legal limit." He shook his head. "He didn't hurt anyone else, thank God for that. He ran off the road and flipped over into a ditch. Wherever he was, there wasn't a lot of traffic. But a passing motorist saw it this morning and called it in. Aiden was there all night."

"Fuck," Ashton muttered.

I squeezed his hand, letting him know that he wasn't alone.

"I know." Asher glanced in the rear-view mirror, his gaze meeting mine before he looked at his son. "We got in another fight last night. He left and I thought he was going home. I shouldn't have assumed. I should have followed him or insisted that he stay. I—"

"Don't." That single word coming from Ashton, ended the conversation. Did he blame his dad? I didn't know Aiden well but any time I had any sort of interaction with him, whether he was drunk or sober, he was always nice to me. But I wondered if something else was going on that I didn't know about.

Pulling my hand from Ashton's, I grabbed my phone.

"What are you doing?" he demanded.

"Just texting the guys to let them know I won't be home today." *Or however long you need me*, going unsaid. Once the text went through, I placed my hand back in Ashton's. His body relaxed then. It was almost like he had been waiting for me to touch him once again.

Before we could say any more on the matter, we pulled up in front of the hospital. Asher parked in some random spot, probably not even thinking clearly knowing one of his sons was only just hanging on. Something about the situation seemed off to me. He appeared calmer than most would.

While Asher walked in front of us, leading the way to where Aiden was, I tugged on Ashton's hand.

When he looked down at me, I nodded toward his dad. "Is he okay? He seems too calm."

"He's been through a lot of shit, Kitten. Our dad and his friends were Navy SEALs. Aiden was working toward being one himself but something happened while he was deployed and he won't talk about it. That's why he drinks. None of us know what happened though. My dad has tried contacting people he knows to see if he could get something to help my brother but the information is classified." Ashton shrugged. "I think the only way Aiden is going to stop drinking, is if he takes a life, takes his own life, or is forced into rehab. Even then, I'm not sure it'll work."

My heart hurt for him. For all of them.

I only wished there was something I could do. Battling cancer didn't seem big enough. Even though it was and I was beyond proud of the fact that I was able to conquer the disease when a lot of people hadn't, it still seemed as if it was petty in comparison to Aiden's problems.

We took the elevator to the third floor. Once it stopped where we needed to go, I could hear voices as soon as the doors opened.

"Is everyone here?" Ashton asked his dad.

"Yes, your brother needs all the support he can get right now and so does your mom." Asher left the elevator, not waiting for us to follow.

"Listen." Ashton pulled me out into the hall, looking both ways before down at me. "I don't know who's all here but I have a feeling it's everyone I grew up with."

I frowned, not really sure what he was getting at.

"I didn't want you to meet everyone this way." He took a breath, shaking his head. "I can explain more later but just in case, I want you to know that I had a brief thing with two of the women I grew up with. Meadow and Piper. We were childhood friends and things led...well, it doesn't matter."

"Are you telling me that you fucked two of your friends and you wanted to be the one to tell me so I don't find out from someone else?"

He nodded slowly.

I almost expected to be jealous but I wasn't. If Ashton wouldn't have told me himself and I ended up finding out from someone else, I was sure jealousy would have reared its ugly head.

"You were jealous when you found out that I live with my foster brothers," I reminded him.

His jaw clenched. "I know."

I stood on tiptoes and kissed his cheek. "I'm not jealous. I know where you're sleeping at night."

A breath left him, his shoulders sagging with relief. "I fucking love you."

"I love you too. Now go to your mom and make sure she's okay."

He nodded. "Are you okay to meet my friends while I do that?"

"Of course.

(Ashton)

The waiting room was packed with people I knew and had grown up with. I shouldn't have been surprised but a part of me was. Even though we spent at least one night each month having dinner, we all lived our separate lives. I had been a shithead toward my friends, if you could even call them that, but I would still do anything for them.

"Ashton." Meadow Allen came up to me with her husband, Shade, at her side. "Anything you need, we're here." She wrapped her arms around my middle, hugging me tight.

"Thank you," I responded, my voice cracking. Hugging her with one arm only, I made sure to keep my other hand locked in Tabatha's. I didn't need her to freak out over the fact that I had fucked Meadow and Piper once upon a time. I probably should have told her sooner, and definitely not at the hospital, but I didn't need any issues from the guys I knew. Not that they would cause a scene, given the situation and all, but one could never be too careful. Especially when I had caused so many problems for them.

"We're here for both you and your brother," Shade added.

Meadow released me, glancing at Tabatha. "Hi." She held out her hand. "I'm Meadow. An old friend of Ashton's."

"Tabatha." She returned the handshake, taking a step closer to me.

I raised an eyebrow, looking between the two women.

Meadow was beautiful, with her curves and pale complexion, but she no longer did it for me. There had been a time where I thought she could have been the one but once she met Shade and his partner, Sunny, before he passed, I knew I no longer stood a chance.

"Meadow, can you keep Tabatha company and introduce her to people? I need to see my mom."

Meadow nodded, giving me a small smile. "Of course." She linked arms with Tabatha. "Come. I wish I could introduce you under better circumstances but I'm assuming you'll be around for the long run, so I'll introduce you again at one of our dinners." She led Tabatha away, moving around the room. When they stopped in front of Piper and Jaron Mercer, Jaron looked my way.

My body stiffened, expecting a fight. But when he only nodded, I let out a breath of relief. I nodded in return, thankful that he was smart enough not to cause a scene here. Sleeping with his girl for half a second never sat well with him and I couldn't say I blamed the guy.

Before I could dwell any more on it, I went in search of my mom and dad in hopes that I could get some answers.

I looked around the room but couldn't find my mom anywhere. I was about to ask where she was when she and my dad entered the room. "Mom."

Her head snapped up.

I rushed to her and threw myself around her small body, careful not to hurt her by hugging too tightly.

She wept into the crook of my neck.

"What do you know?" I asked my dad who kept his hand on the back of her neck.

"Nothing much yet. He's still in surgery." A dark shadow passed over his face. "It was his fault, Ashton."

A sour taste filled my mouth. "Maybe he didn't drink as much as they say he did."

"Ashton." Mom pulled away from me. "You know he did. You know…" Her chin wobbled. "It doesn't matter. When he's out of surgery and on the mend, we'll have to be there for him." She looked up at Dad. "No matter what."

Meaning, Dad will have to put his feelings aside and help his son whether he wanted to or not. I understood the tough love shit but right now, it wasn't what Aiden needed. He needed us. Our support. Our love. He needed anything else we could offer him too.

"Meeka, he's fighting for his life. He was drunk and…" Dad swore under his breath and left the waiting room.

"I understand that he's furious but we can be angry later. When we know that your brother is fine." Mom's eyes welled. "He has to be fine, Ashton."

I pulled her back into my arms because what more could I do? I didn't know what to say or even how to console her, so I just held her instead.

Her shoulders shook with silent sobs. "I'm so angry and I feel guilty." Her words were muffled by my shirt, but I could still hear every word, every painful syllable. I felt them down to the bottom of my soul because I felt the same.

TWENTY-THREE

Tabatha

I DIDN'T HAVE A lot of girlfriends, so when Meadow took me around the room and started introducing me as Ashton's girl and her new best friend, I couldn't help but smile.

I wished I had more time to get to know her and everyone else but given the circumstances, that would have to wait. I appreciated Ashton's honesty when it came to two of the women he had slept with.

When I met Piper, I couldn't help but stare up at her. She was beautiful. With long dark hair, perfect skin, and curves I would kill for, I had a moment and wondered what Ashton saw in me.

"I never thought I'd see the day where Ashton settled down," a man said from beside her.

Piper rolled her eyes. "Be nice. We all have our person. It just took him a while to find his."

The man grunted. "It's nice to meet you." He stuck his hand out.

I returned the handshake, his gray eyes holding a coldness that I was sure ran soul deep.

"Kitten." Ashton came up beside me, wrapping his arm around my middle. He kissed my temple, breathing me in. His body shuddered.

"You okay?" I looked up at him. "Do you know anything?"

"He's still in surgery." Ashton lifted his head, his gaze flicking to Piper and the man standing with her. I could only assume that he was her husband. "All we can do is wait."

"He's a stubborn fucker." The man clapped Ashton's shoulder. "He'll pull through this."

"I'm surprised you're here, Jaron," Ashton bit out, tightening his hold on my waist.

"I'm here for moral support for anyone who needs it." The man, Jaron, grabbed Piper's hand. "I can put our differences aside, Ashton. But can you?"

Ashton grunted, rolling his eyes. "That shit is done and over with and now is not the time or place." He pulled me away from Jaron and Piper and led me to empty chairs across the room.

Once we sat, I turned to him. "What was that about?"

"It's nothing. Old shit. Jaron holds a grudge and that's on me. But he has nothing to worry about anymore." Ashton cupped my cheek. "And neither do you. I love you and I want to spend my life with you. You are it for me. All that I need. The only thing I need."

A smile tugged at my lips. "Promise?"

"You bet your beautiful ass I promise." Ashton leaned his forehead against mine. "I wish I could help my brother. I wish I could give him what he needs."

"Maybe *he* doesn't even know what he needs."

A loud sigh left him. "Maybe."

Before we could say any more, a young man in a white coat came into the room. "Mr. and Mrs. Donovan?"

"That's us," Meeka and Asher said at the same time.

Ashton stood, pulling me upright with him.

"Aiden is out of surgery. It went well but it'll be touch and go for the next little bit. He's stable right now," the doctor explained.

"Can we see him?" Meeka asked, her voice small.

"Of course. Just you and your husband right now though." The doctor spun on his heel. "Please follow me."

"Mom." Ashton stepped forward.

Meeka turned. "Can my other son come with us?"

The doctor glanced between them. "Twins?"

"Yes," they said in unison.

"Come with me." The doctor stepped out of the room, followed by Meeka and Asher.

"Go be with your family," I told Ashton before he could say anything.

He nodded, inhaled a sharp breath, and kissed me softly on the mouth. "I love you."

"I love you," I whispered, praying with everything in me that his brother would make it out of this. I didn't even want to think about what would happen if he didn't.

(Ashton)

Heading to the room Aiden was staying in, along with my parents and the doctor, I couldn't help but wonder what my brother was thinking. Add to the fact that he had already caused enough stress on our mom and dad, this was extreme.

Before meeting Tabatha, I didn't treat women well. I knew that. My friends new that. Hell, everyone knew that. Even the women I had fucked, knew exactly how I was because I never led them to believe any different. I never made them feel like they could have a relationship with me because it was never what I had wanted. Not until I met Tabatha.

Aiden treated women better than I ever did but I knew, because I could feel it deep in the pit of my gut, that he was never interested. Not in women anyway. Not that I cared but it seemed to change him in a way. Besides the fact that whatever happened while he was in the Navy, not understanding his sexuality sent him over the edge, so to speak. That was my theory and if Aiden didn't make it out of this, I would never know.

But besides all of that, I was pissed. My mom was crying. Dad was beside himself. And I was furious. How could he do this to them? How could he be so fucking selfish to drink, knowing he had to drive somewhere? He could have called me. He knew that. Even after I met Tabatha, he knew he could always count on me. Unless I was too wrapped up in her where he thought he couldn't depend on me anymore. Was this my fault? Did not being able to depend on me force him over the edge?

"Please remember that Aiden isn't awake. He's stable. But it could be a while yet before he comes to. Also, the next twenty-four hours are critical." The doctor went on to explain other shit, but all I could focus on was the fact that my brother might not make it out of this.

Once we entered his room, my stomach sunk to the ground beneath me. I was vaguely aware of Mom crying even harder. Her sobs reaching the deepest parts of my soul. They were sounds I never wanted to hear. Ever again.

Before I knew what I was doing, I was standing at the head of the bed, staring down at my brother. "Fuck you, Aiden," I blurted, not even realizing I had spoken out loud until my mom gasped.

"Ashton," Dad said, his voice calm. But when I looked at him, I could see the same rage in his eyes that I felt.

"No. He's a selfish bastard." My heart started racing. "He knew not to drink and drive. He should have called me. He always calls me. Why didn't he call me this time? Why, Aiden?" I looked down at him. "Why the fuck didn't you call me?" My knees shook, a tremor of unease rushing through me. "Were you trying to kill yourself?" I was vaguely aware of Dad coming up to my side. "Were you wanting to destroy our parents and everyone else who loves you? You could have killed an innocent person. Did you not even think of that? No. I bet you didn't. You're so stuck on these demons that you can't think of anyone but yourself." My eyes welled, my words coming out rushed and forced. "Fuck you. Fuck you. Fuck you."

Heavy arms wrapped around me from the side.

"Fuck you," I sobbed, my legs giving out from under me.

Dad caught me, hugging me to him.

"I can't." My cries hardened. "I can't lose him."

"I know," Dad murmured, his voice thick.

Mom joined us, wrapping her arms around my waist. "He'll make it out of this. He has to. I refuse to believe otherwise."

I appreciated her words but a part of me still didn't believe her. If Aiden did in fact make it out of this, it would be a long time before he was forgiven. He needed to make some changes. I wasn't sure if he had been charged. I imagine he would be. Hopefully they could force him into rehab, because this shit needed to end. If going to rehab wasn't a condition, then I would drag him there myself. I would find a place that would take him even if he wasn't willing. Even if I had to take him out of the country.

We stayed with my brother until visiting hours were over. Much to my surprise, when I entered the visitor's area, Tabatha was still there. Along with everyone else.

Tabatha looked up, a small smile splaying on her beautiful face. "How is he?"

"He didn't wake up." I went up to her, needing her touch.

As if she could sense it, she stood, closing the distance between us.

My hand reached the back of her head first before my mouth came down hard on hers.

She latched on to my shirt, pulling me closer, a soft moan leaving the back of her throat.

"Thank you," I whispered, breaking the kiss and leaning my forehead against hers.

Mom and Dad thanked everyone for staying and for their support. Over the next hour or two, the room started clearing out.

Meadow came up to me and gave me a hug. "I like your girl." She cupped my cheek. "And I'm happy for you. If you need anything, Shade and me are here."

I nodded, my throat working over a hard lump.

"Ashton."

I turned at the sound of my name, finding Piper coming toward me.

"We have to head out but if you need anything, we're here for you too." She gave me a hug, much to my surprise.

I returned the embrace, catching Jaron staring our way. Part of me expected him to lose his shit but when he only came up to me and stuck out his hand, I realized that maybe things could be different now. Maybe we had all grown up and moved past the fact that I had once been an asshole who tried to cause problems for several people I knew.

Piper released me, looking up at her husband.

My gaze dropped to Jaron's outstretched hand. I returned the handshake, thankful that they were there. Even if it wasn't for me and my parents but Aiden instead. I still appreciated the support.

"I know we've had our issues but I agree with Piper. Whatever you need, we are here," he reiterated.

I nodded because what could I say? My throat closed up, my heart began racing again. I couldn't deal with these emotions rushing through me and I needed a release. I needed to get them out before they consumed me completely.

We said our goodbyes and, as everyone left, I prayed that Aiden could feel the love and support surrounding him.

"Ashton?" Tabatha wrapped her arms around me, leaning her head back to stare up at me. "I imagine you want to stay?"

"I should." I looked back at my parents sitting across the room. Mom had a wad of Kleenex in her hand while Dad had his arm around her shoulders and his forehead against her temple. They were talking softly amongst themselves. As much as I wanted to go and lose myself in Tabatha, I couldn't leave them or my brother.

"I'm going to call Scooter and tell him I can't make my shift tonight." When Tabatha pulled away and fished her phone out of her bag, I almost told her not to worry about it but changed my mind. Having her there with me, would calm this incessant rage inside of me.

"Ashton." Dad came up to me. "We're going to go back to Aiden's room."

"Okay. I'll stay here with Tabatha for a bit."

"She's good for you." Dad hugged me. "She's really good for you."

"No. She's perfect for me." I hugged him back. We weren't touchy feely kind of people but I always appreciated his hugs. Aiden and I were big and we got that from our father, but Dad was huge. He was wide in the shoulders and tall as fuck. Aiden and I used to tease our parents at how different they were in size.

"Do you think we'll ever find that?"

I looked at my brother. "What do you mean?"

"The sort of love Mom and Dad have." Aiden didn't meet my gaze but only continued with the video game we were playing.

"I don't know." I shrugged. "It's not really my thing."

And it hadn't been. Not until I met Tabatha.

Once my parents left the waiting room, I went and joined her. I wrapped my arm around her shoulders, pulling her into my side.

She yawned, coughed, and snuggled into me.

When she yawned again, I cupped her jaw. "You good?"

Tabatha nodded. "Yeah. Just tired." She leaned her head against my shoulder, her eyes fluttering closed.

A sudden feeling twisted at my gut. I couldn't explain what it was. Nervousness. Anxiety. *Fear.*

I had been so focused on Aiden, I never took a moment to see how Tabatha was. Ever since she told me she had battled cancer, a part of me worried that it would come back. I was sure she felt the same way, along with her brothers, and everyone else who loved her.

Wrapping my arm around Tabatha's shoulders, I pulled her closer to my side. Maybe she should have gone home but at the same time, I didn't want her to leave. I needed her strength. Her fire. Her need to tell me to get my shit together.

I thought over the past couple of months. Could the universe be that cruel and take her away from me? The first time I fell in love. The first time I actually wanted to settle down and have a family of my own. The first time I wanted to be with one woman and one woman only. Could God be that evil and give her cancer again? I didn't know much about that horrible disease, but I knew that chemo and radiation weren't good for the body. I wasn't sure if Tabatha was strong enough to fight it off again.

"Kitten," I murmured, needing to hear her voice.

"Yeah?" She lifted her head, her beautiful eyes meeting mine.

I looked her over. Dark bags sat beneath her eyes. Her pale skin, almost ashen in a way.

"I'm sorry," I blurted.

She frowned. "Why are you sorry?"

"It's my job to take care of you and I haven't been doing that. With Aiden and then now with his accident…" I cupped her cheek, her skin warm. "Are you not feeling well?"

She shrugged. "I'm just really tired."

My stomach twisted. "I don't know much about…" I swallowed hard. "Have you been to the doctor's lately?"

Tabatha looked away. "No."

"Maybe you should go."

"I can't." She pulled away from me but before she could get very far, I grabbed her arm and tugged her back against me. "Ashton."

"No." I kissed her temple. "Don't pull away from me. Whatever it is, we'll deal with it together."

She looked at me then, her eyes shining. "Really? You mean that?"

I stared at her, taken aback by her words. "Of course. You don't think I would be?"

"Listen." She turned her body toward me, taking both of my hands in hers. "I love you. You are persistent and wouldn't take no for an answer but in the best of ways. You were determined and I love you even more for that. But this…if the cancer is back, I understand if you want to end things."

"Fuck no." I placed a hard peck on her lips. "I don't think so."

"Ashton."

"Stop." I fisted her hair, holding her head in place. "I know before you, I went through women like it was a damn job. I'm not proud of the shit I did before you, but I hadn't found my person. I hadn't found you, Tabatha. You told me weeks ago that you battled cancer. I could have left you then but I didn't.

Because I love you. I know I proposed to you the first night we met but I actually meant it. If you would have said yes, I would have taken you to Vegas so we could get married."

She laughed.

I raised an eyebrow. "You think I'm kidding?"

Her smile fell. "You're not?"

"I'm many things but that proposal was not a joke. I never believed in this instant love shit. Yes, I've been attracted to women at first sight but it never went more than just being physical." I tightened my hold on her hair, forcing a soft whimper from the back of her throat. That single sound made the hairs on my body tingle. "The first night we met, I remember going to leave and then I saw a flash of your pink hair. I needed to know who you were and when you called me an asshole, I knew you were the one. I was all in before I even knew your name."

Her breath caught. "I…God, I love you."

"Good. Now be a good girl and stop with this crazy talk about me leaving you if you get sick again. I am yours. Only yours. Don't ever doubt my feelings for you."

Tabatha nodded. "Okay."

"That's better."

She laughed lightly. "Thank you, Ashton. For everything."

If only she knew. She didn't have to thank me for anything. Besides, it should be me thanking *her*. She saved me from going down a dangerous path. While my brother had an addiction when it came to alcohol, I was bordering on becoming a sex addict because I had been bored. With Tabatha, sure the sex was often but she saved me from losing myself. And I couldn't thank her enough for that.

TWENTY-FOUR

Tabatha

"*THE CANCER IS BACK.*"

That was all I heard as I walked like a zombie out of the hospital. I hadn't been feeling well over the past few weeks, but I just chalked it up to not sleeping the greatest. It wasn't fair. None of it was fair. Just when I found a man who broke down my walls, this shit happened.

Ashton had been dealing with his brother, being there for his parents whenever he could and taking care of me just the same. He had left me alone too, not taking things further even though I had often hinted whenever I kissed him. He would make an excuse and tell me that I needed my rest. I appreciated it but I needed him just the same.

He had often brought up about me going to the doctors. He was right but at the same time, I was scared for what I would find out. And with good reason. But the other night when I almost fell asleep at the table while playing poker with my brothers, I knew before they even reacted, that something was wrong.

"Tabby." Beck shot out of his chair just as I almost fell out of mine.

I shook myself, rubbing at my eyes. "I'm fine."

"You are not fine," Jonah insisted. "You need to go see your doctor."

"No." I rose from the chair and went to the kitchen. "I'm fine." But I knew I wasn't. I didn't know how I knew but I wasn't stupid. When I had found out that I had cancer the last time, it stemmed from me being exhausted more than normal.

"You're not fine," my brothers said all at the same time.

"I haven't been sleeping well. I just need some coffee." But we all knew that it wouldn't help.

That had been a few nights ago. I went to the doctors like my brothers and Ashton wanted but a part of me regretted it. It was like I was in denial. Maybe if I hadn't been tested for the cancer and didn't see my oncologist, I could live the rest of my life pretending that I was healthy.

My phone pinged in the back pocket of my jeans, but I ignored it. I needed some time to myself before I faced the guys and Ashton. God, Ashton. This was going to break him.

I already knew they wouldn't be able to save what I had left of my kidney. My doctor had run more tests just to see how aggressive the cancer was and it was coming on fast. But I had already beat it once, I could do it again. Right?

Somehow, I ended up in front of Ashton's apartment building. It was during the day, so he should have been working. After Aiden woke up, Ashton went back to work and continued running the business they owned together.

Aiden ended up in rehab after getting charged with impaired driving. I prayed for him and his family's sake that it helped him.

After Ashton had found out that his brother was awake, he had visited him at the hospital. But when he got home, there was a darkness to him. I never asked how that conversation went but I imagined it hadn't been good or Aiden finally told him why he started drinking so much.

That had been a few weeks ago but Ashton still never talked about it. I would ask him how his brother was and all he would say was that Aiden was finally getting the help he needed.

I was due to go back to the hospital the next day, so I could start chemo and all the other shit they do to try and save me. I scoffed. Ashton had been the only thing to truly save me. He broke down my walls. No, he fucking shattered them.

He had given me a key to his place and told me to come and go as I pleased. I could feel the key burning in my purse and ended up changing my mind. I wound up on the rooftop of the apartment I shared with the guys. I used to go there often to collect my thoughts and to just be by myself. I had set up a little cozy nook type area. With a patio set, a table, and even a cooler that was currently empty. There was a fire pit as well. As much as I wanted to feel the heat of the fire on my skin, I sat on the patio lounger and laid back, staring up at the late afternoon sky.

My phone continued to buzz but I ignored it. Fishing it out of my pocket, I placed it on the table beside me and watched it vibrate lightly as each call and text came in. My brothers would figure out where I was but Ashton, he would have no idea. But I knew him. He would contact one of them and demand to know where I was. My brothers also knew that if I wasn't responding, it was because I wanted to be alone after getting some horrible news.

My thoughts traveled to my dad. It had been a long time since he came to mind. Ashton had helped me realize that not everyone in my life would leave me. Even though I had my brothers, it wasn't the same. They could have left me long ago, but they never did. They were stubborn as hell anyway, so I would have to be the one to leave first.

My chest constricted, my eyes welling. Every emotion ran through me.

Fear. Anger. Rage.

I missed my dad, but I had been pissed for years that he was stupid enough to cheat. The game and idea of winning was more important to him than his own daughter.

A sob left me. I sat up, my body shaking with hard cries.

I had cried when I was a girl and found out my dad had been killed, but I hadn't cried since. Sure, I missed him terribly but that was it.

Now with the cancer being back, the possibility that chemo wouldn't work, all of these pent-up emotions I had pushed away for so long, came to the surface.

Every feeling I had left me on a hard sob.

Bringing my knees up to my chest, I wrapped my arms around them and cried. God, did I cry.

The hairs on the back of my neck tingled, indicating that I was no longer alone but I couldn't be bothered to see who it was. As this person came closer, I could smell the hint of cologne. It was Ashton and that fact alone made me cry even harder.

He sat behind me, pulling me between his legs and wrapping himself around my trembling body.

He didn't offer words of encouragement. He didn't tell me that it would okay. He didn't say anything. He just held me while I let it all out. Emotions I had bottled up for most of my life. Even when I found out I had cancer the first time, I didn't cry. The doctor said I was in shock but I didn't react at all. Obviously, that was a problem but everyone ignored it. Because I ignored it, they felt they had to do the same.

Once my sobs subsided, I lifted my head, wiping my cheeks.

I turned, placing my hand on Ashton's thigh but was unable to meet his gaze. "I'm scared. I knew this whole time that the cancer was back but I was terrified to find out. I..." My chin wobbled. "I'm sorry."

"Stop." Ashton pulled me onto his lap. "What did I tell you?"

"Ashton." I struggled against him, suddenly needing to get away.

"No." His hold on me tightened. "What did I tell you?"

"That was before we found out that the cancer is back, Ashton." I went to pull away from him but like normal, he was stubborn and refused to let me go. "Seriously."

"Stop." He pulled me tighter. "Stop this shit right now. It's you and me against the whole fucking world. It's only ever been you and me. I told you that I wasn't going to leave you no matter if the cancer came back or not. I also told you that if you need a new kidney, I'll give you mine as long as I'm a match. I told you that before I fell in love with you."

"Why?" I threw at him. "Why would you want to be with someone who's sick? I don't know how many years I can give you—"

"Stop this shit, right the fuck now."

Before I knew what was happening, he had me on my back. I gasped, my body heating even though it wasn't the right time. But it had been so damn long since I felt him or even got this side of him, that my body didn't care about the timing being inappropriate as hell and wanted him anyway.

Ashton tilted his head, raising an eyebrow. "Even now?"

"I can't help it when you haven't touched me in weeks," I grumbled.

"I haven't touched you because I'm trying to be a gentleman. You've been exhausted and not feeling well. I know I can be a controlling asshole but that's crossing a line. Even for me."

"I don't want...I just want to feel something other than this fear. I hate being scared. It makes me feel weak and I know that's not true, but it's how I feel. I'm scared that I'll be taken from you before we experience life together. I'm pissed at my father for leaving me. I'm just..." My eyes welled again. "I need a release. I need something. I have to go to the hospital tomorrow but I want to feel normal before that. Even if it's only for a few hours. Please, Ashton."

He placed a soft peck on my head, letting his lips gently trail down the bridge of my nose before capturing my mouth in a hard kiss.

I sighed, breathed him in, and wrapped myself around him. As much as I just wanted him to get on with it, I needed his control. I needed him to take me out of my head. I also didn't care that anyone could come up to the rooftop at any time. It didn't matter. None of that mattered because Ashton was there. He was with me. He loved me and took care of me. Even though the guys in my life had taught me to look out for myself, sometimes a girl just needed to be taken care of.

The kiss deepened, pulling me from my thoughts.

Ashton slid his hands down my sides to the waist of my leggings. With some maneuvering on my part, I helped him slip them down my legs, letting them hang off one foot.

He broke the kiss, leaning back and pulling his hoodie up and over his head. It left him in a white t-shirt and his jeans. The shirt showcased muscles and a wide body I could never get used to seeing.

I frowned, wondering what he was doing when he handed me the hoodie. Taking the hint, I put it on. It was long enough that it was more like a dress, so if anyone came up to the roof, they wouldn't actually see anything.

Ashton towered back over me, slipping his hand beneath the hoodie and my shirt, until it reached my breast. With his other hand, he undid the zipper of his jeans.

I wrapped my legs around his waist at the same time he sank into me. Pleasure shot up my spine, forcing my back to bow off the lounger.

He didn't let me get used to him being back inside of me after weeks of not having him make love to me. His hips powered forward and back, forcing that pleasure higher and higher. Slipping his hand from my breast, he pulled the fabric of the hoodie back down so it covered me and began fucking me like I wanted.

His eyes never left mine. The only sounds we made were my own and our bodies connecting. I was beyond wet for him and he knew it. It wasn't something I could control anyway. Not when it came to him.

A hard whine left me as I slapped my hands against his chest, needing him closer. "Please," I heard myself beg. "More."

Before I could beg for him to go faster and harder, he pulled out of me and flipped me onto my stomach.

"Hold on, Kitten," he murmured in my ear, slipping his hands beneath the hoodie and up to my breasts. "I was trying to be nice and leave you alone since you haven't been feeling well."

"Once I start chemo, I won't feel up to having sex," I explained. "So, I need this. God, baby, I need this."

"I know." He pinched my nipples, sinking his thick cock back into me. "I know that now."

I whimpered, my body clenching around him.

He pushed into me as far as my body would allow and stopped. "I'm marrying you. As soon as—"

"Tonight," I blurted.

His cock twitched inside of me. "What?"

I pulled away from him, turned, and straddled his lap. Cupping his face, I lowered my body onto him. "We'll find a chapel and get married tonight."

"Don't fucking tease me, Kitten," he growled, nipping my jaw.

"I'm not. I need to go into tomorrow as your wife. Please, Ashton." I leaned back, running my fingers through his hair. "Make me your wife."

(Ashton)

I almost thought she was kidding. Making her my wife had been something I had wanted since the first night I met her. But when she was serious and no smile adorned her beautiful face, I pushed her back onto the lounger and gave her what she wanted quickly.

Once she screamed my name, my own release followed. It had been fast and something neither of us wanted, but making her my wife was more important.

"You sure you want to do this?" I asked her once we were in her bedroom. Her brothers were playing poker and as much as I wanted to ask them for her hand in marriage, first, I needed to make sure that she was fine with this.

"Yes." Tabatha went to the bathroom and came back a moment later, stripping out of her clothes. "We can have a big ceremony and reception another day but tonight, I just need to be yours. Please let me be yours."

"You are mine, Kitten, but I need to be sure that you're not just agreeing to marry me because of what's happening tomorrow."

Tabatha stared at me, chewing her bottom lip before letting out a soft sigh. "I'm not going to lie and say that it's not part of the reason I want to get married tonight but I wanted to marry you even before finding out I have cancer again. You know that."

"I do." I sat on the edge of her bed. "But I don't want you to regret anything either." Why the hell was I questioning this when I had wanted it all along?

"Baby." Tabatha moved to the spot between my knees and knelt at my feet. "I love you. I want to spend my life with you. Am I scared that I won't be able to give you a lifetime of happiness? I'm fucking terrified. But I need to marry you as a just in case and if everything goes well, Lord knows I'm praying it does, I'll marry you all over again."

I leaned forward, cupping her cheek. "Well then, Kitten, I guess we need to make some calls."

TWENTY-FIVE

Tabatha

THERE WEREN'T ANY DRIVE-through chapels in our city, even though it was getting bigger and bigger as the years went on. So, after making some calls, Ashton found a chapel in a city that was an hour away.

He called his parents and friends and I called Sarge and my brothers. Much to my surprise, none of them seem surprised that Ashton and I were getting married, and so soon. Looked like it was meant to be more than I thought.

When I got off the phone, I looked around my bedroom and wondered if Ashton would move in with me or if I would move in with him. Even though his brother was now in rehab, I didn't think Ashton would want to leave him alone. There were so many things we had to figure out to make it so we had a stable marriage. Were we making a mistake? Even though it had been my idea, I couldn't help but wonder if this was the right thing to do.

"Kitten." Ashton placed a gentle kiss on my temple. "I can practically hear the wheels turning in your head."

"How are we going to live together?" I asked him.

"Move in with me. I know my apartment's small but I'd love to have your stuff everywhere. I also know that Aiden won't care if you live with us."

"I wish he could join us." I cupped Ashton's cheek, running my thumb along his bottom lip.

"Me too, but his health is more important to me. If he gets the help he needs, that's all I care about."

"I hope rehab helps him."

Ashton sighed. "Me too."

"I don't have a fancy dress or anything but I'll pack something that I think will be good enough." I left the bed and started rummaging through my closet.

"Babe, you could wear a snowsuit and still be hot as fuck."

I laughed, blowing him a kiss.

While I packed a bag and started getting ready, a hard knock sounded on the door. Ashton answered it, letting me finish packing my bag.

"You sure you both want to do this?" I heard Beck ask from the doorway.

"We are," Ashton told him.

Once my bag was packed, I tossed it on the bed. "I know this is fast but with having to go to the hospital tomorrow and starting chemo, I just...I need this. We both need this."

Beck nodded, coming into my room and wrapping his arms around me. "You won't get any issues from me. Not anymore. This fucker's stubborn anyway. Even if I didn't approve, I don't think he'd give a shit."

I laughed.

Ashton grunted. "That's the truth."

"You're just pissed that he beat us last time we played poker," Jonah called from the hallway.

"You should be pissed too," Beck threw at him.

"Nah. I know I'm not that good at the game. I had more fun watching him kick your ass." Jonah laughed. "It was epic." He joined us in my bedroom, gently pushing Beck out of the way so he could get a hug in.

I wrapped my arms his middle, leaning my head against his chest.

"Careful." Phoenix took that moment to join us. Looked like we were having a party in my room of all places. "Ashton's going to get jealous and kick *your* ass."

"It'll be worth it." Jonah held on a little longer than necessary.

"Before that happens, it's my turn." Phoenix shoved Jonah aside and pulled me into his arms.

I sighed, my eyes fluttering closed as I wrapped myself around him. "You good?"

"Yeah, Sis." He kissed the top of my head. "Scooter and Natalie have been helping me deal with my demons."

I leaned back, staring up at him. A breath of relief left me when I didn't see any new piercings. "I love you. I love all of you."

"We love you too." Phoenix squeezed me.

"Are you happy?" I asked him softly.

"I am," he whispered, holding me a little longer.

"Alright." Ashton shot up from his spot on the bed. "That's enough."

Phoenix chuckled, pushing me into Ashton's arms.

"Better?" I asked him.

Ashton wrapped himself around me, pushing all of him up against me. "Much better."

While the guys continued to banter and talk about how I was going to be a married woman in only a couple of hours, I held on to Ashton.

I thought back to the beginning and how stubborn he was. How persistent he had been. If it wasn't for that, I probably never would have even let things go further between us. Even though I had pushed him away, I noticed him before he opened his mouth. My heart hurt that his brother couldn't be with him, but I got it. Aiden had a long road ahead of him. I just hoped that he could find his person. If that was what he was looking for anyway. But he needed support and I would be there for him as much as Ashton. I didn't know him well but I hoped that one day we could be close. For Ashton's sake at least.

(Ashton)

I was damn near vibrating with the need to make Tabatha my wife. Ever since she said yes weeks ago, it had been on my mind constantly. But I knew her health had been a problem. Now that the cancer was back, marrying her was the only thing that made sense. I was just thankful that she agreed.

Once we were sitting in my car and driving to the next city over, I kept my hand locked firm on Tabatha's thigh.

I thought back to the last conversation I had with my brother, my chest tightening over the fact that he wouldn't be with us. Even though Tabatha and I had plans to have another ceremony and a big fucking party after, Aiden should still be at both.

Aiden was awake.

Dad came and told me so.

If it was under any other circumstance, I would have jumped at the chance to see my brother. To make sure that he was okay. To see that he was fine and very much alive. But the fact that he did this to himself, I wanted to make him stew a bit.

"You should go see your brother." Tabatha stood, holding out her hand. "Trust me, I know you're furious, but it'll make you feel better if you see him."

As much as I wanted to argue with her, I knew she was right.

I slipped my fingers in hers and stood before placing a hard peck on her mouth. "I love you."

"And I love you." She patted my stomach. "I'm going to head home. Come find me when you're done."

I nodded, kissed her again, and went to face my brother.

I knew when I entered the room that Aiden would be hooked up to tubes. But I still wasn't expecting to see what I walked in on. He almost seemed vulnerable and small in a way with the big hospital bed around him.

CONSUME US

I hadn't noticed over the weeks how much weight he'd lost. His cheeks were sunken in and dark bags sat under his eyes.

His hair on the top of his head seemed almost thin in a way. Like he was much older than being in his early thirties. He was also pale and ashen. I wished I would have noticed sooner.

It was like I had pushed my brother aside and even though I was mad that he drank and had gotten an accident, I still blamed myself that he took it that far.

Did something set him over the edge? I wished he would talk to me or at least speak to someone about it. Anyone for that matter. But while he laid in the hospital bed with bandages on his face, a cast and a sling on his left arm, and a cast on his leg, I thanked whoever listened up above that he was still alive. Even though he'd be forced into rehab, maybe it was what he needed. Because I knew even though he was really the only alcoholic that I was close with, that sometimes some people needed to have something drastic happen to them before they made any changes. I just wished it wouldn't have come to this. I wished he would have come to me or my parents, or even one of our friends. But were they really friends? It was like we were just thrown together because our parents were friends. In another life, if our parents didn't know each other, would we actually hang out? I had my brother, so I instantly had a best friend. I would never have to worry about being alone. But now that I had Tabatha, maybe Aiden felt like he was alone.

We didn't really talk much anymore. I looked out for him as best I could. Taking him to the bar and bringing him home. But I couldn't be there twenty-four seven. I wasn't his babysitter. And as selfish as it was, maybe he needed this accident. He didn't kill anyone, and he didn't kill himself. And as far as I knew, no one else got hurt. Thankfully he was the only one to get hurt. Because I knew that on top of whatever happened in the Navy, if he would have killed someone, he wouldn't have been able to live with himself.

I stood there staring down at my brother, my twin. The other half of me. The best part of me. We didn't look alike much anymore. Especially now that this disease had taken over. But maybe once he was in rehab, he could gain some weight back and get healthy again. This would be a lifelong battle between him and his addiction. And no matter how mad I was at him, I would always be there. He didn't have to worry about that.

But I wasn't sure if that would be enough. Maybe he needed someone else. Maybe he needed his person.

Why would you do this to yourself?

When Aiden stirred, his head turning and his eyes meeting mine, I realized I had spoken out loud. Eyes that mirrored my own, stared up at me. They were vacant. No longer a bright blue like mine were. They were dull and held so much pain. I could feel it even though he didn't talk to me and tell me what had happened. I could still feel everything he felt. Call it a twin intuition. You could call it whatever you want. But there was something there. Something that we would share forever. Something that only twins understood.

"Why would you do this?" I asked again.

Aiden looked away.

My stomach churned, a sharp tremor racing down my back. Fury erupted through me that he had the audacity to look away from me, to not look me square in the eye and answer my question.

"Why did you do this?" I asked again, my voice louder.

When Aiden looked at me that time, my stomach sunk.

His eyes had welled with unshared tears. His throat bobbed up and down, working over what I could only assume was a mixture of emotions. I fell to my knees beside his bed, grabbed his hand, and held on to him, wishing I could help him. Wishing I could take away his pain. Wishing I could help him carry it, so he didn't have to face it alone.

His agony seeped from him, forcing all breath from my lungs. It was suffocating in the way that he finally let me feel what he was feeling.

I wished I would have helped him sooner.

"Ashton." My name left his lips on a sob.

I jumped to my feet, throwing myself around my brother.

"I'm sorry," I said, pushing my face into the crook of his neck.

His sobs only hardened, and they were so powerful, I could feel them shake through me.

I muttered over and over again how I would do anything for him. How if I could, I would take away his demons. How I would help him battle whatever he was going through. I knew it wasn't enough. It could never be enough. No matter how hard I tried.

I knew he would always battle this alcoholism. But he didn't need to face his demons alone.

"I'll be there for you."

"Ashton," he said my name again. Almost like he didn't believe me. To be fair, I hadn't really given him much of a reason to believe me. Not over these past few weeks.

When Aiden's cries subsided, I leaned back, staring down at my brother.

"Do you feel better?"

He shrugged. "Am I supposed to feel better?"

I shrugged that time, mirroring his movement. "I don't know but I heard that when you have a good cry, it can make you feel better."

"I guess." Aiden didn't look at me. But he picked at a piece of fuzz on his blanket.

"Did you want to talk about it?"

"Not really. But I know I should. I probably should have talked to someone right away. That's what I was told anyway. And I might even still be in the Navy if I had spoken with someone. I've tried ignoring what happened. But every time I close my eyes at night, I see them. I hear them. I can still feel their pain." A shuddered breath left him and I wondered if he was having survivor's guilt. I didn't know exactly what had happened because he never talked about it but something had hit the news at the time. It was very vague. Saying that a few Navy personnel had died. I even asked my dad and he only said that it was bad. But he didn't know exactly what had happened either. It was all hush-hush. And now that our fathers were retired, they didn't have as much pull as they used to which I was sure they were thankful for, in a way, because who wanted to relive those moments for the rest of their lives?

"Did you want to talk to me?" I asked Aidan.

"We were deep in the thick of things. We had a squad of Humvees surrounding us. We were looking for a known terrorist. He hadn't made his way over to the States yet, but we were trying to prevent that from happening or prevent him from going somewhere else. He was becoming dangerous and quickly, and we knew that if we didn't catch him, that it would get worse and it would end up being like 9/11 all over again. So, we searched him out, spent weeks trying to find this guy. When we finally got information on his whereabouts, we started driving to his location and the Humvee in front of us, hit a mine. Thankfully they survived but one guy lost his leg, another lost his arm but it definitely could have been worse. They were alive and that was all that mattered. But the vehicle I was in, we were second. We had stopped. We shouldn't have stopped. I remember saying that we shouldn't have stopped. Everyone agreed but we did it anyway. We wanted to check on our team. So that's what we did. Next thing I knew, and it was like it came right out of an action movie. We were surrounded. Things exploded. Shots rang out. It's *all I can hear when I close my eyes at night. These bastards shot and killed anything they could. They didn't care if it was their own people. They didn't care if it was women or children. They shot anything that got in their way. I was able to call it in but I wasn't fast enough. That wasn't even the worst part." His breath caught, lost in the memories of his nightmare. "They took our vehicle over. I remember a bag being shoved over my head. The two women on my team screamed. I couldn't see what was being done to them. But it all happened so fast. When the bag was finally ripped from my head, I saw them and their vacant eyes. Their dead stares. The women, my Navy sisters, family, they were gone. They were right in front of me, but they were gone and I felt guilty. That for having a dick, I was saved. But because they didn't, they were raped and tortured, sodomized anything else you can imagine, it was done to them. And there was nothing I could do. I was hog-tied with barbed wire. And I wasn't the only one. It took a while but we were finally saved. Those bastards were shot and killed and we were able to complete our mission, but not without risk."*

When Aiden stopped speaking, I couldn't believe what he was telling me. No wonder he had nightmares and had become an alcoholic. Any sane person would search out any way to take away that pain. I was sure some people would even take their own lives.

"Can I ask you a question?" I didn't want to ask but I needed to know.

Aiden looked at me then. "Of course."

"Were you trying to kill yourself? Is that why you drove drunk? You've tried driving before but you never have. What happened this time, Aiden?"

A shuddered breath left him, his shoulders sagging. "I honestly don't know. I thought of it many times, but I can't leave you. I can't leave Mom and Dad. Maybe I'm a pussy. Maybe I'm just not brave enough. But I'm terrified to take my own life. Maybe it's why I drink. Maybe I hope that the alcohol will take me instead. But I know I need help. Especially after what happened tonight. If I could make the judge throw me in jail, I would."

"If you went to jail, it would destroy Mom. You remember how Jaron's parents were when he went to jail?" Even though I didn't like the guy much, I still wouldn't wish that on anyone. And after saving Piper from getting raped, he really should have been given a medal.

"I know," Aiden said, "but it's how I feel."

"Thank you for telling me. I wish there was something I could do."

"Just you listening has helped. If I could go back in time, I would have spoken to someone right away. But I thought I was fine. I thought I could get over it."

"How were you found?"

"It was noticed rather quickly that we were missing. So even though I felt like we were there for years, it was only a couple of days. When we were found, we were taken home right away and those we lost were given proper burials. But I never went to the funerals and I feel guilty for that. I do send flowers often though."

"What happened to make you drink so much? And to drive? You should have called me. You always call me."

"I know. I do know this. Trust me. I know this. Something in me snapped. I can't explain it. But I think it's the guilt of surviving. I think it finally broke me."

I didn't know what to say to that. I was thankful that he finally told me what had happened. I just wished that he would have told me sooner so I could have helped him. But I got it. I understood.

"So what's new with you?" Aiden asked.

"Really? After what you've been through, you want to know what's new with me?"

"Of course. It'll get my mind off of my sorry excuse for a life."

I sighed, grabbing his hand and held it in mine. "I'm getting married to Tabatha."

"Good. I like her for you. She doesn't take your crap." He smiled.

"No, she doesn't and that's one of the reasons I love her. She makes me want to be a better man."

Aiden and I continued talking for the next hour or so. It was nice to just talk to him about anything. And nothing really at all. We talked about Tabatha and talked about if he was interested in anyone. He said he didn't really care to look for a relationship, especially now that he was probably going into rehab. But what stuck out the most to me was the fact that in the beginning, he said that he wished that he would end up in jail. He thought maybe that would force this addiction to go away. But we both knew that with addictions, they never went away. No matter how hard you forced them. They would always be there. He had told me that he tried quitting drinking several times. But he always relapsed. As soon as he heard the voices, the screams from his friends, that he has spent years working beside, he drowned himself in a bottle. The fact that he did this all on his own and never told anyone, forced this ache in my chest. It must have been lonely. I imagined that even if he went and told people about his alcoholism, I was sure he would still feel alone. Everyone battled it differently. I was sure that no two alcoholics were the same. They all had different reasons for drinking.

When the nurses came in to check on Aiden, they told me that visiting hours were far past being over. Mom and Dad came in, said their goodbyes, and left. But before they did that, they told him that if he needed anything, to call them. Dad specifically said this.

I could almost see the overwhelming emotion between them. They had butted heads for so long. I was sure that it would be hard to get back to that place. Both of us looked like dad. But Aiden had his personality.

I strived to be the man for Tabatha that Dad was for Mom and if I was half as good as him, then my job was done.

I wished my brother could join us, but he needed to get better. That was all that mattered to me.

Tabatha and I were now on our way to the next city over. Mom and Dad were following with Tabatha's brothers behind them. I wanted to invite everyone I knew but we had to make this quick. We would celebrate more and party later. Once I knew that Tabatha was healthy enough to do so. Before then, we would get married, and I would give her one of my kidneys if needed.

The most important thing out of all of this was that she battled this awful disease. If she didn't, I wasn't sure what we would do.

TWENTY-SIX

Tabatha

ASHTON AND I WERE married. It was a quick ceremony. It was small and romantic. It was just me and him, my brothers, Sarge, and Ashton's parents.

Ashton had called Aiden and told him the good news. He had him on speaker and he actually did seem excited for us. He also sounded different. Even though I hadn't spoken to him much over the months I knew Ashton, he sounded solemn in a way. Maybe he was sad that he could no longer drink or maybe he was waiting until he was out of rehab so he could drink again. Maybe that was what everybody expected from him. For him to fall deep in the pit of a bottle and never come out. I didn't have much experience with alcoholics or even drug addicts really, but I had done my own research. And still, I didn't know enough. I had asked Ashton if I could talk to Aiden for a moment and turned off the speaker. I stepped out of the room even though Ashton gave me a look. Probably wondering what I was doing.

"Aiden."

"Yeah."

"I know we don't know each other well but I just want you to know that if you ever need to talk. I'm here. Maybe having an unbiased opinion and someone who hasn't known you your whole life, it might be easier to talk to me. I don't know. That probably doesn't even make sense. But I just want you to know that the offer is there."

He cleared his throat and cleared it again before muttering a thank you. The call disconnected shortly after. I was sure most would think that it was rude that he just hung up on me. But I knew that with Aiden, he meant his thank you. He was obviously thrown off guard by my offer. I just hoped that he took me up on it one day. If it came to that.

"Where did you go?" Ashton had asked me when I made my way back out to him. I told him that I spoke to his brother and wanted to do it privately.

Ashton only kissed my temple. He didn't ask me what I talked to his brother about, which I appreciated.

After that small ceremony, we drove back home. It was almost three in the morning by the time Ashton tucked me into his bed.

As much as he insisted on me getting some rest since I had to go to the hospital in a few hours, I convinced him to make love to me even if it was quick.

"We have to consummate our marriage, Ashton."

"As much as I like that idea, you do need your rest," he had said, but once I started kissing him, his mind had changed. Now it was the next morning, and I was sitting on the edge of the tub waiting. For what, I wasn't sure. I still had an hour before I had to go to the hospital.

Even though I had been down this road before, besides my brothers and Sarge, I never had someone that I wanted to fight for.

They always asked me how I was doing.

I loved them. They were a piece of me. But those questions also drove me crazy because I didn't know how I was doing. Ashton never asked me. He would just kiss my temple, or cheek, or squeeze my hand a little longer. Held me like he knew it was what I needed without me having to ask. But he never asked how I was doing.

How did I feel?

Was I scared? Of course, I was scared.

Was I worried? Obviously.

The hospital offered counseling for cancer survivors. But I never took them up on their offer. Maybe this time I would. I didn't feel too bad physically. Just tired. But I've been tired for weeks. It felt normal to be tired lately.

Once we arrived to the hospital, Ashton and I sat a little longer in the car.

If I was older, I wouldn't even go into the hospital.

I would live out our days together instead and die at home where I was safe and happy. But I was young, way too young to give up.

I knew what was coming with the chemo and the radiation and the side effects that it would most definitely cause, I still had things to live for. I wasn't sure if I could ever give Ashton babies. The doctors weren't sure either and I never wanted them to officially check.

"I don't know if I can give you children," I blurted, braced myself, and looked at Ashton. "I mean... no, that's exactly what I mean. I'm sorry, but I really don't know if I can have babies. Or even one baby, let alone several."

"That's not the reason I married you," Ashton said, grabbing my hands. He brought them up to his mouth. Kissing my fingertips, the gentle movement forced a lump in my throat.

"I know it's not the reason you married me, but I just want you to know that it might not happen. I should have told you sooner. But honestly, with everything going on with your brother and dealing with my own family and then dealing with myself trying everything I could to push you away, I never thought to tell you that we may not be able to have kids."

"That's fine, Kitten. I only want you and you are all that I need. I don't need children to feel complete. Society makes us think that once we get married, the next step is to have children. I think a lot of children would be better off if they were never born at all. I think parents resent them because they felt like they had to have them."

I knew he wasn't talking about his own personal experience, but from mine and my brothers instead. None of our parents wanted us except for my dad. But even then, he made stupid choices that cost him his life and left me without either parent.

"You won't resent me if I can't give you at least one child?"

"Tabatha, I proposed to you the first night we met. I only knew your name and I still wanted to marry you. I knew nothing else about you. I knew what you looked like and that was it. The fact that you gave me attitude and shot me down right away, I knew I had met the one."

I scoffed. "There was no way you could have known that. You're just trying to say that to make me feel better."

"If you don't know by now, I say exactly what's on my mind. And I don't really care what people think about that."

"I know but—"

"No buts, Kitten. I proposed to you and if you would have said yes, I would have driven us to the courthouse. Out of the city to a chapel. I would have hired some priests even if we weren't from their religion, and I would have paid them to marry us."

I stared at him. The man that I was now going to spend the rest of my life with. I realized he wasn't kidding.

"So, you would have married me? Before knowing anything about me?"

He tilted his head, raising an eyebrow. "You seem surprised by that."

"I'm not. Not really, maybe. I don't know. I guess I shouldn't be. I've been with you for a few months now and we're already married." I lifted my hand looking at my ringless finger. "Speaking of which, you owe me a ring, buddy."

He laughed. "I owe you two rings technically. A diamond and a wedding band."

"And I owe you a wedding band."

"We'll figure that out later. Right now. I just need my girl healthy."

I sighed, wishing he could take me out of there. Wishing we could go somewhere just the two of us and have an actual honeymoon and not spend our first few weeks as man and wife at the hospital.

"Listen, I know this is going to be hard. I don't know many cancer survivors. Not personally anyway. But I do know that you're strong. You will get through this."

I frowned. "You don't know that. I've already battled it once. A body can only handle so much chemo before it shuts down."

"I told you that if you need a kidney and if mine is a match, I will give you one. Call it a wedding present."

I looked at him then, rolled my eyes, and tried not to laugh but I couldn't help it. Not that the situation was funny, but the fact that he offered his kidney as a wedding present, it made me shake my head, but still made me smile nonetheless.

"Well, I guess we should go in and get this done and over with."

Ashton left the vehicle and went around to my side. He opened the door, held out his hand, and waited.

When I slipped my hand in his, he helped me out of the car. But before I could walk away, he wrapped his arm around me and crushed his mouth to mine. The kiss deepened, forcing a moan from somewhere within us. I wasn't sure who made the noise but before it could turn into more, he released me.

"Whatever happens," he leaned his forehead against mine, "whatever the outcome is, I want you to know that I'm here. And I want you to know that whatever happens, no matter what the outcome is, I am not going anywhere."

"I appreciate you being here."

He gave me a small smirk, but it never reached his eyes. It was different for him. He had never experienced this before. But I had.

"If you end up losing hair, and you decide to shave your head, I'll shave mine with you," he offered.

Even though it was something simple, a kind gesture, it forced a sob to escape me.

He muttered a curse, throwing himself around me. "I didn't mean to make you cry."

"I know. It's not you. It's the situation. We should be on a honeymoon. We should be enjoying each other."

"We're going to have lots of time to enjoy each other. I promise you. And at any time, we can't enjoy each other over these next few weeks, we'll make up for it when you're feeling better."

I leaned back, wiping under my eyes. "Promise?"

Ashton kissed my nose. "Promise."

EPILOGUE

ASHTON

IT HAD BEEN OVER a year since Tabatha battled cancer for the second time. She ended up needing a kidney transplant. And by some sort of a miracle, I was a match. So, I gave her one of mine and thankfully her body didn't reject it.

It was a long road of recovery. But she made it through and never once complained. Even when she spent hours with her head in a toilet.

I had never seen someone so sick, but was thankful that she came out of it and survived.

One afternoon, I was sitting at Scooters in the back corner of the bar, waiting for someone I had known my whole life, to join me.

Much like Aiden who had a twelve-step program that he had to go through, I made amends as well with people. Even if they never accepted my apologies. I still did it. I still let them know that I was sorry for how I had acted.

I had contacted an old friend who I didn't see much anymore.

Luna Porter was married and had children of her own. But there was a time in the beginning where I had hinted for more from her. Not for a relationship but just sex. And I still felt bad for doing that. She obviously deserved better and she did get better when she finally admitted her feelings for Zach.

The ones I felt the most guilt about, were Jaron and Piper. Aiden and I had slept with Piper at the same time over the course of a few weeks but it had never amounted to anything more than that. When she broke things off between us, my little ego was hurt. So, I lashed out and tried causing problems for them. Nothing major, thankfully, but my mouth got in the way sometimes. I was surprised Jaron never punched me.

While I waited for an old acquaintance to show up, I looked over at the bar. Tabatha was serving drinks and chatting with customers, her coworkers, and even Scooter as he came out and stocked up.

One of her coworkers saw me staring and nodded toward me. Tabatha turned her head, her eyes meeting mine.

I nodded once, giving her a little wave.

She blew me a kiss, her hand dropping to her swollen stomach.

Every cell in my body stirred that my baby was growing inside of her. She was around six months along. And it came as a surprise. A wonderful surprise since we both assumed that she couldn't get pregnant. But she did and she was being constantly monitored as a result of it.

We ended up having another wedding and reception and invited everyone we knew.

Even though she had already been pregnant by the time of the reception, you would never know with the way we had consummated our marriage a second time because my wife was a dirty girl.

That was several months ago, but my dick still ached from time to time with memories of that night and what my wife did to it.

Before I could get caught lusting after my wife, my date for the evening showed up. When Jaron entered the bar, he stopped and looked around the room.

When his eyes met mine, that permanent scowl on his face seemed to deepen even more.

I was so happy that he was excited to have a date with me. I gave him a wave and signaled the waitress over, ordering a beer for him and another for me.

Once Jaron sat across the table from me, he crossed his arms under his chest.

"The only reason I'm here is because Piper told me to come. Other than that, I wouldn't be here."

"I figured as much," I told him "Our ladies do like to tell us what to do from time to time because they know what's best for us. Even though we like to deny it."

"What do you want, Ashton?"

"I wanted to apologize."

"You're wanting to apologize? For what?" Of course, he was going make me say it.

"For how I acted when you and Piper finally got back together after you got out of jail. For sleeping with her in the first place."

"We all have a past, Ashton. Things we did before we finally found our person."

I looked at Tabatha then, remembering how, in the beginning, she had called me out on my shit, accusing me of being a womanizer. And knowing just by looking at me and hearing me speak only a handful of words, how I had gone through women like she went through underwear.

"Most of us aren't proud of our past," Jaron continued. "But some of us just don't care. And we don't learn from them."

"If you're hinting that I haven't learned from my mistakes, I have." I sat back, mirroring his pose. I nodded towards Tabatha. "Right there. She's proof that I've learned from my mistakes."

Jaron followed my gaze. "Yes, Piper told me that you and Tabatha are still together and that you even married her."

When Tabatha turned back around, her swollen stomach was on full display.

Jaron's eyes widened. "But I didn't know she's pregnant. Piper didn't tell me that part."

"To be fair, I haven't told Piper because I don't see any of you much anymore and Tabatha likes to stay at home a lot. Besides working, she doesn't get out much which is partially my fault, because I really don't mind if she stays at home with me all the time. But I also don't want her to turn into a homebody."

Jaron nodded. "I actually know how you feel."

"So, yeah, the reason I called you to meet up for a beer was just so I could apologize. So here I am, apologizing for how I was and for being a dick. And for treating Piper like crap when I should have been there for her when you couldn't be and yes, my ego was bruised. Even though I knew she wasn't my person. I knew I wouldn't end up with her. It still bothered me. I was jealous, I guess, knowing that she had found someone."

"I never liked you," Jaron said. "And I think it's because I knew that if I never came back, Piper could have ended up with you. Or Aiden."

I grunted. "Definitely not Aiden."

"Would do you mean?" Jaron frowned.

"It's not my place to say. And I don't even know all the details anyway. But I think it's going to take a special person to capture Aiden's heart." And I couldn't wait to meet them.

"How's he doing? Besides that?"

"He's still in rehab. Even though he could have left a few months ago. I actually think he likes it there. I think it's safer for him having a routine. Not being around alcohol. He actually started working there. And helping in any way that he can. I don't know a whole lot. I haven't seen him in a while or even talked to him on the phone, but he seems to be getting better slowly."

"Good. I'm glad."

It was on the tip of my tongue to ask him if he really was glad. But I thought better of it. Tabatha was teaching me that I didn't have to say exactly what was on my mind without thinking about it first. She told me often that I was lucky I didn't get a shot in the head with the things that came out of my mouth sometimes. My argument was that she never minded my words when I was between her legs.

Jaron and I sat there in silence for what felt like a lifetime when I was sure it was only a matter of minutes.

"How are you and the family doing?" I asked him, figuring that was safe.

"Good. Piper's well, I'm well, the kids are growing quickly. We're happy. Finally. That's all that matters."

Much like him, I had never liked Jaron but maybe now we could at least be civil. Maybe now things wouldn't be so uncomfortable.

"You never came to my wedding," I pointed out.

"You never came to mine," he threw back at me.

"True. But I was also dealing with a wife who was battling cancer."

"Fair enough. You win. I guess I didn't go to yours out of spite."

"Well, I appreciate your honesty." We continued chatting like that. About nothing at all really. His kids, my future kid. If I was excited, scared. He even threw in some advice that I never asked for but appreciated just the same.

About an hour later, he checked his phone.

"I appreciate you reaching out. I really do actually. I don't think we can ever be friends. But at least I can now say hi to you and not want to rip your face off."

A laugh boomed through me. "Well again, I appreciate your honesty."

Jaron shrugged, a deep chuckle leaving him. He stuck out his hand, waiting.

I returned the handshake.

"Thank you for your apology. I accept it. But I'll never forget." And with that, Jaron left the booth and made his way out of the bar.

Just when I was thinking of going to the bar to see my wife, Tabatha joined me in the booth.

"Hi."

I chuckled. "Hi."

"How was your visit?"

"It went well actually. Much better than I thought it would."

Tabatha's smile grew. She reached across the table for my hands. "I'm glad."

"Me too." I paused. "So…" I raised an eyebrow

She giggled, her cheeks turning rosy. Her eyes held a hint of mischief.

"It looks like my wife is hinting for something."

She grinned. "I'm done my shift."

Before she could say any more, I jumped from the booth and grabbed her hand. I all but dragged her out of the bar with her laughter following behind us.

Once we were seated in my car, I grabbed her face and kissed her.

(Tabatha)

Later that night, Ashton was rubbing oil on my stomach. Even though I was completely naked, he never hinted for more. He would whisper words to my belly that only he could hear. Almost like he was talking to our baby. Which I still couldn't believe that we were actually having a baby in a few short months.

I always assumed that I could never have children with my health issues, and chemo and everything. But the day that we found out that we were pregnant, was a day I would never forget. It had been the month before our actual wedding and I was throwing up anything that I tried putting in my stomach. After doing some math, I made Ashton buy me a few pregnancy tests.

Next thing we knew, we had a doctor's appointment and found out I was pregnant. It was a happy day. And I strived for that same happiness every single day. I wanted to live it over and over again.

"Are you happy?" I asked Ashton.

His eyes snapped to mine. "Of course, I'm happy. Are you?"

"I am very happy."

"Good." He kissed my stomach, laid down beside me, and pulled the blankets up and over us. He kept his hand on my stomach and kissed my cheek. "Talk to me."

"I don't know exactly what to say. But I do know that I just want to thank you."

"For what?"

"For not giving up on me. I know I had abandonment issues and maybe I still do. Even though my dad was taken from me, and he didn't actually leave me himself like my mom did, I still blame him for getting himself killed."

"I get that it's hard. You were young. Do you know who killed him? I never thought to ask until now."

"No, it never came out. And I never really looked into it. The news just said that a gambling game had gone wrong. And a life was lost because of it."

"That's very vague," he grumbled.

"Usually is."

"So..."

"So..."

I laughed.

Ashton moved his hand from my stomach to the spot between my thighs.

"Now that you're pregnant with our first baby, I think we should practice making a second one." He waggled his eyebrows.

"I can't get pregnant with a second baby at the same time that I'm pregnant with the first baby, Ashton. That's not exactly how it works."

"Nope, you can't but it is a fun thought. And we can still practice anyway."

I only laughed and pushed him on his back. I knew that he could have overpowered me if he really wanted to. But he didn't. From time to time, he liked it when I dominated him. Also, from this angle, he could see my swollen stomach which he seemed to enjoy quite a bit.

Later that evening, once we were both sated, satisfied, and exhausted, I curled against Ashton, my husband. A man I had never looked for and found just the same.

His love consumed me.

It kept me safe.

He kept me safe.

And I knew there would be moments where maybe I questioned his love, or at least the fact that he'd want to stay with me and not leave like my parents did, but he was patient.

I appreciated his persistence and his patience and his love for me.

I had never been the romantic type. But with Ashton, I wanted the romance. I wanted the flowers, the hearts, and the chocolates.

I wanted to be swept off my feet. I wanted him to open doors for me, and just hold my hand, and kiss me, and tell me that everything would be okay.

As if he could read my thoughts. He pinched my chin turning my head to meet his mouth. "Everything is okay."

"Everything is okay," I repeated.

THE END

The Next Generation Series:
https://www.aboutjmwalker.com/next-generation-series

ACKNOWLEDGEMENTS

We are at book #9. 9! That is so crazy to me. This is my biggest series to date and probably my only big series I'll ever write. But I say this now and we all know that things could very well change. If you've read this far, I really can't thank you enough. I know my books aren't for everyone but I can't thank you enough for taking the time out of your busy schedule to read my little stories that my brain conjures up.

My team: Angie, Jennifer, Christina and Joanne – I truly can't thank you girls enough for helping me fix this book up. I struggled something fierce with this one but you helped me through it. I can't tell you how much I appreciate you.

My Jems: We are almost done this series! I can't wait but at the same time, I'm super sad of course. BUT at I truly can't wait to give you books with brand new characters with tropes I've never written before and so on. Just wait. Some super craziness is coming your way. I also can't thank you all enough for being by my side and for your never-ending support. Best reader team ever!

Authors, bloggers, readers and everyone else! Thank you for sharing my cover reveals, release posts and so on. While this community has some ups and downs, I wouldn't want to walk through this book journey with anyone else.

Here's to books, our love of romance and more!

Happy reading!
xx

ABOUT

J.M. Walker, a Canadian author, is an Amazon bestselling author who also hit USA Today with Wanted: An Outlaw Anthology and the Dissent Anthology. She loves all things books, pigs and lip gloss. She is happily married to the man who inspires all of her Heroes and continues to make her weak in the knees every single day.

"Above all, be the HEROINE of your own life..." ~ Nora Ephron

Find me!

https://linktr.ee/authorjmwalker